Leia Stone is the *USA Today* bestselling author of multiple series. She's sold over three million books and her Fallen Academy series has been optioned for film; her novels have been translated into five languages and she even dabbles in script writing. She lives in Spokane, Washington with her husband and two children. Follow her on Instagram @leiastoneauthor and on TikTok @leiastone and find her on Facebook at facebook.com/leia.stone.

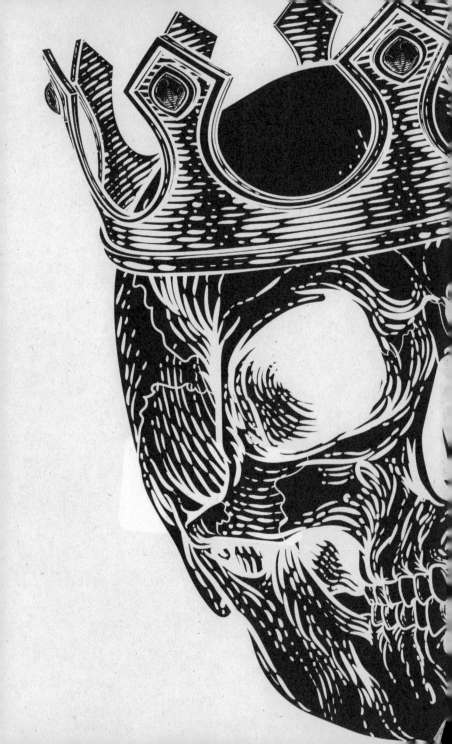

THE
BROKEN
ELF
KING

LEIA STONE

ONE PLACE. MANY STORIES

HQ
An imprint of HarperCollins*Publishers* Ltd
1 London Bridge Street
London SE1 9GF

www.harpercollins.co.uk

HarperCollins*Publishers*
Macken House, 39/40 Mayor Street Upper,
Dublin 1, D01 C9W8, Ireland
This edition 2023

8
First published in Great Britain by Leia Stone LLC 2022

Copyright © Leia Stone

ISBN: 9780008638504

This book is produced from independently certified FSC™ paper
to ensure responsible forest management.

For more information visit: www.harpercollins.co.uk/green

Printed and Bound in the UK using 100% Renewable
Electricity at CPI Group (UK) Ltd.

Fallenmoore

Cinder
Village

Archmere

Gypsy
Rock

NIGHTFALL

Thorngate

Middle
Bridge

Jade City

EMBERGATE

Grim
Hollow

Necromere

AVALIER

The covered wagon jerked to a stop and my shoulder slammed into the person next to me. I mumbled an apology, and then the back canvas flaps opened.

"Out!" the slave trader barked, and we all stood. It took quite an effort considering our hands were tied behind our backs.

I followed the line of my fellow captives, and when I got to the edge of the wagon I jumped, wincing at the sting in my heels. I peered around quickly to find that we were at the golden gates of Elf City, the capital of Archmere. I'd never been outside of Nightfall, and although my current predicament was dreary, I wanted to at least sightsee before I was sold into a life of servitude. My father, a full-blooded elf, spoke fondly of his motherland, and I could see why. Tall trees with white blooms lined the outer castle gates, and rolling hills and mountains surrounded us on all sides. It was breathtaking.

"Head down," the trader snapped at me, bopping me in the back of the skull.

My feet suddenly caught on my long cloak and I yelped as I went down. With my hands tied behind me there wasn't much I could do but brace for the fall. Turning my face to the side, I squared my shoulders, hitting the ground hard and smashing my breasts against a rock. Pain splashed across the entire front side of my body, but I'd mercifully kept my nose from breaking, so I was calling it a win. The other servants stopped and peered down at me as I rolled to my side and glared up at the slave trader. He was tall and thickly built, a human but still strong enough to cause some damage if I pissed him off.

I groaned, and then seconds later the trader reached down and hauled me up by the armpit.

"If you can't even walk straight, I won't get proper money for you," the trader spat.

I wanted to throat-punch the bastard, but that was impossible with my current predicament. I'd settle for a headbutt, though it would probably get me killed. The best I could hope for now was for my new master to be a decent person—er, elf.

The line of my fellow indentured servants started walking again, and I was forced to follow, all thoughts of the glorious headbutt behind me. This time I was more mindful of my footing.

I wondered what my aunt was doing right now. When they'd taken me she'd been screaming and crying. She was probably worried sick. I'd lived in Nightfall all nineteen years of my life, and as an elf-human hybrid I was blessed with short-cropped ears. So the queen, nor anyone else in Nightfall had any idea I wasn't human.

"What's your debt?" the girl beside me whispered.

Pulled from my thoughts, I shook my head, not understanding what she meant.

"Gambling. I owe two gold coins to Bino," she offered, looking sullen.

Bino ran the poker ring at the tavern. Now I understood her question. She wanted to know why I was being sold.

I should never have borrowed the money for my aunt's medicine knowing I wasn't going to be able to pay it back. But I'd been desperate to stop the seizures that plagued her. I'd never been taught to use my elvin healing, so we were at the mercy of the human doctors and what they had available. My aunt was a human, same as my mother, and my father had been an elf. Mom died in labor with me and my dad was killed in the town square to make an example out of trespassers. He'd been coming to see me. Now my aunt was all I had, the only family I'd ever known.

"Five gold coins. To the chemist," I told her.

She looked surprised by the amount, no doubt wondering if I had a pill problem. I wished it were that—it would make more sense than the queen charging an arm and a leg for life-saving medication. Sometimes I thought it was her way to weed out the sick. Make all of the weak, poor people dependent on medication die off and strengthen her perfect society. Most of us hated Queen Zaphira. Her sick plan to humanize the entire realm meant that all of the magical races would need to be culled first. The necros, elves, fae, wolvens, and even the dragon-folk would eventually be wiped from Avalier if the queen had her way.

"My aunt is sick. She needs expensive medicine," I explained to the girl.

My aunt's seizures started when I was twelve, little fits here and there, but this latest one had been so bad her leg hadn't worked right afterward. She had to drag it now when she walked. She would need more medicine in a month's time to keep them away.

4

"Quit yapping!" the trader yelled, and the girl and I parted, looking ahead and taking in the city.

The elvin city was beautiful. It was carved of alderwood with gold inlay and semiprecious stones. The high-pointed arches were breathtaking. The sunlight hitting the gold inlay and precious stones made it look like they glittered as we walked. But we'd passed through the entire city and I'd barely noticed, lost in my thoughts and talking to the girl. Now we stood at a doorway on the side of the large white castle.

"Servant entrance," a guard said, and I looked up at the voice.

Don't let anyone tell you that all elves are tall and skinny. The man guarding the servant entrance to the castle was the opposite of that. A short, squatty man with a beaky nose and ice-blue eyes glared at me. His golden-white hair was tied into a ponytail and braided at the sides. I noticed the sword at his hip and wondered if he even knew how to use it.

There was no way he was a part of the king's royal guard. The Bow Men were known for their silent and deadly treetop assaults. This man didn't look like he could climb a tree.

The trader came out of nowhere and grasped my neck, forcing my head down so sharply that pain exploded in my neck. "I'll pluck those pretty eyes out of your head if you can't keep your face down."

I hissed, balling my hands into fists behind me. This rat bastard was really starting to piss me off. I'd been sold into servitude yes, but that didn't mean I was a punching bag. I was about to give him a piece of my mind when he let go.

I stumbled forward. My face felt hot, I was so angry, but I inhaled sharply, taking deep breaths to calm down.

We were funneled through a hall which was as ornate and decorated as the outside of the castle, and then into a large open storeroom with towering ceilings that rose two stories high. Bags of flour and rice sat in the corner, and piles of pots and pans were stacked in another. We lined up against the far wall and I looked upward at the windows atop the second floor to see some people staring down on us.

Our new masters?

I didn't know the first thing about being a servant. I'd never had one. But I knew how to cook and clean, so it couldn't be much more different than that.

Right?

"You will be unbound so that the lead maid can check you for diseases, then you will be assigned into your new jobs here in the palace," the trader yelled, snapping me from my thoughts. "If you try to run, I will kill you and your debt will fall to your next remaining family member."

We were going to work here in the palace? That was kind of exciting. I eyed the stack of flour and rice and hoped I wasn't relegated to the kitchens. I didn't mind cooking, but doing dishes was Hades. Soggy food creeped me out. I'd love to be assigned to the library or even to work with the healers. As a half elf with zero training I had no healing ability myself, but I'd love to learn and help in any small way.

At Nightfall University I'd been studying biology so that I could find a cure for my aunt, but that was all gone now. Almost two entire years of classes and home-work and studies, all for nothing.

My shackles unclicked and I rolled my shoulders, groaning at the painful release in my chest from being tied like that for several hours of the journey. For a split second I wanted to run, wanted to bolt like a bunny rabbit across the room, outside and into the woods. I eyed the doors and there, on each side, were two Bow Men. They stood tall and silent, barely moving to breathe, with an arrow already nocked into their bows.

I gulped.

An old woman entered the room then, her white hair tied into a sleek bun atop her head. She wore a blue cotton maid's uniform with a white apron, and held a small stick in her hand.

"My name is Mrs. Tirth. I am the lead maid here at Archmere Castle. I will be checking you for lice and making sure you don't have any deformities that would keep you from doing your job here."

Lice? *Gross.* I eyed the girl next to me, who scratched her head.

There were nine of us in all, a mix of elf, fae, and human—the castle must have purchased us in bulk for various jobs. I didn't want to overstep, but I really wanted to work with the healers or around books if possible.

Biting my tongue, I waited until Mrs. Tirth used her stick to poke and prod everyone's hair and check in their mouths and peer closely at their hands and feet, until she got to me. When she did, I deeply curtsied. "Mrs. Tirth, would it be inappropriate to offer a list of strengths so that you might best fit us with our jobs?"

The old woman raised an eyebrow at me and then glanced up into the viewing box, where a few hooded figures still looked down on us.

"Strengths?" she asked as she began to dig through my brown hair with the stick.

"Yes, ma'am. I can read and write. I'm adept at calculus and organic chemistry, and have a passion for reading and healing."

The stick froze, tangled in my hair, and the woman stared down at me. I braced myself for her reaction but she just burst out into laughter. The trader cackled too, as well as the other slaves, and now everyone was laughing at me.

"Honey, I just need you to make bread or clean the toilets," Mrs. Tirth said, and my stomach fell.

Well, it was a worth a shot.

I felt the trader move behind me. "Want me to check her for pubic lice?" He huffed and then his hand landed on my ass and squeezed.

Hard.

Mrs. Tirth looked affronted at the trader's comment, but I knew she'd do nothing about it.

Every angry, repressed feeling I'd been holding in since the bankers had come and taken me away from my aunt exploded out of me then. A vengeful rage washed over me and I snapped. Spinning, I faced the ugly trader. He gazed down at me with lusty eyes and I snapped my palm upward into his nose just like my auntie had taught me, and was rewarded with the crunch of bone. He bent forward to grab his face and I reached up with my knee, smashing it as hard as I could into his man parts.

A wail cut through the room and he fell to the side, red-faced.

"Oh dear," Mrs. Tirth said behind me.

I spun to face the head servant. "He touched my backside without permission. Is that encouraged here?" I asked her, hoping to talk myself out of whatever punishment was about to come my way for retaliating against the trader.

Her face flushed and I noticed movement above in the window. One of the hooded figures was leaving the room. I knew I'd gone too far, but *dammit*, what the trader did wasn't okay and I was hoping Mrs. Tirth would agree. Woman to woman.

She swallowed hard. "It is not," she finally said.

The two Bow Men were suddenly behind me, hooking me under the armpits and dragging me towards the doors.

Crap, where did they come from?

I tried to struggle in their grasp but it was no use. They lifted me into the air, pinched something in my armpit to cause a whimper from my throat, and carried me as if I were made of parchment.

My heart pounded in my chest and I turned to one of them. "He grabbed me, you must have seen. I didn't kill him or anything," I pleaded.

The double doors opened and then I was being walked down the ornately decorated hallway and into another room, this one smaller and with a man sitting behind a desk, a gray cloak pulled up to obscure his identity.

"Okay, I'm obviously new here, so now that I know the rules maybe we can give me a free pass," I begged. I didn't want to be hanged for kneeing the trader in the balls, but I couldn't let that fly. The Bow Men dropped me before the desk and then left the room.

I stood there, frozen, as I stared at the person in the cloak. "I—"

"You talk too much. We will need to work on that." His voice was gruff, powerful, and I immediately knew I was in the presence of someone in charge.

"Yes... sir. I can do that. Assuming you let me live?" I wasn't sure what was going on here.

The man reached up with long slender fingers and pulled back the cloak, revealing the strong jaw and handsome face of the freaking king of the elves.

"Raife Lightstone," I breathed, curtsying deeply.

His blue eyes ran over my body as if assessing my curtsy, and my cheeks reddened.

"Your curtsy indicates you come from a highborn family," he observed.

We didn't really have highborns in Nightfall. Educated and uneducated was what we called it, and ninety percent of the people were educated in Nightfall because the queen mandated it and made it free. I was considered poor but highly educated, so for all intents and purposes a highborn in his mind.

"Yes, my lord," I said, trying to keep my answers short since he'd said I spoke too much.

He stood and I froze, taken aback by how lanky he was, at least a head and a half taller than me, and that was saying something as I was tall for a woman. He stepped out from behind the desk and faced me. "What's your name?"

"Kailani Dulane, sir."

"Are you aware of the one gift that all the kings of Avalier share?" he asked, and I knew where this was going.

Oh Maker.

I swallowed hard. King Valdren of the dragon-folk, King Lucien Thorne of the fae, King Axil Moon of the wolven, and King Raife Lightstone of the elves, all had the gift of smelling a lie.

"You can smell a lie," I said.

He looked surprised. "You *are* well educated."

The Nightfall library had books on every magical race. It was all to aid in the queen's plot to eradicate them. The more we knew about them, the more we could hurt them and eventually wipe them out.

"I'm going to ask you a series of questions, and based on your answers it will determine your fate," he said, walking in a slow circle around me.

Dizziness washed over me but I nodded.

He inhaled through his nose. "Half elf?" he asked, sounding pleased.

"Yes, lord. My father," was all I said, trying to be brief as possible.

"His name?"

I swallowed hard. "Rufus Dulane. He lived in the fishing village of King's Burrow."

He nodded, seemingly pleased with that answer.

"Why were you sold into servitude?" he asked.

I sighed. "I took a loan I could not repay."

"Obviously." He sounded annoyed with my shallow answer. "What for?"

I didn't like the intrusiveness of the question but knew I must answer and truthfully. My life was in his hands. "For life-saving medication for my aunt."

His brow knotted in confusion. He would be perplexed at that. People in Archmere didn't need medication. If they got sick they were healed. For free. It was as easy as breathing for them.

"Did you know you would not be able to repay the loan when you took it?" he questioned.

I growled slightly then, my gaze flicking to his and holding it. "Yes," I said with annoyance. "To save my aunt."

He seemed to consider my response.

"What are your thoughts on the elvin race?"

I frowned. "That's a broad question. I—"

"I need to know if I will be hiring someone who hates me and my people," he clarified. "You grew up in Nightfall under the queen's rule."

So he was thinking of hiring me? Not killing me?

That excited me. Maybe this wouldn't end in my hanging.

I nodded. "I think they are lucky. They have no sickness and can easily heal. I am jealous of the healing ability and wish them no harm."

He frowned. "Jealous of an ability you have?"

I felt my cheeks redden. "I never bloomed. My father died before he could train me and... my magic never came."

Blooming was what the elves called it when your magic surfaced, usually around age five when you started your training.

He stepped before me then, squaring his shoulders and looking me right in the eyes. "Alright... and what are your thoughts on the Nightfall queen?"

I stiffened, holding my breath. It was no secret that the queen had murdered the elf king's entire family when he was fourteen. Seven siblings; only he survived. He hated her, that much I knew, and so did I, but to say that out loud was treason.

I looked over my shoulder, checking if the door was closed. Speaking out against the queen was met with a swift response, and I'd never done it, not even to my aunt. We grumbled about the lack of accommodations, or treatment—we spoke ill of some of the army's deeds, but never of her. His eyes narrowed to slits.

"What do you think about the Nightfall queen?" he pressed again.

I took in a deep breath. "I hate her. I wish she'd just die so we all could live in peace," I said in a rush, and then clamped my hands over my mouth.

A halfcocked grin spread over his face for a second and then it was gone. "Very well. I'd like to hire you on as my new personal assistant. My last one got married and left," he declared, and went back behind his desk to scribble on a piece of parchment.

I sagged in relief. Personal assistant to the king? That sounded like a big deal. Not like cleaning toilets or making bread. "I... I'd be honored."

"I need someone well educated," he stated, still looking down at his parchment. "Fast at taking notes, able to read books, and learn about new things and inform me."

I nearly jumped out of my skin with joy. "I love reading. I read a book a day, all kinds of subjects, and even fiction for fun."

He looked up then and pushed the piece of parchment he'd been writing on across the desk, handing me a quill and ink. "Do it quickly."

I had no idea what it was, a test of some sort? I worked well under pressure, and so I sat at the chair across from his desk and grabbed his ink quill and the piece of parchment.

It was a test. And it was in three different languages!

Thank the Maker I spoke them all.

"I haven't seen written Old Elvish in years," I admitted. I dipped the quill in the ink, grateful I'd had such a curiosity for languages across the realm and studied them all.

His first question was written in Old Elvish and was simple. It gave a problem of a fishing vessel sinking out in Fallenmoore territory. The question asked whether the elf king had the right to retrieve the boat or would need King Moon's permission before doing so. It seemed mostly like a question to make sure I understood the language.

I answered and then moved on to the next. This one was written in New Elvish. Another simple question, which I answered. The last one was a detailed arithmetic problem written in Avalerian, which was the language shared among all peoples of Avalier.

I finished it easily, and handed back the parchment.

He raised his eyebrows. "That was fast."

I shrugged.

He glanced at the parchment, took the quill, and made a few notes next to my arithmetic problem as if checking my work. "Well done."

I beamed.

He folded his hands before him. "My council is insisting I get married. The courting process starts soon. I will need you to keep detailed notes on each woman I meet with and help me decide which one to choose."

My eyes nearly fell out of my head.

"You... you want me to help you pick a wife?"

He nodded nonchalantly. "It's the only way to get the council off my back."

Wow, lucky lady. He seemed *really* into marriage.

"Well, sure, I can do that." If it kept my head attached to my neck I'd do just about anything. "What are my other job duties? I'd like to write them down," I told him.

He looked impressed at that. He handed me a clean parchment and quill. I jotted down what he'd already told me.

Find wife.

"You'll accompany me to meetings, remind me of people's names and jobs. I like to know my staffs' birthdays but I can't be bothered to remember them."

"Of course."

He leaned back in his chair. "Oh, my old taste tester died, so I'll need you to fill in until I can hire a new one."

I froze. A taste tester to royalty was one of the most

dangerous jobs in the realm. They were constantly poisoned.

"You... couldn't heal them?"

He frowned. "Not in time. It's a common misunderstanding that elves can heal anything and never get sick."

"What about one of the other slaves you just bought?" He had eight of them.

He shook his head. "I don't trust any of them."

Did that mean he trusted me? If so, why?

Okay, it was only part-time until he could find a more permanent one.

Find wife.

Remember names, birthdays.

Attend meetings.

Taste tester.

"Anything else, my lord?"

He nodded. "If I am to trust you and you are to work closely with me, I will need you to take a Vow of No Harm."

My eyebrow raised. I didn't know what that was, but I knew the elves and fae took vows seriously.

"Okay," I said timidly. Ten minutes ago I'd kneed my captor in the balls and now I was in a job interview with the king of the elves.

What a day.

He cleared his throat. "One more thing..."

I braced myself. He looked slightly uncomfortable.

"Are you unmarried?"

Oh, easy question. "Yes. Unmarried. Never met a man I could tolerate long enough to marry."

The halfcocked smirk was back and he nodded. "No children?"

I shook my head. "Nope."

He looked relieved. "This is a demanding job, round the clock. I fear that having a family would impede your ability to serve me properly."

I nodded. "Fully able to serve, sir."

I was an indentured servant working off a five gold coin debt. It wasn't like my family could move here with me anyway.

I cleared my throat. "How does the pay work?"

He dipped his head, looking more comfortable, as if talking of money didn't bother him. "I pay your debt today to the trader. Then you work off a gold coin a year."

Five years. It would take me five years to work off three months' worth of medicine for my aunt. Anger roiled through me. Not at him but at the chemist who'd charged so much for the life-saving medication.

"How much is your debt?" he asked.

I sighed. "Five gold coins."

He didn't look shocked. Maybe people came here with higher debts and worked their whole lives for him, but I wanted my own life. I was grateful for the position, but working five years here tasting food for poison and helping him court a wife wasn't exactly my passion. I'd be twenty-four years old when I left here. Too old to try to become a doctor?

"You're disappointed with the five-year assignment?" His eyes narrowed; there was a distrust there. I couldn't fathom why. It's not like I could lie to the guy.

"A little surprised at the length of time to pay my debt," I said honestly. "I had hoped to become a doctor... I left university for this, and I'm excited to go back to school." I rubbed the back of my neck and winced, forgetting the pain the trader had caused earlier.

Dawning understanding shone in his eyes, and then a little pity. "We don't study medicine here like they do in Nightfall, but you can shadow me on my healing rounds and ask a few questions so long as they aren't too intrusive and distracting."

Hope bubbled up inside of me. "My lord, that would be wonderful."

All elves had some sort of healing ability, no matter how small, but it had to be taught and practiced in order to bloom. Because I'd never bloomed, my magic was all but dead, but working in an infirmary in any capacity would be amazing.

"One more thing." He stood, stepped around the

desk and reached out, brushing his hand across the back of my neck. A shiver ran down my spine and the pain the trader had caused vanished. Raife winced for a second and then sat back down, picking up the quill and scribbling a note.

Did he just heal me? With a single touch?

"Uh, thanks," I said.

"You may retire to your rooms," he said, not looking up from his parchment. "Get settled. I will call on you first thing in the morning. Give this to Mrs. Tirth." He handed me the letter he'd scribbled.

I stood, understanding I'd just been dismissed, and took my piece of parchment with me.

Personal assistant to the king?

Score.

Mrs. Tirth was waiting for me outside of the king's office. I handed her the letter and she frowned.

"This isn't the king's handwriting," she said.

I looked over her shoulder and blushed. I'd given her my list of job duties. Snatching it out of her hands, I handed her the letter the king had written.

She scanned it quickly and then a look of surprise passed over her face. "New personal assistant."

"I know. I thought after dropping the trader it might get me hanged."

Mrs. Tirth shook her head. "That's probably what got you the job."

Now it was my turn to look surprised. "What do you mean?"

She glanced back at the office and lowered her voice to a whisper. "The king hates the traders. And he likes strong women. He won't have to worry about you getting killed easily."

What an odd thing to say. I just nodded.

"Do you have any belongings?" she asked.

I shook my head. "Debtors didn't let me take anything."

"No matter, a clothing allowance, meals, and free room and board are included in the job."

That was a relief.

"As a personal assistant to a high-ranking royal, you will be expected to dress the part. You are now a reflection of his monarchy. No cotton. Only silk and chiffon. Lace trim preferred. You'll work with the palace seamstress," Mrs. Tirth said as we traversed the halls.

I loved fancy dresses. You didn't have to twist my arm to wear silk and lace.

"Let's talk about behavior," she added. "As a staff member of the king, you will be required not to drink while on the job, and no cursing or otherwise unlady-like behavior."

I nodded. "Of course."

There was a story there, a reason she needed that disclaimer, and I was tempted to ask it.

We passed another long hallway and then stopped at a set of black lacquered double doors.

"We will just do the Vow of No Harm and then you can settle into your rooms." Mrs. Tirth smiled sweetly.

Oh. Yeah. I'd forgotten I had agreed to that. "Very well."

Reaching up, Mrs. Tirth rapped on the door with her wrinkled fist and then it opened.

I gasped when I saw the king behind the door.

What the...? I peered over my shoulder, wondering how he could have left his office and beat us here. My mouth opened, then closed, then opened again.

He winked. "Secret tunnels."

That wink did something to my insides but I brushed it off. Secret tunnels. Yes, that made sense.

The king backed away from the opening and stepped deeper into the room, giving me a view of it for the first time.

Wow. I hadn't expected to see crystal light beds! My father spoke of them in his journals he left behind for me. It was the only way I could learn about his life in Archmere and what it was like growing up here. Crystal light beds were healing and regenerative. But somehow I thought today they might have a different purpose.

The king walked over to a dark black bed, carved

from a transparent, smoky-colored stone, and lay down flat inside it. There were six crystal beds in here, pink, purple, and black, two of each, large enough for a grown man to sleep in. The room felt tranquil and healing, with white stone floors and light purple wall parchment that had specks of gold in it.

"Lie down in the other black crystal bed," Mrs. Tirth said, and gestured to it.

My heart pounded wildly in my chest as I approached the bed.

What exactly did this vow entail?

I thought it would be more of a pledge, but now I was worried there was some magic involved. I really wanted this job, and I didn't intend to hurt the king, so I guessed I'd just have to deal with it.

I lay back in the bed, surprised that although it was hard it wasn't uncomfortable. It molded to my body.

The moment I fully laid back in it, it glowed a deep blackish purple.

"Uhh," I said.

"Perfectly normal." Mrs. Tirth hovered over me. "It's just synching up yours and the king's energy signatures for the vow."

Synching up our energy?

Okay, just breathe, I told myself, trying to calm down. *They are healing elves, it's not like this can kill me. Right?*

Mrs. Tirth glanced over at the king, and he must have seemed satisfied, because then she looked down at me.

"State your full name," she said in a serious voice.

I let out a shaky breath. "Kailani Rose Dulane."

Mrs. Tirth peered at me with an unwavering gaze. "Do you, Kailani Rose Dulane, vow to never harm Raife Lightstone, King of the Elves?"

"I do," I said, relieved that this was more of a verbal vow.

Mrs. Tirth then kneeled so that she was right beside me, the purple light casting creepy shadows across her face. "Do you vow to never *help* in the plotting of his harm, or the harm of his monarchy? To never seek to injure even a hair on his head lest you suffer the very same fate."

Her questions were more ominous this time, and the blackish-purple energy that had been glowing around my body now tightened to bands and started to squeeze me.

Suffer the same fate? So if I hurt him, I would in turn be hurt? That was more than a vow, that was magic. But as I said before, I had no intention of harming the king, and I was from Nightfall, his sworn enemy, so I knew that if I didn't do this he wouldn't trust me.

"I vow it," I said and the bands released, the light

faded, and Mrs. Tirth stood, stepping away as if all suspicion of my character was forgiven.

I sat up, looked at the king who was now standing, and wondered just what in the Hades I'd gotten myself into.

The next morning I woke up with purpose. I was going to change my outlook. I wasn't an indentured servant, I was the hired hand of a royal. My contract was five years and then I could pursue my career in medicine.

This was just a blip in the road map of life.

After washing up, I found a beautiful silk lavender-colored gown waiting on the dressing bench outside the washroom. Slipping into it, I braided my long brown hair over one shoulder and applied some light blush and lip stain.

Personal assistant to the king.

All my days of studying, reading books, learning languages, tackling challenging mathematics and the sciences, it was all about to pay off.

I puffed my chest up.

There was a knock at the door and I was greeted by Mrs. Tirth.

She looked flustered, sweat beading her brow and hair falling from her bun. "You look pretty," she told me.

"Thanks." I smiled.

She exhaled as if catching her breath and then handed me a piece of parchment. "I'm late for orientation for the new hired help. Here is the king's schedule for the week and meeting notes from last week. You are to brief him of last week's meeting before he goes in so he remembers what was talked about."

I nodded. How busy did someone have to be in order to forget what they spoke about just a week ago?

"The king is hungry. You must taste the food. Come!" she barked, and then took off down the hall.

Food taster. I almost forgot.

I finished strapping my right heel in the silver sandal and then took off at a brisk pace after her. As we rushed to the kitchens, I skimmed the schedule.

Farmers' Union meeting.

Elder Council meeting.

Prospective wives family meeting.

Hospital rounds.

Bow Men meeting.

Lunch.

Treasurer Tax meeting.

Land Survey meeting.

Mining Union meeting.

Dinner.

I felt tired just looking at the list of meetings. My head spun as I imagined how much information would be crammed into them. I hoped the king had a typewriter, but by the look of the quill and parchment on his desk yesterday, I doubted it. My hand was going to hurt by day's end.

The humans of Nightfall excelled in engineering and machinery. Inventions were encouraged and the queen paid bonuses for useful things, but I knew outside of Nightfall those things were not encouraged and so they lived "behind the times," as we liked to say.

Mrs. Tirth burst into the kitchen, where the chef was waiting, looking down his nose at me.

"Kailani, this is Chef Brulier," she said.

He took one look at my nice dress and braided hair and raised an eyebrow. "New taster?"

"For now, until the king can get someone else," Mrs. Tirth explained.

The chef held the plate out to me and I took it, eyeing the delicious meat pie slice and fruit compote.

"How much do I eat?" I asked Mrs. Tirth.

"A large bite, but try not to disturb the food too much. It must still be presentable. If you notice anything bitter or foul, speak up. If you feel sick, dizzy, or off in any way, say something immediately."

Nerves rolled through my stomach. I was about to taste food for poison. Suddenly my job didn't look so rosy. Though it could be worse. I could be washing dishes like the girl at the back of the kitchens. I remembered her from yesterday, the one I had conversed with. We'd never even traded names.

Taking the fork, I dug under the beautiful browned top crust and poked a large hunk of meat and potatoes dripping with gravy. I was careful not to disturb the top crust, but I made a point to cut into the bottom crust. If the crust were poisoned I'd have to sample it to see.

Placing the food into my mouth, I chewed slowly. A burst of flavor splashed across my tongue, peppery, creamy, and delicious.

"Yummm," I moaned, and the chef perked up, looking pleased.

"Bitterness? Throat burning? Dizziness? Stomach cramping?" Mrs. Tirth asked.

I shook my head and then she pointed to the fruit compote.

I was handed a fresh fork and grabbed a sizable chunk of melon dripping with honey. I popped it into my mouth and chewed. Sugary goodness filled my mouth and I waited for any taste of bitterness, but there was none.

Mrs. Tirth consulted a pocket watch. "One more minute."

It hit me then—*They're waiting one minute to see if I've been poisoned.*

My heart picked up as I too waited for any symptoms. After a moment, she looked me over. "Good?"

I nodded, giving her a thumbs-up.

"You are to serve him the plate. If a waiter does it, you have to taste it again," Mrs. Tirth said.

Wow. This guy was paranoid. I knew most kings and queens were, but this was next level. I nodded, grabbing the plate, and then Mrs. Tirth pointed to two double doors. "Brief him for the first meeting over breakfast. And good luck! I've got to run," she said, and then took off, leaving me holding a plate of poisonless food and the stack of notes from last week's meeting.

Walking across the busy kitchen, I neared the double doors and a waiter opened it for me. He was holding a plate almost identical to mine.

Raife was sitting at the head of an extravagant table just inside of the room. Alone.

I eyed the waiter suspiciously.

"*I* have the king's food," I said loudly and forcefully. Why did he have an identical plate? Was he going to switch them last minute? Was I going to foil an assassination plot on my very first day?

The waiter nodded. "And I have yours."

Heat crept up my cheeks and I muttered an apology, stepping into the room.

"Good morning, my lord," I greeted the king, who was looking over some parchments.

He stared up at me, his eyes slowly raking over my dress in a way that caused even more heat to creep up my cheeks.

The waiter placed my plate in front of the seat next to the king and left.

I set down the plate I held in front of Raife. "No bitter taste and no sickness have befallen me," I told the king before sitting beside him.

He nodded, leaning forward to smell the food slowly. As the realm's most powerful healer, I knew he could smell most poisons, but I also knew there were a handful of odorless ones.

"Did you think the waiter was trying to poison me?" he asked suddenly, and I swallowed hard, knowing I couldn't lie to him.

Great, he'd overheard me.

"Yes. I'm sorry if I offended him. I just—"

"Don't ever apologize for trying to protect me. I don't care who you offend in the process."

Oh, well, that was refreshing.

I nodded, and he picked up his fork, staring at his plate.

I grabbed mine as well, having enough proper manners to know that I needed to wait for the king to eat first. He looked... nervous.

Did he fear the food wasn't safe? "My lord, are you okay?"

Maybe it wasn't right of me to ask such a personal question, but he seemed to be lost in his mind right now, frozen with the fork over his plate like a man stricken.

He released a breath, shaking himself slightly. Piercing a piece of the fruit, he popped it into his mouth and chewed. I relaxed a little, taking a bite of my own food.

"I'm sure you know that the Nightfall queen killed my entire family?" His question was so blunt I actually gasped, not prepared for it.

Why was he bringing that up now? Over *breakfast*. I set my fork down and met his eyes. "Yes, my lord. Everyone knows."

He nodded. "Do you know how she did it?"

I winced. Of course not. No one asked for such a

detail when they found out that an entire royal family had been slaughtered. All I'd heard was that the queen had taken them all out and left only one. *Him.*

He took a deep breath and looked at his food once more. "Poison. She poisoned them all in front of me."

My entire body froze. I couldn't move, didn't breathe.

The king pierced a piece of fruit and placed it in his mouth and chewed robotically. "I don't enjoy mealtimes. It's something you should know about me."

I could feel tears welling in my eyes, but I didn't think he would appreciate my pity, so I blinked them back and nodded. He watched them all die of poison? Clutching their throats as their stomachs burned? I'd heard his youngest sibling was six years old at the time. It made me sick. A few tears spilled over onto my cheeks no matter how badly I tried to keep them held back.

The king watched me, saying nothing as I processed his pain as if it were my own.

He cocked his head slightly to the side. "Do you cry easily?"

Embarrassment flushed through me. I wouldn't say that, I was tough, but... sometimes if someone was in pain I couldn't help but sympathize.

"I'm sorry, my lord." I wiped my cheeks.

He stood, took two steps until he was looming over

me, and then bent down until he was right beside my face. A wave of sadness crept into my heart, nearly crushing me, and I gasped. He gasped as well, and then stumbled backwards. I turned to face him. His eyes were wide and he was clutching his chest.

"What's wrong?" I asked. This casual business breakfast had taken an unexpected turn.

"You're an... empath," he stated, stepping farther away from me, and my sadness and despair faded with every step.

"A wh-what?" My head finally cleared and I was able to focus on the now and not think of the haunting memory of his dying family.

His brows knotted together and he stepped closer again, this time coming right up against me so that his right arm brushed against my left.

My sharp intake of breath matched his. Guilt, sorrow, agony, anger, revenge, so many emotions warred within me, threatening to eat me alive. But when I stared up at the king I saw... peace. He looked like he could breathe for the first time. A contented sigh escaped him as my stomach tied into knots with all of this sudden emotion.

"I forgot what it felt like," he said wistfully.

I was so confused I could only breathe through whatever was happening.

The doors to the dining hall opened then and he

stumbled backwards away from me, taking four huge steps to create distance.

"The Farmers' Union has assembled in the meeting hall," a young Bow Man said.

Raife cleared his throat. "Thank you, Cahal."

The king sat at the table and began to eat again, letting out a shaky breath between bites. "Brief me on this meeting," he said as if he hadn't just walked over and downloaded all of his sadness into me.

I wanted to laugh, I wanted to ask him what the Hades an empath was, but I also wasn't sure I was ready for that information. All the wheels were turning in my head now. The times my aunt's seizures would come on and I just knew a moment before and could position myself behind her. When passing the town drunks my mind felt hazy. The rage I felt when near the boxing matches.

I—

"Kailani?" The king looked at me sternly.

I snapped out of my thoughts and picked up the meeting notes from last week. "I'm sorry, my lord. The Farmers' Union is demanding you divert more water from the Great River, which contradicts with the Elvish Land Survey Council. They say it will affect the fish and other regions. They recommend boring a hole and building a well instead."

He nodded. "Cost and length of time to bore the well?"

I scanned the notes. "Ten gold coins and... three months' time."

Three months *by hand*. You could bore a well in a day with a machine in Nightfall, but I didn't say that. Ten gold coins seemed like way too much, but I kept my mouth shut about that too.

His eyes narrowed. "Ten gold coins for three months' work?"

I inclined my head. "I also feel it is excessive, my lord." Considering I was making one gold coin a year as the king's assistant.

"Find more information on the well digger. The crown's coin purse will not bleed for the farmers no matter how much they threaten low crop yield," he snapped.

"Yes, my lord." I jotted down a to-do list.

Info on well digger.

Get more estimates?

He placed one last bite of food in his mouth and then stood. "Very well, let's go."

I popped a melon cube in my mouth and gathered my things, following the king as he led us out of the room.

ALL THROUGH THE FARMERS' meeting, I kept thinking of only one thing.

Empath. Empath. Empath.

Did he mean it casually or as a thing? Was an empath a thing? An elf thing? A magic thing?

"Kailani?" King Raife looked at me and I blushed. I never zoned out like this; it was embarrassing.

"I'm sorry, my lord. Yes?" I kept my voice pleasant and my pen poised on the parchment.

The lead farmer, Mr. Wilco, nodded to me. "I was just saying how nice it was to meet you."

I bowed my head slightly. "And you, sir. I look forward to our next meeting."

He stood and the other half dozen farmers stood with him, seeing themselves out.

I immediately turned to the king. "I'm so sorry, sir. I hope I didn't embarrass you. That won't happen again."

I did not want to get fired on my first day and then be relegated to washing dishes for five years. Or probably ten, since that job most likely paid much less.

He nodded. "It better not, because my council is next, and there is something you should know about them."

I physically flinched a little at the verbal reprimand but dipped my chin. "What is it?"

He leaned in closely, lowering his voice. "They

have been threatening for two years to overthrow me if I do not marry and start a family."

Shock surged up inside of me. "That's treason," I growled.

He appraised my sharp response with interest and I found myself studying his face at this close of a distance. I'd known this man all of twenty-four hours and yet I felt like I'd known him longer. It was hard to explain. There was an ease in his presence, something comfortable and familiar.

His face looked much like one printed in our Nightfall history books, but more manly. Those were a few years old when he still had some boyishness to his features. The strong jaw I now peered at, the shadow of a beard and full soft lips, the arresting blue eyes, were all man.

"Normally, it would be treason yes, but there is a clause in our founding laws." He pulled me from my thoughts. "If the entire royal family is killed, or cannot, or does not, have children by a certain age, then the council can unanimously vote them out and then vote in a new four-person quorum."

A quorum? End the monarchy? It was a wild idea. Every territory in Avalier had a king or queen. I couldn't imagine anything else. Either you were born with royal blood or you weren't.

I nodded. "So you really do need my help finding a wife." I pulled out a fresh piece of parchment.

He looked wistfully out the window as if the idea of having a wife saddened him.

"But you don't want that, do you?" Maybe it was an overstep but I couldn't help it. If I was going to find him a wife, I should know why he didn't want one. He was over twenty winters old! That was ancient in royal terms. He should be married with two or three heirs by now.

He swallowed hard, and then looked at me with an expression that made chills rise up on my arms. "Why would I want to fall in love and bring children into this world just so that the Nightfall queen can kill them too?"

His words sliced through my heart so fiercely that I felt a physical ache. I must have winced in pain, because he leaned backwards and away from me.

"But I must marry if I am to keep my position as king, so you will have to help me find someone tolerable," he added.

"But not too lovable?" I asked. His look was a warning and I immediately lowered my head. "I'm sorry, my lord."

"Once the council is off my ass, I can plan the war to take down the queen."

I froze. "Overthrow the Nightfall queen?"

He nodded, looking pleased with himself, as if the act would bring him great joy. I was sure it would, but it was also the most dangerous thing I'd ever heard.

"No one gets near her unless they've served in her army for at least five years. She's got contraptions and gadgets that make her have powers akin to the magic users in the realm. My lord, she's untouchable."

He appraised me with pride. "And it seems I have chosen the best assistant to help advise me in matters of the queen."

It hit me then. One of the first things he'd told me: *"You grew up in Nightfall under the queen's rule."*

"That's why you hired me?" I tried to hide the hurt in my voice. I'd thought it was maybe the organic chemistry or the fact that I'd kicked that trader's ass and impressed him.

He inclined his head. "Mostly, yes. You're the best candidate for the job."

I simply nodded, feeling stupid for having thought that he might have been impressed with my other qualities. It didn't really matter anyway. I was paying off my debt and he was a decent man. He didn't seem like he would beat me or anything, and I wasn't washing dishes, so all in all I was still counting this a win.

The meeting hall doors opened then and I turned

in that direction. Four tall male elves entered the room and bowed deeply to the king.

"You may be seated," the king told them.

Their eyes flicked to me and I gave them a small smile, which was not returned. They all sat with stiff posture and clasped hands. Their ages varied from thirty to sixty years old, and as I looked closer I could tell one pair were father and son. The two men had black hair, though one was feathered with gray, and both had the same hooked nose. The other two elves were both brunettes. All of them had the typical long hairstyle with braided sides.

"Council, this is Kailani Dulane, my new personal assistant," the king said and gestured to me. "Kailani, this is Haig, Aron, Greylin, and Foxworth." He pointed to each one.

The eldest, Haig, the black-haired one with gray running through, raised an eyebrow. "I wasn't aware Joana was leaving. We would have helped you in your search for a new staff member," he said.

The king leaned back casually in his chair. "I wasn't aware I needed to tell you the ins and outs of my private staff, Haig. Nor that I needed help hiring staff."

The man's jaw grit at the reprimand. "You do not, Your Highness. It was simply an offer to help make sure you had the highest caliber candidate possible."

His gaze flicked over to me and his nostrils flared.

He was smelling me and I suddenly felt uncomfortable.

"Half human?" Haig looked affronted at what he'd scented. "Can you really trust a human on your staff?"

The king groaned as if he was already tired of this question. "She's taken a protection vow. I'm not an idiot!"

Haig reeled back at the snap and I kept quiet.

Haig's son, Aron, the one who looked just like him but younger, stared at the quill in my hand. "She can read and write?" He sounded surprised.

Okay, I'd had quite enough of this.

"Yes, *she* can," I said in Old Elvish. "In *three* different languages," I finished in New Elvish.

The king grinned and the council looked flustered at this turn of events. A long silence stretched out and I cleared my throat. "The king has informed me of his excitement at taking a wife and I am eager to help," I lied, which caused the king's grin to fall. He knew I'd just lied but I was hoping the council didn't. The king was anything but eager.

Haig nodded. "Yes. A wife and heirs are of the utmost importance now."

"Unless of course he no longer wants to rule, which is why he's delayed taking a wife?" Foxworth said. I remembered him by the nervous eye blinking he kept doing.

The king's eyes narrowed. "I am eager to shut you all up."

Ouch. The king was kinda hot when he was laying a smackdown on his council.

Haig cleared his throat and pulled a folded letter from his robes, handing it to the king. "A list of a dozen of the most influential families in Elf City." Haig nodded. "Their daughters are all single, cleared for breeding, and eager to meet you."

I choked on my own spit at *cleared for breeding*, coughing and smacking my chest wildly. The king looked mildly concerned but I waved him off and took a sip of water.

"Apologies," I said.

The king opened the letter and glanced down at it briefly before handing it to me.

The names looked familiar. Frowning, I flipped to the schedule of meetings today. Right after this conference we had one called the *Prospective wives family meeting.* The attendees' names were the same.

"My lord, we have a meeting with these families next," I told him.

He looked surprised, but then covered it.

Haig nodded. "I took the liberty of inviting their parents to a roundtable. They can tell you about their daughters and you can pick the top five to invite to a joint dinner."

My eyes widened. "Dinner all together?"

Haig looked down his crooked nose at me. "Yes, in the interest of time. What would you know about courting a queen?"

It was a challenge; he'd been rude to me since the second he walked in here. I needed to nip it in the bud now or he'd forever think me a pushover. My gaze flicked to King Raife, and he nodded the slightest bit as if saying *go get 'em*.

I shrugged to Haig nonchalantly. "Oh I don't know, considering I'm the only one in this room with breasts, I guess I know more than any of you."

Now it was King Raife's turn to choke on his own spit. It sounded like a laugh which gave way to a cough.

Even stuffy old Foxworth cracked a grin. I'd gained the respect of one of them, I guessed I couldn't ask for more.

Haig opened his mouth to rebuke when the king spoke: "It's settled, then. Five different dinner dates. Getting to know each woman separately. I wouldn't want my future wife to feel as if I chose her in the same way I choose my cattle."

I gave a triumphant nod, making a meeting note and ignoring the icy glare from Haig.

I wanted whichever woman Raife chose to have a fair shot at winning his heart. She deserved dinner with the king alone.

Haig stood, prompting the others to stand as well. "I want an engagement by next month. We have counseled you since you were a new king at the tender age of fourteen. This is what's best for all of Archmere and you know it. No more messing around!" Haig pounded his fist on the table and then they all left.

My eyebrows rose, and when the door closed I looked over at the king. "If they talked to the Nightfall queen like that, she'd behead them."

He gave me a cool stare. "I'm not the Nightfall queen, and I know they seem disrespectful and over-controlling, but you have to understand I became a king before I could even grow a beard. They've all become somewhat of father figures and uncles to me."

My heart pinched then, and I saw the whole thing in a new light. Haig was like the overbearing father who forced you to do what was good for you, even if you hated it.

I nodded. "Well, time to meet the families and pick our top five. This could be fun." I tried to lighten the mood. "What kind of things are you into? I can try to match someone with common interests. You don't want to be stuck with someone forever who hates reading if you love it. Or who talks too much if you like quiet time," I said.

He looked at me and chuckled. "I like quiet time and you talk too much."

It was playful so I laughed. "Well, it is a good thing I am not in the running to be your wife. What else?"

He shrugged. "I like chess when I have time. Archery of course. Fine cuisine. Reading. Walking through the lily gardens, and most of all healing my patients."

I'd heard only rumors, but the elf king had an entire infirmary erected in his name and was the greatest healer in all the realm. I'd love to see him work with his patients, and hoped that was still part of the job description since he'd all but promised it to me if I stayed out of the way.

I jotted it all down.

Quiet time.

Chess.

Archery.

Gardens.

Food.

Reading.

Healing.

"What about looks? Are you into blondes? Redheads? Tall? Athletic?" I asked.

The king raised an eyebrow and his gaze traveled down from the tip of my nose to my cleavage and back up. "Pretty is pretty, I don't care what color package it comes in," he said, and I felt my cheeks heat.

Okay...

Pretty, I added to my list, and then there was a knock at the door.

"Enter," the king said.

A servant entered with a cart of pastries and tea, and right behind him Mrs. Tirth wearing her crisp housemaid uniform. "My lord, I introduce you to Miss Agatha Trulin, mother of Gertie Trulin."

A lithe fae with wild curly blond hair and a sweeping gold cloak entered and curtsied deeply. "Your Highness, it is truly a pleasure."

She sat down at the table and was served tea and given a cookie.

Another mother entered, who was also introduced by Mrs. Tirth, and I started to take notes.

Agatha Trulin—Gertie's mother. Curly blond hair.

Billie Gillhard—Bronwyn's mother. Long nails.

When all dozen women had been seated at the table, it was officially full. The king introduced me as his new personal assistant and all the women smiled kindly at me. When the waiter got to me, he served me two cups of tea and two cookies. It took me a moment to understand why.

Oh. Food taster.

As the king made boring small talk with the high-born mothers of Elf City, I sipped his tea and waited. Heart palpations? Headache? Stomach cramps? Nope,

nope, nope. I watched my pocket watch as Raife cast worried glances my way.

How much anxiety it must cause him at every meal, wondering if the queen would come back to finish him off.

After a full two minutes, I felt totally fine and ever so casually slid the tea over to the king. He stared at it warily while I nibbled on the cookie.

It's okay, I wanted to tell him. *It's safe.* But you could see the concern in his face as he pulled the cup to his lips and then looked at me. I gave him an encouraging smile and he drank. After I'd tasted the cookie, which was delicious because almond was my favorite, I gave that to him as well and then focused on the women.

"My daughter, Gertie, loves to read and garden. She's also a master archer," Agatha stated.

I put a star next to Gertie's name. Sounded like a good fit off the bat. King Raife met my eyes in agreement.

"Would you say your daughter Gertie is a strong and silent type, or a social butterfly?" I asked her, my quill poised over the parchment.

She swallowed hard, looking down at my parchment, which I kept at an angle so that only the king and I could see it.

"She can be both," Agatha said diplomatically.

I nodded, giving her a smile. It must be hard to be called into a room with a bunch of other mothers—all of them trying to get their daughter to be the next queen.

"My Bronwyn is quite shy, I must say. She also likes reading and will play chess for hours until you pull her away. She won the ladies' classic tournament last year."

"I heard that," the king said, "Congratulations, you must be very proud."

I placed a star next to her name as well. The meeting went on with each mother giving a little snippet of information about their daughter and respectfully allowing the others to speak. I was surprised at the civility here. No speaking over the other or trying to tear another's daughter down. I was also surprised the daughters themselves were not here. It must be the custom.

"Did any of you bring a picture?" I asked, and then immediately cursed myself. Box cameras were a human Nightfall thing. "Or a portrait?"

The women nodded their heads excitedly and one by one pulled small eight-to-ten-inch hand painted portraits from their satchels. The artisans of Elf City were the best in the realm. Their paintings were amazing, and that was shown true here.

I glanced at them at the same time the king did.

"They are all so beautiful," the king said diplomatically.

I wished I could have a moment to confer with the king on which ones he thought the prettiest, but instead I made hearts next to the names of the ones I thought the most stunning. He looked at my parchment and nodded to me.

I was just about to ask another question when the door burst open, startling us all. A woman who wore the white robes of a healer looked to the king. She was speckled with bits of blood. "My lord, I'm sorry, it's just that one of your patients—"

He stood so fast the chair knocked over and then he fled from the room, following her without another word.

"Thank you all for coming. The king's patients are so important to him. We will be in touch about dinner dates for some of your daughters," I said to everyone and stood, running after the king.

I had to bolt down the hallway to catch up with them.

"Who is it?" King Raife was asking the healer as we jogged at full speed down the hall.

"Corleenaa," she said, and the king's face fell.

He cursed. "The bleeding is back? It makes no sense!"

I riffled through the notes for our infirmary rounds, and stopped on the name Corleenaa Yahmeen.

Corleenaa Yahmeen.

Age: six.

Bleeding disorder of unknown cause.

We ran across the palace lawn at breakneck speed over to a giant brick building I assumed was the infirmary. My sandal strap cut into my heel but I ignored it. If a six-year-old was bleeding out, it wasn't worth caring about foot pain. We passed the infirmary sign and I barely noticed the name.

Raife Lightstone Healing Infirmary.

We burst into a busy intake room and then down a hallway, to a set of double doors marked *Operating Theatre*. I knew that this would be nothing like our human operating rooms, but an elvin one full of wands and crystals and light.

"Stay here or go to the viewing room," Raife said to me, and my heart fell.

"Yes, lord," I obeyed. I'd wanted to be a doctor after my schooling; I wasn't squeamish with blood, or the sick, but he didn't know that. I veered to the right and then followed the sign that read *Operating Theatre Viewing Room*.

I pushed open the double doors and was immediately confronted with a weeping woman. She was in her early thirties, and a man about the same age clung to her, holding her tightly as he stared stony-faced at a wall of glass.

I stiffened, guilt worming through me at intruding on their moment just to watch the king operate. They must be the girl's parents.

The woman looked up at me, her chin shaking. "Who are you?"

I bowed slightly. "King Lightstone's new personal assistant. I thought the room was empty. I'll leave you—"

Before I could finish, she left her husband's side and grasped my hand, pulling me into the room.

"Maker bless the king! He's here?" She dragged me over to the far wall, which was made purely of glass. Now that I was closer to her, I was overwhelmed with a strong smell of sweet blackberry syrup. Blackberry jam was my favorite candy as a child and it instantly made me nostalgic.

As we stepped closer to the glass I noticed that I was given a perfect view of the operating room. My gaze flicked around the space, taking it all in.

Unlike the human operating rooms we had at Nightfall, there were no gadgets or blades or machines trying to keep someone alive. There was just a nurse, an elvin wand, and *a lot* of blood.

The little girl Corleena was a small elf, and her pale face was rolled to the side, her eyes closed as if she were sleeping, but blood dribbled out of the corners of her lips and onto the floor. I'd never seen an elvish child; her little ears were pointy and adorable and her face was like a porcelain doll. Her white hair was long like her mother's, and in two braids that hung down the sides of the table. Her body suddenly jerked, her mouth opened and she vomited more blood.

Her mother fell to her knees beside me, letting go of my hand, and that's when King Raife entered the room. He wore a white physicians coat and barked an order at the nurse with the healing wand.

At the sight of the king, the mother pressed her hands and face to the window and stared down at her dying little girl. I was rooted to the spot, unsure how the king could do anything in this dire of a situation. That blood needed cauterization or stitches or something, and yet I saw no tools to do so. Although I was half elvish, I knew nothing of elvin healing other than it was magical. I'd read a few books on it but never seen it in person. My father was an artisan trader selling healing-infused pendants and other things across the realm. His journal didn't cover healings of this nature. If I had known how to heal, I'd have healed my aunt years ago.

I waited for the king to blast her with light or something, but he simply knelt beside her and placed his hands lightly on her tummy. Taking a deep breath in, purple light emanated softly from his palm and he coughed, a small spray of blood dotting his chin.

I gasped, looking around in alarm, but the mother stood, giving me a hopeful gaze. The king winced, doubling over and releasing the girl as he grabbed his midsection.

I froze, watching him wide-eyed as I processed what I was seeing. No one else seemed alarmed by the king's grave appearance, including the nurse, so I watched on. Suddenly the little girl's eyes blinked open and she looked around the room.

"Mommy?" she said, all paleness gone from her. A healthy pinkness shone on her cheeks as she looked around frantically for her mother. The mother bolted from the viewing room with the father, leaving me to my thoughts.

Did the king... did he take on her illness and then heal it within himself? If so, that was *very* dangerous.

The little girl reached for Raife, grasping his fingers as he stood. He froze, staring down at her with a compassion that melted my heart. He truly loved his patients. Watching him with her caused something to blossom inside my chest. It was a weird feeling, nothing I'd ever felt before. It confused me so I pushed it aside.

King Raife spoke to the parents briefly and then left the room. I scurried out of the viewing hall to meet him back at the entrance to the operating theatre.

The second he stepped out, I rushed up to him. "Are you okay?" My gaze fell to the splatter of blood on his chin. He seemed to notice and reached up and wiped it, his hand shaking slightly.

"It keeps happening. It doesn't make sense. I don't feel a chronic bleeding issue. It is acute," he mumbled, ignoring me.

Corleena, he was still stuck on her case even as I was asking about *him*.

"You healed her. It was the most amazing thing I've ever seen," I told him.

He looked up at me with worry in his gaze. "It's the *fourth* time I've healed her of internal bleeding. If I don't find the cause I might not get here fast enough next time. They live on a large blackberry farm an hour's horse ride away."

A heaviness fell over our conversation. It explained why the mother smelled of blackberry syrup. She probably grew and made it from scratch. I lowered my voice, leaning into the king. "You don't think the parents would... have done this to her on purpose?" I felt awful for even suggesting it, but four times was a lot.

He sighed, and at this closeness I felt the unease

and worry roll through him and into me, so I stepped back a foot.

"I considered it of course, but they are always so worried for her. The mother seems to fall apart in tears and then the father is in genuine shock. He carried her limp on horseback the entire way. I just don't see that."

I nodded; it was unfair of me to suggest it. The mother seemed more than genuine, and in shock was exactly how I would describe the father.

Oh how I hated something unsolved. My mind would chew on this for hours.

"Could I get a sample of her blood? Before she goes?" I asked.

His brow furrowed. "We don't have any of your fancy human gadgets here, and there is nothing in her blood I would not smell." He looked offended.

I relented, nodding. I was thinking some type of poison or a clotting issue, but she was six, and that would have been present at birth.

"You have to let it go." He sighed and reached up to rub the bridge of his nose. "I've been over this case hundreds of times in my head. There is nothing that stands out other than she smells of blackberries every time I see her, which isn't unusual considering they own a blackberry farm. I have other patients to see. Come on."

He turned and fled down the hall, leaving me to my thoughts.

After doing a round of his patients and checking on them or healing their wounds, we made our way back to the castle to the Bow Men meeting.

The Bow Men were the elf king's loyal elite army known for being soundless when walking, and deadly with an arrow. The meeting was a brief rundown of the city's defenses, and my introduction to the top four commanders on his force.

Cahal, Ares, Tanin, and Arok.

We broke for lunch, in which I tasted all the food first, and then we were thrust into another three meetings. A tax meeting, land survey meeting, and the mining council. These meetings were the most boring things I'd ever had to sit through. I almost wished I was washing dishes. In the final minutes of the mining council meeting, I looked to the king to catch him nodding off, so I used my ankle to kick him awake slightly.

"Okay, I think I have a handle on the situation. Thank you," King Raife said to the mining council and stood.

Oh thank the Maker!

I stood as well. "We will be in touch about the labor shortage issue," I told them kindly.

They bowed their heads deeply as the king and I left.

My stomach rumbled as we walked down the hallway to the king's private dining hall, causing me to blush nervously.

"I'm famished," I exclaimed.

His lip curled in amusement. "What did you think of your first day? Honestly."

Honestly—as if I could lie to him. I thought it was kind of cute he wanted to know what I thought of the job. "I like it. It keeps my brain active. The tax and land stuff are boring, but what job doesn't have some snooze times? The food tasting thing still freaks me out. I keep waiting to feel ill—oh, and I can't stop thinking about Corleena and how you healed her." I said it all in a rush, completely forgetting I was talking to my boss, the king of the entire elf race. He was so... personable, and humble, and easy to be around.

He made a noise in his throat I couldn't quite decipher. A *hmm* or *hrphm*.

"Oh, and your council is really not fun," I added.

That caused him to belly laugh, and a warmth trickled down my body.

I made the king laugh. It was a sound I liked hearing from him.

"I don't think fun is in their job description," he added. "And you have to let Corleena go or it will keep you up all night. Step one of healing is to keep yourself healthy. You cannot pour from an empty vessel."

I frowned. "I know, but what if—?"

"And you're not a healer," he added sharply.

I bit my tongue as we entered the dining room. Two plates of food sat there with domed steel lids.

"Maybe it's hard for me to let go because I'm an empath?" I asked coolly.

He stiffened. I wanted to know what that meant, what our whole interaction at breakfast was all about.

"After you taste my food, you may eat yours in the kitchens," he said suddenly. "I'd like to be alone tonight. I have much to think about after the day full of meetings."

I pushed down the sense of rejection and nodded. It was like I'd been slapped. The king had some mood swings, that was for sure.

"Yes, lord." Lifting the lid on his plate, my mouth watered as I stared at the meat and potato stew with a buttered roll, and green beans topped with slivered almonds. There was even a slice of sweet potato pie. Picking up one of the three forks, I took a hunk of meat and potato from the stew and popped it into my mouth. A moan of pleasure escaped me.

"Your chef is seriously amazing. You should give him a raise," I said.

He watched me intensely. "Should I?"

I popped an almond covered green bean in my mouth and moaned, then I set the fork down and grabbed a clean one, cutting into the sweet potato pie.

"Maker have mercy on my soul," I cooed as the sweet maple syrup splashed across my tongue.

The king's eyes bored into me so deeply then that I straightened a little, wondering if I was doing something wrong.

"And the roll?" I asked, clearing my throat.

He swallowed hard and nodded. I tore off a small piece and chewed it, making no noise for fear I was breaking some royal protocol. I had manners, but probably not *noble* manners.

"I would like to enjoy food as much as you do," he said wistfully, and my stomach dropped.

He feared every meal would be poisoned? What an awful way to live. "My lord, do you really think Queen Zaphira would try that again?" It was a serious question. I knew the queen actively wanted to wipe out all of the magical races, especially their kings, but to poison again? It seemed too obvious.

His eyes narrowed, and he stared at me like I was a complete simpleton. "Why do you think I am in need of a new taster?"

I froze, the hairs on my arms raising. "The other one is getting married?" I hedged.

He looked at me point blank. "That was my

assistant. My former taster is dead. Once a year since I was crowned, Queen *Zaphira* tries to kill me. I never know when it's coming so it always keeps me in an active state of worry, which I'm sure is her intention. Always a flavorless, scentless poison that I cannot detect until my taster is dead."

Pure terror gripped me and I swayed on my feet, swallowing hard. "Are... are you not able to heal them?"

He sighed. "Poison is a tricky thing to heal. I have to take enough into myself to filter and allow the other person's healing to kick in, but not so much that I myself become ill. Impossible to do blindly with a scentless, tasteless poison. Whatever she is using isn't something we grow here."

And just like that I wanted to be assigned to dish-washing.

"Sir, I recommend we find a new taste tester immediately."

He chuckled, and then just looked sad. "As you can imagine, not many want the job, but I'll keep looking."

Zaphira was still actively trying to poison him after keeping him alive all those years ago? That was some seriously psychotic behavior.

"Feeling okay? I am quite hungry," he asked. I checked my pocket watch. It had been two minutes and I felt fine other than the sense of impending doom pressing in on me.

"I'm fine. Enjoy your meal, sir." I curtsied, taking my plate and leaving him be.

As I reached the door he called out to me: "Kailani? When we're alone you can call me Raife."

I smiled, trying to see that as a good thing, but all I could think about was that I'd taken a five-year job post that I might not even live a year to see. First thing tomorrow I was interviewing for new tasters.

My mind was an insatiable thing, and when I gave it something to chew on that it couldn't figure out, it didn't rest.

I lay awake in the early morning hours, unable to sleep all night. I tossed and turned thinking of Corleena. *Blackberries. Vomiting blood.* Why did those things feel connected? They shouldn't, blackberries didn't make you vomit blood. If they did, the mother and father would be too.

I decided to get up early for the day and hit the library. Maybe something in there could help me solve this riddle. I dressed in a pale pink chiffon gown with the back cut out, and braided my hair down my back, applying some pink lip stain to finish the look. I liked the status the title of my new job gave me, and dressing the part for it was important and fun. Every day a new dress arrived from the seamstress in a beautiful color or pattern and fit my body like a glove. It was any little girl's dream.

Over the next hour, as the sun began to rise, I pored over books. The palace librarian wasn't here yet but I was sure we'd become fast friends eventually. Reading was my favorite pastime. I dug into herbology, poisons, horticulture, bleeding disorders. It was only when I flipped to a chapter called invasive species that my entire body went rigid.

Corlia Mortifia or "nightlock berries" are invasive to Archmere and grow only in Nightfall. These berries look and smell similar to Archmerian blackberries but cause internal bleeding in children and mild stomach cramping in adults.

It was like my soul left my body in that moment; the shock of this truth rang throughout my being. The parents weren't poisoning her. She was doing that herself! She must be eating berries from the field that weren't blackberries.

Without another thought I burst from where I'd been sitting in a reading chair and ran across the small library, book opened in my hands to the page about the nightlock berries.

I barely remembered where the king's private sleep quarters were when he'd told me, but luckily I had a map. Pulling it out, I consulted the giant palace floor-plan and headed in the direction of his private wing. When I got to the giant double doors of his room, I noticed a Bow Man on either side. They gripped their weapons as I approached, which was ridiculous considering I'd just met them in the meeting yesterday. Cahal, the giant one with reddish hair and a beard, and Ares, the dark-skinned one with dreamy eyes, looked at me suspiciously as if my book would knock them out or something.

"I need to speak with the king. It's urgent!" I told them, and rushed forward to knock on the door. They held out their arms to stop me, and then squeezed together to block my way.

"He's not to be disturbed," Cahal said.

"This is life or death!" I screamed. "If you don't let me knock on this door, a little girl might die and then I will—"

The door wrenched open and the men moved out of the way, heads down. My eyes fell on the taut muscles of the tunicless king. His hair was fully down, scattered around his shoulders, and his trousers were hanging half way off his hips, barely tied.

Holy Maker of all things beautiful.

His skin draped over taut muscle; not an ounce of fat graced his trim, chiseled body.

Someone moved in the room behind him and I startled to see a woman with blond hair streak past behind him and into a washroom. She was fully dressed and looked like she was crying, which was weird.

Oh. *Oh.*

The king is not to be disturbed. Now I knew why. Heat crept up my cheeks as I realized I'd just interrupted him bedding a woman.

"Kailani, what it is?" His voice was gruff and thick with sleep... or arousal from the obvious lovemaking I'd just disturbed.

Maker, kill me now.

I couldn't find my words, so instead I handed him the book, page open to the nightlock berries. I watched as his eyes widened the more he read. A growl rumbled in his throat and then he looked at one of his Bow Men. "Cahal, saddle the horses. We're going to Briar Ridge."

Without another word, his lead Bow Man took off like a stallion down the hallway.

Then Raife looked at me, seemingly for the first time. His gaze ran the length of my pink gown and then back up, eyes hooding. "You ride horses?"

I just nodded, still unable to speak. I was afraid if I

did say something it would be gibberish, or worse—I'd tell him how amazing he looked half naked.

"Meet me in the stables," he said, handing me the book back and then shut the door in my face, breaking the hold his pecs had over me.

My chest was heaving as I looked sideways at the single Bow Man who now guarded the door. Ares. If he knew I was blushing, he said nothing about it. A true professional.

Pushing all thoughts of what I'd just witnessed out of my mind, I consulted my map and then rushed out of the castle and to the stables. I was surprised to see the king was already there. He must have a second exit to his room or an underground tunnel or something.

A medium sized white female horse was already saddled and waiting for me. In Nightfall we had mostly motorized horseless carriages, negating the need for horses, but I'd still learned to ride for sport. Hooking my leg into the stirrup, I hoisted myself up onto the mare and sat sidesaddle, fanning out my dress.

"We have to get there before she eats any more of these berries," Raife said, and I nodded in agreement.

—————————

We rode fast and hard through the early morning

to the small farm village of Briar Ridge. I wasn't used to riding for so long. My butt was numb and my legs felt bruised by the time we arrived. The sun was just peeking over the clouds as we pulled our horses up to a small blue farmhouse with a thatched roof. The sun cast illuminated shafts of light over fields of blackberries that spanned out as far as the eye could see.

I recognized the mother immediately, her white hair flowing behind her. She was milking a goatin in an open field, and must have just noticed us. She stopped what she was doing and stood, setting her bucket down as she realized she had guests. Wiping her hands on her apron, she ran over to greet us.

"My lord." She fell into a deep curtsy. "Is... everything okay?"

She was no doubt wondering why the king of the elves was here. We dismounted and the front door to the farmhouse opened. Corleena's father walked out to greet us as well.

"My king. We didn't know to expect a visit," the father said, dropping to one knee and dipping his head in the deepest bow possible. A true sign of humility and respect in the elvin kingdom. In Nightfall, one would go fully flat on the floor to gain the queen's utmost respect.

The king launched right into the heart of the

matter. "My assistant may have found what's been making Corleena so sick."

The mother went rigid, grasping her apron and looked up at me. "What is it?"

"Where is she?" I asked, praying she hadn't eaten any of the berries in the last twelve hours since I'd last seen her.

"She's in the fields, probably eating berr—"

I took off like a rocket, lifting my elegant dress to run for the blackberry fields. "Corleena!" I shouted her name in panic.

"Corleena!" the king's voice came from behind me. Her mother and father had no idea what was happening but they began to scream her name in panic too. They clearly caught on that this was a serious situation.

I hit the densely packed rows of blackberries and slowed, my heart racing. What if she was passed out, bleeding in this very field? What if we were too late?

"I'm here!" a small voice called to my left.

I pivoted, turning and following that voice, coming upon her with a handful of black berries in her hand, one was raised to her mouth.

When she saw me, she frowned in surprise, and I reached out, lightly smacking the fruit from her hand.

"Don't eat those!" I told her.

Tears filled her eyes and I instantly felt bad for scaring her.

"What's going on?" Her mother, the king, and her father ran up behind me and stopped.

I pulled the book from my cloak pocket and opened it, handing it to the mother, spread to the page about the nightlock berries.

"We think she's found some of these and been eating them instead of the true blackberries," I said.

Corleena ran to her parents, clinging to her mother's side. I watched as her mother's eyes widened. The father read over his wife's shoulder, mouth opening in shock. He spun from the book, looking at the bushes around us. He began to scrutinize them, then pulled a few off and inspected them. He moved to another bush, pulling off a leaf and a berry, bringing it to his nose.

His eyes went wide as he dropped them from his hands. "These aren't blackberries." He pointed to the bush to his right. "Those are." He then gestured to the left. He shook his head. "My family has been growing the berries for five generations I... I don't understand how I didn't know."

The king nodded. "You didn't think to look too closely, it's understandable. Have you mass harvested yet? Started making any syrup?"

The farmer shook his head. "Picking season just

started, so not many. Thank the Maker. Just a few locals."

"I'll need a list of who they are so my staff can check on them and warn them," the king said.

They both nodded. "Of course." The wife looked near tears and kept holding tightly to little Corleena.

The father suddenly appeared stricken. "The fields... we'll have to burn them and start over to be safe."

My heart fell into my stomach. Their home was humble, their clothing worn; they did not look like the kind of people who could easily miss a whole season of income and start over.

The king inclined his head. "I have reason to believe this was an invasive species planted by the Nightfall queen. Therefore, it is my responsibility to take care of it. I'll pay you for this season's berries and cover the cost of burning the fields and planting a new lot next year."

The mother grasped her chest, tears rolling down her cheeks, but the farmer shook his head. "My king, I could not accept that. Not after what you've done to save Corleena's life. It's too much."

The wife smacked him lightly in the back of the head and I had to hide a grin.

"My husband is a proud man," the wife explained. "We *humbly* accept your offer, my lord, and next season we will be more watchful now that we know what to look for. We'll spread the word to other farmers too."

Raife nodded. "Very well. My castle treasurer will be in touch." He then bent down to Corleena's level. "Miss Corleena, have you eaten any of those berries last night or today?"

She nodded. "Just one."

Raife reached out and placed his hand on her shoulder. A purple glow emanated from his palm, and for a split second I saw a blackness travel up the vein of his wrist and into his body. He released her and winced slightly.

The mother reached out and held tightly to Corleena, shaking her head. "We didn't know. How could we not have known?"

My heart felt for this family. To be farming black-berries for so long and not realize a fake was in your midst. Even now, I looked at the two different bushes that the farmer had pointed to and could barely see a difference. The points of the leaves on the fakes appeared a tiny bit rounder, the berries a bit plumper, but it was nearly impossible to tell the difference between them.

The king straightened. "Well then, I think you're going to be just fine now."

After another five minutes of the wife and farmer

profusely thanking the king and I, we finally mounted our horses.

I winced as my sore muscles ground into the hard saddle.

Raife noticed. "Hurt?"

I blushed. "Not used to riding."

He looked at me for longer than was socially appropriate and I cleared my throat.

"You saved her life, Kailani. Even after I gave up and told you to put her case out of your head. You should be really proud..."

It was as if the air charged around us. I could feel it as a tangible force.

"I'm proud," he added.

Proud. He was proud of *me*?

It was a silly thing to say, something a teacher said to a student or a father to a child, and yet it unlocked something inside of me. It warmed my heart and made me choke up a little. I hadn't really thought of it as saving her life, but we'd caught her eating the berries and so... I guessed I did.

"It's something anyone would do. If you have the chance to save a life, you should save it."

He chuckled, displaying his handsome smile. "It's not always that easy." He was staring at my forehead and I wondered if there was a bug on it or something.

"Your mind works in a beautiful way, that's why she's healed," he said.

Did he just call my mind *beautiful*? Because that was doing warm things to my insides.

"Have you ever heard of the healing caves?" he asked.

"No."

He kicked his horse and then took off, Cahal following after him, and then myself a moment later, wincing as my butt pounded the hard saddle.

Not another word was spoken. We rode for an hour in a direction I didn't recognize, and I was ready to prop up on my feet to give my backside a rest when the king pulled his horse up to the base of a large mountain. Cahal tied up his horse and went to the mouth of a cave, disappearing inside.

I raised one eyebrow at the king and he dismounted, looking up at me. "Come on."

I sort of loved how informal we'd become over the whopping three days we'd known each other. It would be exhausting to *Yes, my lord, No, Your Highness* every sentence for the next five years.

I slipped off my horse just as an old elvin woman stepped out of the caves with a towel wrapped around her.

Were we at the healing caves he'd mentioned?

The old woman saw the king and bowed deeply

before scurrying off some stone path that led away from the cave opening. I peered past her and noticed a village just beyond it.

Cahal came out and nodded to him. "It's all clear now, my lord," he said.

My mouth popped open. "Did you just kick that sweet elderly lady out so you could go in?"

Raife gave me a mischievous grin. "She could be an elderly assassin."

I moved to playfully slap his shoulder but then thought better of it.

"The village benefits from use of the healing pools. Each time I go in I leave a hefty donation." Raife gestured to a small stone bowl by the opening of the cave. It held copper and silver coins, even a few bottles of honey. The king placed a stack of silver coins inside and then stepped through the opening.

I swallowed hard, looking back at Cahal to see what he was doing. He stood like a sentinel on the side of the door, an arrow nocked in his bow.

"Am I supposed to go in?" I whispered to Cahal.

"Kailani," the king beckoned, and I charged forward into the darkness, unsure what I would find.

After stumbling in the dark a few feet and then turning a corner, I noticed a bright light ahead, which outlined the king's body. He disappeared from view and then I walked into an open cavernous space.

"Holy Maker," I gasped, after moving into the hidden oasis.

The top of the cave was actually open to the outside, so sunlight shone down onto the turquoise liquid. A stream of water trickled down the sides of the mountain rock, filling the pool below.

"It's incredible." There was a splash to my left and I startled, turning to see the king poke his head up out of the water. He was without his tunic but wearing his trousers; the water was crystal clear and I could even see his bare toes. A huge sigh escaped him as he slowly treaded water.

"The only place I can heal," he muttered.

I frowned. "What do you mean?"

He looked my body up and down. Heat crept into my cheeks every time he did that—which was often I was noticing. "Come in."

I blushed. I was wearing a beautiful and expensive silk gown. There was no way I was getting in the water with this on, and wearing just my undergarments would be inappropriate. They were white and totally see-through when wet.

"You can wear my tunic," he said, and then turned to give me his back. "Trust me. You won't feel any pain riding home after a dip in these pools."

Would it heal my sore butt? Now I was curious, and that got me moving. Unlacing the back of my dress

I slipped out of it and folded it onto the rock nearby. I looked up to make sure he was still turned and padded over to his dark tunic, slipping it over my head to cover my small bralette and cream undershorts.

"O-okay," I told him, and then dipped my feet into the water, sitting at the edge. A small tingle worked its way up my legs and I sighed. "Oh wow." It was like the weight my body normally felt from carrying my own skin and bones around all day had left. I just felt... nothing.

"Come all the way in." He was suddenly before me as my legs dangled over the edge, and I chewed on my lip.

"I... never learned to swim and it looks deep."

Reaching up, as if it was no big deal, he hooked his hands under my armpits and plopped me into the water before him. "I've got you."

I've got you.

Those three words did something to me. They worked their way into my soul and I was starting to get really confused about how I felt about my new boss. I swallowed hard, at the same time trying to tread water and also experience the utter and deep relaxation the waters provided. His hands left my armpits and went to my wrists, keeping me above water as my feet kicked around a bit frantically.

"Don't worry. I won't let you drown," he told me.

Being this close to him, to those blue eyes and his long blond hair, his tunicless body, I instantly wondered what it would be like to bed him. I also wondered who he'd been bedding this morning when I interrupted him. Maybe he was a serial seducer just hoping to bed me casually over the next five years I worked for him while he also bedded half of the castle! All while married!

"What are you thinking right now?" he asked, eyes narrowing.

Oh Maker, tell me he can't read my thoughts.

"I'm wondering why you said the pools are the only thing that can heal you," I lied.

His eyes narrowed further at the lie but I didn't care. A woman was entitled to her own thoughts!

"I'm the greatest healer in the realm. There is no one who can match my power. That's how elvin healing works. Someone inferior to your healing power cannot heal you. It's why I'm brought in to the hardest cases and the smaller ones are left with the less capable healers who still need wands."

I'd seen the healing wands and wondered why he didn't use one. I guessed he didn't need to.

I frowned, treading water more slowly now that I knew I wasn't going to drop to the bottom of however deep this pool went.

"So if you fell ill? A palace healer couldn't help

you?" I asked.

He shook his head. "I don't even have a palace healer for that reason. If my staff falls ill, I heal them."

Shock ripped through me. "I didn't know that. Is that well known?"

He eyed me curiously. "No, I probably shouldn't have told you that."

That stung a little, but I knew what he meant.

"How's your backside?" he asked. "Still sore?"

It wasn't. I felt amazing, truth be told. "No, but you could have healed it," I told him.

He smirked. "Would you have let me?"

No. No, I wouldn't have. I would have said I was fine and then suffered. He knew that? Such little time together and already he knew how I worked? Was that why he came here? For me? Surely not, surely for himself as well.

"It didn't hurt that bad," I lied, and then regretted it, forgetting he could tell.

He shook his head. "Two lies. Shall I start keeping count? We might rack up quite a few over the next five years."

I sighed. "Sometimes lies are good. You don't want to know what I was thinking earlier."

That intrigued him; an eyebrow raised and his lips curled. "Oh, I most certainly do."

Okay, he wanted the truth, he could have it.

"I was wondering about the woman you bedded this morning and if you did that often to many women," I said boldly. "If you were going to get married and continue to do it."

His Adam's apple bobbed. "You're right, some lies serve their purpose," was all he said.

He wasn't going to answer me and that was okay, he wasn't entitled to. I opened my mouth to speak when he cleared his throat.

"I would never bed another while married. Dara is a friend that I had an agreement with," he said plainly.

A bedding agreement? I suddenly wanted a male friend who looked like he did to have an agreement with.

Had, he said *had*.

"Had?" I raised an eyebrow.

He sighed. "I'm looking for a wife now, so when Dara came into my room this morning and woke me, I told her the agreement was over."

Jealously flared to life inside of me so strongly I was shocked by it. She woke him for sex? That meant she had access to his room and did that on a regular basis. That also must have been why she was crying. Oh how I wished I could smell a lie!

"Would you like to interrogate me further about my private life?" he asked stonily.

Oops. I'd forgotten I was talking to the king of the

elves. I did that often. He just seemed so normal.

"So," I went for a change in topic, "were you always the greatest healer of your family?" I diverted to hopefully a safer topic, but instantly knew I'd done wrong when I saw a storm brew in his gaze.

Hades! Why did I bring up his dead family? It was just the first thing that I thought of and I was trying not to ask him any more sex questions.

"I was not," he said softly, looking far off at the cave wall as if trapped in a memory. "My sister Trini was, then my father, then me."

The royal family had the most potent healing bloodline. It's how they became royal in the first place.

Pain and sorrow slammed into me so harshly then that I gasped. A vision of dead bodies littering the dining room floor with white foam coming from their mouths flashed into my mind and I whimpered. The elvin king, the queen, Raife's siblings, all with their moonlight-colored hair and fancy clothing. They littered an elegant dining hall, clutching their throats as a young Raife screamed, shooting bursts of purple healing magic at each of them. But it wasn't enough, he wasn't strong enough, and there were too many. I felt his sanity slip away as darkness took him, and now it took me.

In the healing pool, the king's hands ripped away from me and I immediately started to sink, the water coming up to my ears and then covering my face. I kicked my feet frantically but was forced to hold my breath as my head submerged. Just when I thought I might drown, the king dove under the water and grasped me by the waist, pulling me upward.

I breached the water and gasped for air, coughing.

"Hades!" he cursed. "I wasn't thinking. I'm so sorry," he said, pressing my body to his as he rapped on my back and I sputtered for air.

"I'm fine," I muttered, my heart hammering in my throat as he held me smooshed against him. My breasts were pressed against his chest with only a thin piece of material separating us and we seemed to realize it at the same time. He pushed me away from him, holding me at arm's length but not letting me go.

His face looked panicked and I felt his disappointment seep into me. "You trusted me and... I nearly drowned you. I'm sorry, I was trying to give you space because I knew you were feeling... my emotions."

"It's okay," I told him again as he dragged us to the edge of the rock grotto. Once I reached it, I tore away from him and gripped the edge for dear life, hauling myself up over. I lay on my back, panting as my frazzled nerves settled.

He pulled himself out in one elegant move and went to stand but I grasped his wrist, forcing him to look down at me.

When his eyes reached mine, they were steel gray, thinned to slits.

"Tell me what it is." My voice shook.

I didn't need to explain. He knew. I had just felt what he was feeling through touch. I *saw* his family dead for a split second in my mind. This wasn't normal.

He sighed, removing my grip from his, and seated himself next to me. I sat up, turning to face him, and decided to stare him down until he unloaded the entire truth.

He watched me as if wondering how much to tell me.

"This will be like helping Corleena for me," I warned. "I won't rest until I know everything. No book about empaths will go untouched in the library."

A halfcocked smile pulled at his lips and my stomach did a summersault. "Are you threatening to read all the books in my library?" He shook himself. "I'm scared."

I scowled at him and his smile faltered.

"Empaths are *extremely* rare," he said. "So rare in fact that it's believed only a few live at any given time. Like a magical force that the world cannot handle too much of."

Chills broke out onto my arms. "Well, if they are so rare, how do you know about them?"

His whole body collapsed inward and I knew the answer would be painful. "Because my mother was one."

The breath was stolen from my lungs. Even sitting a few inches apart and not touching, I felt the grief from here. He loved her the most. He would never admit that out loud but he did. She was *everything* to him, his protector and nurturer, his inspiration. The grief was all-consuming, cutting into my heart like a physical blow. A tear wobbled in my vision and spilled onto my cheek; he moved to scoot away from me but I reached out to stop him. "Let me take it. Even if only for a moment, let me take the pain," I told him.

He gazed up at me then with such a confused vulnerability I wasn't prepared for it. It was like he was begging me to take it but didn't want to hurt me. Without overthinking it, I leaned in and took him into my arms, hugging him.

Unbearable sadness seeped into me then, but the sigh of relief that escaped him made it all worth it. I had to bite down the sobs that wanted to rip from my throat.

So. Much. Guilt. He felt so guilty for being left alive; it ate at him every second of the day. He'd rather be dead with them than alive alone. Tears flowed down my cheeks unchecked, my throat hurting from trying to keep the wailing inside of me. I wanted to scream, I wanted to pound my chest, I wanted to murder some-one. I was so filled with rage.

Life wasn't fair. I wanted to die. How could one go on living in a dark world like this where six-year-olds were poisoned?

It was at these desperate thoughts that the king pulled away from me and cleared his throat. "We should get back. I have a lot of meetings." He stood, grabbed his boots, and walked out of the cave, taking his sadness with him and leaving me in a tumultuous emotional whirlwind.

What the Hades had just happened?

As I peeled off his wet tunic and slipped into my dress, one thought struck me.

He's so much more broken than I thought.

AFTER OUR LITTLE EMPATHIC EXCHANGE, the king totally closed off to me. He barely looked at me in our meetings later that day. After I tasted his food he asked to dine alone, and now he was getting ready to usher in his first dinner date.

Yes, I was ashamed to admit that while I was thinking of bedding him in the healing pools, I'd forgotten I was also supposed to be helping him find a wife.

After tasting his amazing dinner, I moved to leave the kitchen and return to my room to eat alone.

"Miss Kailani, you have been summoned," one of the waiters called to me.

I frowned, nodding, and then entered the dining hall. The king summoned me? Was he worried I hadn't tasted the food?

When I entered, my gaze immediately went to the woman with the red hair and overly showy cleavage. I recognized her from the portrait her mother had brought. She was talking loudly and I had to force myself not to cringe at her annoying laugh.

Bonnie.

"My lord, is there a problem?" I asked Raife, and curtsied deeply for good measure.

He looked annoyed, all but rolling his eyes. "Miss Harthrop would like her food tasted as well."

I froze, my eyebrows shooting up.

Bonnie nodded. "I am after all an important person in the king's life, and maybe soon the *most* important person. I don't want the Nightfall queen to poison me either."

She shoved her plate over to me and I tried to conceal my shock and disgust for her over-importance of self.

"We wouldn't want that," I said dryly.

Reaching out to one of the empty place settings, I

grabbed a clean fork. Instead of doing my best not to disturb to food, I stabbed the middle of the meat and cheese pie and came away with a huge bite. Putting it into my mouth, I moaned. "It's divine."

Bonnie frowned, looking from me to Raife. I glanced at the king to find he was barely suppressing a smile at my display.

"The roll too," I told her. "I heard the queen likes to bake her poisons in."

Her eyes bugged and she nodded, scooting the roll over to me.

I tore it in half, taking a large bite and relishing the flakiness of it.

"Butter?" she asked, grabbing the small cube of butter from her plate.

I took the entire thing, mushed it into my other bite of roll and downed it.

"Water please," I asked her. "The queen's poison is tasteless."

Bonnie handed me the water with a shaking hand and I drank half the thing in one go.

After setting it down I endured an entire minute of the scared girl watching me and waiting for me to grab my stomach. I was half tempted to, just to mess with her, but would never put the king through that. Not even for a joke.

After my watch showed I was in the clear, I reached out and patted her arm. "Food's safe, my lady."

She all but collapsed into the chair and then looked at Raife. "I don't know how you do that every meal! It's frightening."

I looked down at her plate. It looked like it had been mauled by a catin, and I had to keep myself from smiling.

"Goodnight." I grasped the edges of my dress and curtsied again.

The steel gray-blue eyes watched me all the way back to the kitchen doors.

A mere hour later, I was about to take a bath when a note slid under my door.

Bonnie is a No.

-Raife

For some reason, I felt happy about him immediately rejecting her. She was annoying. Who could live with that laugh forever!?

As I was trying to fall asleep, I couldn't get one image out of my head. The dead people on the ground with foaming mouths, Raife's family. Just thinking of it, and the accompanying guilt that had rushed through me, made my stomach churn. How long could a person live with that guilt before it consumed them?

It was a long time before I slept.

4

The next three days were full of meetings, and healings at the infirmary, and private dates with Raife's top five. Each and every night a note slipped under my door.

They all said the same thing. The girl's name and the word *No*.

Tonight was the last girl, the final night.

Lottie Sherwood.

The council had just left the meeting. Their concern that the king had not announced an engagement after four dates had been evident.

I moved to stand and leave to taste the king's

dinner before his final date, when he let his head drop onto the desk with a loud thud.

I grinned. The king and I had become friendly, showing his personality to me more and more. We didn't speak of what had happened in the healing caves and the deep emotional transference we'd shared there, but he'd been more relaxed around me.

"You look like a man excited for a date," I joked. "I think Lottie Sherwood is the one."

He raised his head to look at me, a red mark on his forehead from where the table had indented it. "When I think of spending the rest of my life with any one of the women I've spent a mere hour with, I want to meet an untimely death."

I snort-laughed and then cleared my throat to cover it. "My lord, they can't have been *that* bad."

He gave me a serious glare. "You have no idea. Come tonight and you'll see. She'll have some flaw that I can't live with—that *you* wouldn't be able to either."

I raised one eyebrow. "You're asking me to crash your date?"

He shrugged. "They aren't *really* dates. Gertie brought her father. It's a formal, stuffy thing. Me bringing my assistant won't be a problem."

Attend the king's date to find a wife? This felt weird, but I was also intrigued, so no way in Hades was I saying no to that.

"I'll be there," I told him and stood.

He nodded and his eyes ran over my red silk dress with black lace. "Maybe dress down a bit. Don't want to make her jealous." He winked.

My entire body warmed at his compliment. It *was* a compliment, right?

I laughed nervously. "Of course, my lord."

After a slight curtsy, I left the room and headed for my sleeping quarters. *Dress down*. That meant I was dressed too nicely, or just that I might show her up? All of my gowns were made with palace approval—I was told to dress this way as the king's representative...

Was he calling me pretty? My mind was so frazzled that I walked past my door and had to circle back.

Twenty minutes later, I wore a navy-blue silk gown with dramatic sleeves that covered my arms to my elbows. The fashion lover in me couldn't allow this outfit to be too boring, so I paired them with lime green high-heeled shoes. The clothing allowance the crown provided me basically allowed for a new dress every other day. I was constantly going to the seamstress to be fitted or look at new fabrics. It was my favorite part of the week.

After stepping into the kitchen, a new chef greeted me.

I frowned. "Where is Brulier?"

"His mother fell sick. He's gone to travel to

Winding Meadow to visit her. He'll be back next week. You the taster?" He eyed me up and down with scrutiny.

I nodded, and he set two identical plates of food before me. I'd taken to tasting the prospective wives' food as well. I might as well get used to it, since no one else had come forward and applied for the job. As the king said, no one wanted a twelve-month clock on their life. I tried not to think about it.

Digging into the large hunk of meat, I cut off a small slice from the corner and ate it. Next I grabbed a green bean and then a half a spoonful of some sort of gravy. I did the same to the next plate quickly, eager to meet this woman and attend one of the king's dates. Once my watch had shown that a full minute had passed since my last bite, I took the two plates through the double doors and spread a smile across my lips.

"Good evening," I greeted the beautiful woman before me, and then curtsied to the king. Lottie was wearing a peach ballgown with white lace trim; her bright blond hair was tied up into a cascade of curls with braids down the side. She was breathtaking. I instantly felt jealous for some reason.

Setting the plate before her and then the king, I made my way to my seat, where I saw a plate of food was already waiting for me.

"This is my personal assistant, Kailani," he told

Lottie. "I thought it would be nice for her to join us. I spend a lot of time with her, so I'd like for you to get to know her as well."

A flicker of annoyance crossed her features, but she turned it into a radiant smile. "Of course. Hello, Kailani."

"It's nice to meet you, Lottie. I hear you like to play chess?" I took a sip of my water, as a dry tickle had formed in my throat.

She nodded, putting the fork into her meat. The king raised a green bean to his lips.

"I do enjoy the mental stimulation," she said.

A cramp formed in my stomach and all at once fear rushed into me.

Dry throat. Cramps.

The king was just about to bite the tip of the green bean when I stood up so fast that the chair fell backwards. Reaching forward, I ripped the fork from his hand and threw it on the ground. Next I reached for his and Lottie's plates and tossed both to the floor.

"What the Hades!?" Lottie yelled, and I doubled forward in agony. My throat was on fire, my stomach felt like it was chewing on razor blades, and I knew I was about to die. Lottie seemed to catch on then, standing and screaming, "*Poison!*" as she fled from the room.

I looked up at the king and there was so much fear and pain on his face that my heart broke for him.

"No," he breathed, rushing forward to take me into his arms. I felt it then, bleeding from him and into me. All the trauma of watching his family die was coming right back to him. Funny how I was the one dying and yet I was worried about him.

"It's okay." I reached up and wiped away a tear that had slid from his eye.

He blinked rapidly, as if shocked that a tear had produced itself, and then he shook his head. Placing one hand on my stomach, he grit his jaw. "That *bitch* will not take another from me," he declared.

All at once it was like the stomach cramping and throat burning was pulled out of my body through my navel. The king's face went red; he started to gag and then he fell backwards.

"Raife!" I screamed, sitting up and throwing myself on top of him. His face was purple as if he couldn't breathe, and I remembered what he said then. Why he never saved previous people who had been poisoned by Queen Zaphira. It was too hard to know how much poison to take from the person if it was tasteless and odorless. He was presumably supposed to take half, but he'd taken it all—the idiot took every bit of poison from me.

"Why would you do that!?" Tears leaked from my

eyes in panic as I beat on his chest. "Give it back. Give it back to me," I pleaded, grasping his sweaty palms as if I could suck the poison back into my body.

My chest felt tight, my stomach burning; thoughts of impending doom took over me. I knew they were his thoughts, not mine, and I wasn't shocked when I felt excitement rush through him as well.

He wants to die. Maybe not actively but for the pain to stop, for the waiting to be poisoned by the queen every day. He was excited to leave all that behind, to be done with it and join his family in the heavenly realms.

Something instinctual kicked in and I sat on top of him, my legs straddling his waist, and started to do chest compressions. It might not be some fancy and magical form of elvin healing, but it worked in the human world. If his face was purple, it meant he couldn't breathe, so I would breathe for him. I would do everything I could to save him because I wasn't ready to let him go.

Leaning forward, I pressed my lips to his, pinching his nose with my fingers, and exhaled. It was as if lightning hit my spine; an electrical charge ripped through my back and the breath I exhaled into his mouth was... purple. Small bits of it leaked from the seal of his lips despite my best efforts. I gasped, taking some of the purple breath back into my mouth, and that's when he coughed, the blue color leaving his face, changing into a violent red, and then peach.

He stared at me wide-eyed, chest heaving as I sat atop him, staring down in complete and utter bewilderment.

"You stupid man!" I screamed, pounding his chest. "I thought you were dying!"

He grasped my hand, catching it midair, his gaze slowly hooding over. "I was, and if you don't get off of me I think my body is about to show you how alive I really feel right now." He looked down at his crotch and my legs straddled over it and I blushed, throwing myself off of him and to the floor beside him.

He sat up, resting his arms over his knees, and ran his fingers through his hair.

"What happened?" I asked. "You... you shouldn't have done that. I'm not worth it."

His life was way more important than mine.

He cast me a long side glance, opened his mouth to speak, and then the doors from the kitchens burst open. It was Mrs. Tirth. "The chef has fled. Lottie said there was poison? Is everyone okay?" She looked frantically from me to the king.

Raife stood, fists balled. "Fled where?" he growled.

Mrs. Tirth swallowed hard. "The gardens, my lord. Minutes ago—"

Raife took off out the dining hall and through the

kitchens, seemingly to give chase to the chef who'd just tried to kill us both.

It was at this precise moment that I had a mental breakdown. Sobs wracked my chest as I processed everything that had just happened.

"Oh dear." Mrs. Tirth crouched beside me and helped me stand. "Did he heal you?" She looked confused as to how I was still alive.

I nodded.

Then I healed him back ... I think, I wanted to say, but didn't. Whatever that purple breath thing was, it was freaky and I was too shaken to process it properly.

"What's happened to your hair?" She reached out and fingered my locks.

I frowned, confused at what she meant, then I saw that in a bed of my brown hair was a thick streak of white.

That was too much for me to handle. I just shook my head and burst into tears again.

"Oh, hush, darling. It's okay." She pulled me into a hug and it reminded me of my sweet auntie. Oh how I missed her and her big strong hugs. I wondered what she was doing right now and if she was worried about me. If she had any idea how close I just came to death, she would have completely lost it.

Mrs. Tirth walked me back to my rooms and I slipped out of my gown and soaked in a hot bath. Afterward, I put on a short blue satin nightgown and decided I'd read by the window to get my mind off of things. I loved science and mathematics, but for times like these only a romance novel would do. Luckily, the king had many in his library, I supposed from his sisters or even his mother.

The one I had my eye on was by J. Hall. It was about a fallen winged being called an angel and her soulmate lover. I stroked the gold feather embossed on the cover and then startled when a small rap sounded at my door.

I set the book down and rushed forward just as the white note slipped under the door.

I held my breath as I opened it.

It was longer than all the others and I brought it back to the couch with me to read.

I HOPE YOU'RE OKAY. *I didn't want to wake you if you were resting.*

Thanks for... saving me.

Lottie is a No. She told Mrs. Tirth she could never live in constant fear of being poisoned.

Back to the drawing board tomorrow? The elders want a meeting first thing in the morning.

-Raife

. . .

I STROKED THE WORDS, *I hope you're okay.* Never in a million years did I think I'd be at the service of a king to pay off my debts, and I hadn't expected him to be a decent man. Kings were jerks, rich bastards who acted above you and never let you speak your mind. Not Raife. It was my job to find him a wife, and *dammit* I was going to. I knew now more than ever how important getting the council to back his war was. The queen wouldn't stop coming after him—his future wife, their children. If Raife and his army really stood a chance at taking her out, then I wanted to help him. It would throw Nightfall into chaos for a small time but then one of her more level-headed sons would take over. Her eldest, the psychopath of the family, was killed several months ago by Dragon King Drae Valdren. Now all that was left were her six sons who seemed decently normal as far as rulers went. Nothing like their monster mother.

I barely slept. Instead I drew up pages and pages of ideas. After crossing them out, I landed on the three most plausible and wrote them in my best cursive script.

1. *An arranged marriage like the fae do, with a highborn family where Raife pays a dowry*

of sorts and the woman agrees without even seeing him.

2. *A grand ball with every single woman in all of Archmere in attendance. He would pick the prettiest one after a night of dancing and propose the very next day.*

3. *And lastly, a totally desperate idea, a fake marriage. A friend or old lover who would agree to a charade to convince the council he was settled and on his way to having heirs so he could fund his war. Dara?*

THE NEXT MORNING, I wore a blue crushed velvet gown with a sleeveless lace-up corset, and clutched my little marriage ideas parchment proudly.

The meeting with the council was in five minutes, and after we heard what they had to say I'd scheduled in some time for just Raife and I to brainstorm my ideas and which one he might like.

I stopped by the kitchens. Mrs. Tirth was there with a frown as the rest of the staff cleaned and did dishes around her. Everyone looked sullen and the mood was low. "He's decided to fast today," she said.

My stomach dropped. He was too scared to eat. After last night he'd rather not eat than be poisoned again. I didn't blame him.

I frowned. "Do we know anything about the poison used?"

She shook her head. "The queen's special blend. Tasteless, scentless, and now takes at least five minutes to kick in."

I picked up an apple and took a bite, deciding to just have the small piece of fruit for breakfast. Surely the poison couldn't be injected into an apple, could it?

After I swallowed the one bite, I wondered if it *could* be injected into an apple and chucked it into the trash. "When will Chef Brulier be back?" I asked her.

She shrugged. "His mother is dying. Old age, nothing that can be done."

He was the only chef I trusted.

"Very well. Until he returns, I will be cooking all of the king's and my meals," I informed her.

Half the kitchen staff stopped then and turned to me.

Mrs. Tirth frowned. "You cook?"

I shrugged. "Kept my aunt and I alive, how hard can it be? You're all excused until further notice!" I said loudly.

They froze, looking worriedly from Mrs. Tirth back to me.

"You heard her," Raife's voice boomed from behind me, and I jumped a little.

They set down what they were working on and

began to leave. Mrs. Tirth sensed this was a private moment, and chose to see herself out as well.

"You can cook?" he asked.

I turned, drinking him in. He wore a high-collared gray silk tunic, and his hair was tied into a knot at the back of his neck. There were dark bags under his eyes indicating he hadn't slept much either.

"It may not be up to a king's liking, but I can make stew and basic flatbreads. I can keep us fed and not poisoned."

He reached up and brushed his fingers across his chin. "I thought you hated doing dishes?"

I nodded. "I do. I won't be doing them. We're calling the maids back every night to clean up."

A grin pulled at his lips and his gaze traveled down my gown. My body heated when he did, and I hoped it was from arousal and not injected apple poison. I wanted to ask him what happened last night, what the purple breath healing thing was, why he looked so good in a simple gray silk tunic...

"Are you okay?" He reached up and ran the back of his finger along the outside of my neck, down my throat and to my collarbone.

I froze, melting under his touch.

He pulled his hand back as if realizing what he was doing. "I mean, my throat is still a little raw," he said.

I shook my head. "I'm fine... physically speaking."

He nodded. "And emotionally?"

"A total wreck inside," I confirmed, which caused him to bark out in laughter.

Hades, I loved that sound. I couldn't help but grin, as his joy was infectious.

"Well, that makes two of us," he said, and eyed my apple in the trash with the missing bite.

I fingered the white lock of my hair at the base of my neck and Raife reached up to touch it.

"I was in the library late last night and read that a traumatic event can cause the hair to go white," he said.

"It can?" I asked.

He nodded, and I tied my hair up in a bun, tucking it away so neither of us had to look at it.

"The council is waiting," I told him. I wanted to ask what that purple breath was, but I honestly couldn't handle the answer. Had I saved him? Was that really what happened? Because if so I was really starting to freak out and I didn't want to think about it anymore.

He nodded, gesturing that I lead the way as his hand came to the small of my back to usher me out of the kitchens. I turned back and looked at the small space. "Post two of your most trusted Bow Men at each kitchen entrance and exit. No one in or out but me and the dishwasher. *No one* else. Not even Mrs. Tirth. This is my kitchen now." I liked the woman, but I didn't trust anyone right now.

He frowned, looking concerned, but nodded.

THE MEETING with the council was more intense than I had prepared for.

"I'm sorry to hear of another assassination attempt," Haig said. "But this is proof we need you to take a wife and start a family lest you be wiped out by the Nightfall queen."

Raife rubbed the bridge of his nose. "I'm working on it."

"Are you?" Aron asked. "Because the mothers say you haven't called any of the girls back for second dates."

Raife looked at me pleadingly and I held up the piece of parchment with my ideas on it. "Actually, gentlemen, I have his short list right here. We are going over it after this meeting. Picking the woman you will spend the rest of your life with is no small matter. You're all married, you should know that," I told them, eyeing the swirled elvin rings on their marriage fingers.

I knew Raife could smell the lie, but he wouldn't care.

The council shifted in their seats. "We want a

proposal by the end of the week. Wedding next month, and an heir by next year. You got it, son?" Haig said with the stern voice of a caring father.

Raife sighed. "I got it."

Geez. That wasn't really leaving a lot of time to fall in love and travel the countryside, to grow together before throwing a screaming baby in the mix. Don't get me wrong, I loved children; babies smelled like new life and joy, but they also took up your entire day and night and your life was never the same after you had one. I wanted at least five years alone with my husband before popping any of those out.

Poor Raife.

His whole life was dictated by this council, this kingdom, this life.

The council bid us a good day then, and left the room, latching the door behind them as they left.

Raife turned to me and eyed the parchment. "Short list, huh?"

I shrugged. "I mean, not a total lie, it's a short list of ideas." I handed it to him.

He read it, his eyes going from the parchment to me and back to the parchment. His gaze returned to me and he rubbed his chin, chewing on his bottom lip. "You might be on to something here, Lani."

The pet name took me off guard.

Lani. It's what my auntie and close friends called me.

"Oh, which do you like?" I leaned forward to see his finger on the third, most desperate option.

Fake Marriage.

"I mean... that's a last resort after the fancy ball and—"

"I don't want a fancy ball or some big, drawn-out thing. I want to get married, get the council off my ass, and then get the funding for my war."

My heart hurt a little that he didn't want the true love option. The big ball would have been fun to plan.

I nodded. "Very well. Do you have a trusted confidant that would agree to such an arrangement? Maybe... Dara?" It killed me to say it. I didn't know why I was jealous of his whore but I was.

His cheeks reddened and he shook his head. "She's not... wife material."

Relief rushed through me but I hid it. "Well, who did you have in mind?"

He stared at me for an uncomfortably long amount of time. Setting the parchment down, he reached out and took my hand. "You."

Complete and total shock ripped through me. "Me?"

He nodded. "We spend all day together anyway, every meal, all these meetings. The council would totally buy it, and you've become like a best friend to me. I genuinely enjoy spending time with you."

Best. Friend. It was like a knife to the heart. I was afraid he'd somehow feel the pain of it, so I gently slipped my hand from his. "Oh," I said, and got up, starting to pace the room.

What is happening?

"You're pacing," he observed.

"I'm processing a fake marriage with the elvin king," I deadpanned.

He inclined his head. "I would of course increase your pay. It would have to be believable. I cannot have the council getting wind of this in the middle of a war with the Nightfall queen and then take my funding."

Increase my pay. A *paid* position. *Ouch.* The knife he'd stabbed in my heart twisted deeper.

"You haven't said anything," he said, nervousness creeping into his voice.

"Still processing." I lapped the small room, wearing lines in the carpet.

A fake marriage to the king. Like... with kisses and sharing a bed and stuff? "Would we... consummate this marriage?" I blushed as I said it.

He looked surprised by that. "No. It's fake. No one needs to know what goes on behind closed doors. But hand holding and the occasional kiss would be required."

Best. Friend.

Kissing him was something I had thought about—before he'd called me his *best friend*. Now I just wanted to die. I was so grateful I was the empath and not him.

"Increasing my pay for it feels weird. I'm not a whore," I finally said, and turned to face him.

He flinched as if I'd slapped him. "I don't think you are—I would *never* think that. I was merely trying to make the arrangement attractive to you."

"How long are we talking?"

Was I seriously considering this?

"However long it takes me to win a war against the queen. I've already gotten the king of Embergate to agree to join me. I'll be working on Lucien Thorne and Axil Moon next."

Wow, he'd gotten the word of the dragon king and would be going after the fae king and wolf king next? "You plan to go after the queen united?" I asked in surprise.

He nodded. "Only way it will work. She's regrettably too powerful otherwise."

He was right. I was feeling more confident about his war efforts now that I knew he had planned to get the others involved.

"I want my aunt healed," I blurted out. "I don't want extra money, but I want you to extradite my aunt and heal her, set her up in a home here. I don't want her living in there if you will bring war to the Nightfall realm."

He stood. "Done. I'm sorry I didn't offer to heal her earlier."

Done? Just like that? I wondered what else I could have asked for.

"The council said they expect a child next year." I blushed.

He nodded. "I'll tell them we are trying. You are half human, so that could be to blame for a few years."

Holy Hades, was I really saying yes to this?

Raife sidestepped the table and took both of my hands in his. "Kailani, ever since I was fourteen years old and the queen robbed me of the privilege of a family, I vowed to get revenge. To get justice for my mother, my father, Trini, Raelin, Dane, Akara, Gwen, and Sabe."

Hearing their names caused tears to line my eyes. I could feel the emotions rolling through him like waves. Excitement at this idea, that it could work to appease the council, anger at the queen, protection and adoration for me.

His hands pulled away and he cleared his throat. "Do me this favor and I will deny you nothing. For so long as I live, whatever you ask I will grant it. Please, Lani."

Whoa. He was all but begging me.

So we would marry, defeat the queen and then we divorce? I guessed there were worse ways to spend my twenties.

"Okay, Raife. I'll do it. For you and for your family."

He grinned, rushing forward to pick me up. His arms came around the back of my legs as he stood, vaulting me into the air and spinning me around. Laughter bubbled out of me as pure elation rushed through him and into my body. This moment right here made being an empath a wonderful thing. Feeling someone else's joy, sharing in their elation, it was beautiful.

He set me down then and slammed his open hand on the table in excitement. "It's time to plan a wedding. And then a war."

I mean, it wasn't what every blushing bride wanted to hear, but I'd take it.

Have you ever wondered how your life got to its current place? As I stood outside the door to the meeting Raife was having with his council, I wondered how mine had come to this moment. I fingered the delicate elvin gold, its swirl shape curving around my marriage finger. I'd just come from the seamstress, giving her ideas on how to design my fake wedding dress to wear to my fake wedding. Now I pressed my ear to the door as Haig bellowed, "She's half human, weak, a liability!"

I winced.

Raife all but growled, "*Don't* speak about my future wife, *your* future queen, like that."

"My lord, I merely mean any children you have might be compromised in the healing gift department if her human lineage were to overwhelm—"

"She's an empath," Raife declared, and the room erupted into gasps.

My heart hammered in my throat at his revealing of what felt like *my* secret.

"You're sure?" Haig asked, shock apparent in his voice.

"Don't insult my intelligence," Raife said.

"Let's focus on the information that the king has in fact taken a betrothed," Foxworth cut in. "This is good news. When is the wedding?"

"Next month. We can't wait to be wed," Raife added quickly.

He couldn't wait to start a war with the queen was what he meant.

A deep chuckle came from the room. I didn't recognize who it was until he spoke. "All this flirting and casting long glances at her, I knew you were falling in love," Greylin added.

I blushed, wishing that were true.

Raife cleared his throat. "What can I say, she's

beautiful and smart and... all the things you would want in a life partner."

Oh, how I wished I could smell a lie!

"We should host an engagement party tomorrow. The court will be thrilled to know you've made a decision. Maybe now the daily questions from the mothers will stop," Haig added with a mild annoyance. Were the mothers seeing Haig and asking about when Raife was going to choose? Now I felt a bit bad about that.

An engagement party tomorrow sounded soon, but Raife agreed immediately. "I'll have my event planner get everything set up."

At the sound of the chairs scooting backwards, I jumped deep into the hallway, at the far wall with my hands clutching my notes and the king's schedule for the rest of the day. When the door opened, Haig was the first to see me.

His eyes raked over me suspiciously before falling on the engagement ring at my finger, and his features softened.

"Congratulations, Kailani. We look forward to the upcoming nuptials."

I gave him a big gummy smile, acting the part of an excited new bride. "Thank you, sir."

The other council members stepped out, each one congratulating me, and then they left down the long corridor to some part of the castle I had yet to explore.

Raife finally stood before me, taking in my lavender dress with a deep V-neck and sheer sleeves. "Foxworth and Greylin are sold on it," he whispered. "But we need to convince Haig and Aron."

I swallowed hard. "Convince?"

Raife nodded casually. "You know, that we're really in love."

Right.

I tossed my hair over one shoulder. "Well, not to brag or anything, but I did get top marks in theatre class my upper-class year."

Raife smirked, looking insanely handsome. "I took theatrics in my upper-class years as well. Top marks."

"Game on, then," I challenged him.

He reached out and threaded his fingers through mine, slowly so that they stroked my palm on their way, which caused heat to flush my chest and cheeks.

"Shall we do lunch now, darling?" he purred, easily dropping into the acting, and my stomach dropped.

I simply nodded, unable to speak for fear of my voice cracking. Being fake married to a troll with warts on his nose would involve superb acting. Pretending I was in love with Raife Lightstone was a little too easy.

AFTER I MADE US LUNCH, Raife offered to do the dishes, insisting that bringing another person into our "safe" kitchen was a risk.

I frowned, setting the plates in the sink. "You're the king. Have you ever done a dish in your life?" I asked.

He shrugged, picking the dirty plate up and eyeing the scrub brush. "I'm the most educated man in this castle, how hard can it be?" He grabbed the bar of soap and rubbed it over the plate, making small circles and causing the food to mash into the soap. I tried to grab my mouth and to cover the laugh, but a snort came out and Raife glared at me.

"I'm sorry, my love..." I practiced the pet name. Raife and I agreed that even alone we should pretend to be engaged and in love so that we didn't get too confused with the roles. "The soap goes on the brush, then the brush goes on the plate and makes bubbles."

He scowled. "There are two ways to do everything."

I nodded. "But this is the only way that keeps the soap clean and free of crumbs."

Reaching into the running water, he flicked some at me playfully, causing me to shriek and stumble backwards. "You're sexy when you're acting like a know-it-all," he said.

My chest heaved. This was above and beyond the acting. Right?

Best friend, he called me his best friend, I reminded myself.

"I try." I shrugged cutely, unsure what else to do. Hearing Raife Lightstone call me sexy had caused all the blood to rush from my head to another place.

Raife looked over at me. "Are you okay with this last-minute engagement party? Sorry I didn't have time to ask you."

He was so thoughtful, checking in with me. I nodded. "Yes, but I have no idea what to wear."

Raife chuckled; he knew how much I loved fashion. "Why don't you take the rest of the day off to go and see Samarah and pick out your design and fabric."

"Really?" I squealed.

He nodded and I rushed forward, popping onto my tiptoes to brush a quick kiss onto his cheek.

I felt his body stiffen beneath mine, and then I tore out of the kitchen in search of the seamstress. I needed a dress that would blow a kingdom away, or at the very least Raife Lightstone.

THE NEXT DAY PASSED QUICKLY. We had meetings and healings up until the very hour before the party. The event was catered by a local company who was delighted to have the honor of doing so in the head chef's absence. Raife and I both agreed it was too risky to eat at the event and that we would eat before, which we just had.

"I need to go get ready," I mentioned.

He nodded, looking over some parchments. "See you there, love," he said offhandedly.

There was a butler in the room taking our plates so I knew this display was for him, but I couldn't deny hearing him call me "love" did strange things to my stomach.

I rushed back to my room to find that two of Samarah's assistants were there, waiting to dress me.

"Oh, bless you," I told them as we all rushed inside.

I quickly stripped to my undergarments as they hoisted the large deep purple dress over my head.

As they began to tighten the corseted back, I peered down at the intricate beadwork and artistry. "You must have been sewing all night," I murmured in awe.

One of them yawned and nodded. "Samarah is asleep now. We will be right after."

I reached out and grasped both of their hands. "Thank you. I really appreciate you."

They both beamed at me. "Of course, Kailani. It's a great honor."

After they had me in the dress, I slipped into some

silver heels and then sat down while they intricately braided my hair.

There was a knock at the door and one of the hand-maidens answered.

"A gift from the king," a male voice I recognized said.

A gift from Raife?

I peered over my shoulder to see one of Raife's trusted Bow Men at the door. The assistant took the gift from him and brought the small package to me.

It was wrapped in pale blue silk. I untied it to reveal a beautiful glass bottle of perfume.

There was a note.

Thought this would smell amazing on you - Raife

My heart hammered in my chest at the romantic gesture. The girls doing my hair must have peeked over my shoulder and read the note because one of them sighed. "That's so sweet."

I smiled, unsure if the perfume gift and desire to smell it on me was genuine or all part of the lie.

When the girls were done, they left and I sprayed two puffs of the fragrance, one on my wrist and one on my neck. Inhaling deeply, I smiled. It *did* smell good.

There was a knock at the door and I strolled across the room, pulling it open.

Raife stood there in a dark gray silk tunic with a

high collar. His hair was slicked back into a ponytail at his nape, and I suddenly forgot to speak.

"Wow," he said, as he looked me up and down.

I grinned. "I got your gift."

Stepping forward, I held my wrist to his nose. He clasped my hand in his and pulled me closer so that I was only inches away from his body. Leaning his nose into my wrist, he inhaled and sent a shiver down my spine.

Emotions were coming off of him strongly, and none of them had to do with grief or anger as they normally did. These were all desire and satisfaction.

"Ready, my lord?" a Bow Man asked in the hallway, and I was snapped from my trance.

Raife dropped my hand and slipped his fingers into mine, again stroking my palm as he did. It was a subtle signature move that I wasn't sure he knew caused me so much delight.

Walking the hallway hand in hand, we nodded to the staff who had lined up to get a look at us.

"Congratulations, my lord," one of them said.

"Wishing you many years of happiness, Your Highness," another said.

He thanked them and smiled and waved until we stepped up to the open doors of the large ballroom. Hundreds of voices could be heard inside, and I suddenly became nervous, my palms going slick with sweat.

Raife looked sideways at me. "Is the woman who once took a slave trader to the ground... scared?" I reached over and lightly punched his arm, causing the Bow Men to tense beside us.

"No. I'm just... nervous."

Raife grinned. "Same thing."

"Is not," I argued.

Before we could talk about it any further, Raife had pulled me into the room. Then over a hundred pairs of eyes were on us.

Maker help me. I hated crowds. I just wanted to go home and curl up with a good book.

As if sensing my desire to bolt, Raife tucked me closer to his side and brought his hand up to wave at the now clapping masses of people.

Everyone was dressed in their finest silks; live music was playing, and two large buffet tables lined the edges of the walls. There were even decorations of silver silk streamers and purple flowers. I was amazed the castle staff was able to put on such a grand event with such short notice.

People rushed to form a line and greet the king and I. They spoke with excitement about the upcoming wedding and wished us happiness and many children.

Raife handled all the talking and smiling like a champion. He was born for this. I, however, leaned into him, smiling shyly and thanking people with as few words as possible.

The entire time, Raife had slowly been leading us to the middle of the dance floor, and once we got there the band stopped mid-song and started up again. This time it was a slower tune, something very romantic.

The crowd took the hint and backed away, forming a large circle around us. Raife clasped my hips and then leaned forward into my ear. "Dance with me," he whispered.

My body melted at his touch. Without a word, I draped my arms behind his neck and pulled back to look into his gray-blue eyes, letting him lead the dance.

He was peering at me with an intensity I couldn't decipher. I could feel the emotions stirring within him. The most predominant one... was fear. I wanted to ask what he was afraid of, but now wasn't the time.

He leaned forward then and whispered against my neck. "Promise me something, Lani," he huffed.

"Anything," I said quickly. I was like clay in his hands, under a spell that I hadn't even realized he'd cast. Everything was blurring. Fake or real, I didn't know. I just wanted to stay like this forever.

"Promise me you won't fall in love with me," he breathed, and I stiffened as he pulled back to look into my eyes.

Fake. This was all *fake.* I needed to remember that. He was warning me of that.

I nodded, and then rested my head on his shoulder so he wouldn't see my eyes tearing up.

Thinking I could be fake-married to Raife Lightstone without getting hurt was starting to look less and less likely.

Oh Maker, what had I gotten myself into?

6

The next morning I awoke in a weird mood. I'd been falling into this betrothal with Raife pretty hard and it all came crashing down when he'd bluntly told me not to fall in love with him. Now I was going to make an active effort to keep this illusion separate in my mind. Raife was my employer. Raife was a business arrangement. Raife was going to be my *fake* husband.

With that in mind, I settled into the day as I always did. Cooking us breakfast, running his meetings, and then breaking for lunch.

After lunch, he did the dishes, an act I once saw as

romantic but now saw as a duty to keep the kitchen poison free.

"The Bow Men are taking me out later for drinks to celebrate," Raife said as he haphazardly scrubbed the plate with the brush. "When we do this, the wives have a social night of sorts. A crafting club or something. Would you like to go?"

Crafts? I mean, I'd rather a book club, but I wouldn't mind making some girlfriends, especially if I was about to become queen.

That fact hadn't really settled into me yet that I was not only marrying the king of the elves but that I was going to become the people's queen. A fake queen but a queen nonetheless.

"Sure. I'd love that," I told him.

He nodded. "I'll take you over to Cahal's wife's house. Just after dinner."

I wrung my hands together nervously, a bit shy to bring up the next topic. "Have you given any more thought to how you will get my aunt here to heal her?"

He set the plates on the drying rack and turned off the water. Facing me, he dried his hands on a towel. "I gave you my word and promise, I will bring her here and heal her soon, but I don't think I can do it before the wedding."

A month? She had to wait another month of worrying how I was? She probably thought I had been sold to the cruel fae king and was in chains all day long.

"The reason for this is that an extraction from the Nightfall territory is not a small feat. It will require a dozen laws to be broken, hundreds of gold coins to be spent, and lives could be lost. I will have to get the council's approval, and I fear they will not say yes until you are queen."

Wow, lives lost, laws broken... I hadn't really thought that through when I'd asked him to do it. My aunt had another month of the seizure medication, which was cutting it close, but I nodded. She'd be okay for another month. "Thank you."

The rest of the day passed with the usual business that was the king's life. He'd been stuck up at the infirmary healing for the past three hours while I made a simple dinner of boiled eggs and seared meat with salad.

I wasn't able to do any of the fancy pastry stuff, but Raife wasn't complaining and I was enjoying not fearing for my life with every chew and swallow.

Dinnertime came and went and still the king wasn't back from the infirmary, so I decided to pack the plated food with stainless steel lids into a basket and go see what was keeping him. After entering the front reception area of the infirmary, I waved to the healer on duty who recognized me. "He's been in surgery for hours. Four-year-old child fell and became impaled, not sure she will make it," the nurse told me.

Oh Maker.

That sounded awful, and I knew the cases with children affected Raife more deeply than adults. They all reminded him of the siblings he couldn't save.

Dropping the dinner basket off with her and asking her to watch it for me, I shuffled down the hallway in search of the king.

I found him in the operating theatre, hunched over the lifeless body of a child with blood *everywhere*. A gasp ripped from my throat at the sight of the gruesome scene as I watched on through the glass.

"I cannot make blood appear out of nowhere!" Raife snapped to a nurse. There was no family in the viewing room and I knew why. This was way too traumatic to watch. They were probably in the waiting room, praying that the Maker protect their child. A sudden calmness came over me, and that same instinctual urge I'd had when the king was dying welled within me now. Walking briskly from the viewing area, I crossed through the double doors into the actual operating room.

Once I was standing under the bright lights and looking at the scene firsthand, Raife's head snapped in my direction.

"Out!" he roared.

The nurse with him looked shocked at his outburst but I ignored it, merely looking down at the lifeless little girl on the table. Somehow I knew that her soul was about to leave her body; she was on death's door. And as freaked out as I was, I couldn't help but follow this instinct inside of me.

"Lani, no!" the king growled, when I crossed the room quickly and reached for the child. Grasping her face, I angled it up towards me and then leaned forward, readying my lips to press to hers.

"I forbid it!" Raife screamed in a panicked shout, and lunged for me.

I didn't know what his fear was about, but it was too late. My lips touched the child's and I exhaled. This time I didn't pinch her nose shut or press my lips hard to make a seal—in fact, they barely touched hers, but the purple magical breath that left me filled her lungs and washed over her face. The nurse gasped at the same time the little girl did, turning it into a sputtering cough.

Raife ripped me away, holding my shoulders tightly and then looking up at my hair with absolute terror in his eyes.

My hands shook. Would there be another lock of white hair? If there was, what did it mean? Stress like Raife said? I didn't feel stressed.

"She's... blessed," the nurse breathed, staring at me in shock.

Blessed? She said that like it was a known thing. A person, a name.

"Mommy," the little girl wept, sitting up easily like she wasn't just covered in blood and dying moments before.

Tears ran down my cheeks as the confusion settled into me. Did I save her life? How was that possible? What was the purple breath?

Raife leaned forward, resting his forehead on mine. "I can't save you from your own heart," he breathed, sending shockwaves of confusion into me.

What? He can't save me from my own heart? What the Hades did that even mean?

He stepped back. "Miss Baka." Raife turned on the nurse, who was consoling the scared child. "I will need you to sign a sworn statement promising that you will keep the nature of my wife-to-be's healing powers a secret. She is to become the next queen, and it is for her utmost safety that this does not leave the room."

Dread settled in my gut. I wondered if maybe in my ignorance healing the child hadn't been the smartest thing to do. Not that I'd known that's what would happen, but also I wouldn't change it if I did.

The nurse glanced from my hair to the king and

back to the girl and nodded frantically. "Of course, my lord."

Raife was pissed; he was flicking glances my way with his jaw gritted. Bending down, he looked the little girl in the eyes. "I healed you. Are you ready to go see your parents?"

The little girl nodded, wiping the tears from her eyes, and Raife slipped his hand into hers. "Miss Baka, can you please take little Oaklyn back to her parents in the waiting room? I'll have a member of my staff bring those parchments by later."

The nurse appeared shaken as she nodded and then pulled the girl from the room. When the doors shut, Raife stared up into the viewing room seemingly to make sure it was empty.

"Why are you mad?" I asked nervously, pulling at the fabric of my dress.

Raife sighed, pinching the bridge of his nose. "You've just put a target on your back, a target we don't need."

I swallowed hard. "What do you mean? What was that? Raife, tell me what I just did. You're hiding something."

He walked over to me, placing a hand atop each shoulder, and looked me right in the eyes. "You're what they call *blessed*. You can perform the *Breath of Life* and bring someone back from the brink of death, or heal them from otherwise unhealable things."

I didn't have a reaction, I just blinked at him in shock. "Is that an empath thing? Your mom could do it too?"

Bring someone back from the brink of death? That wasn't possible.

He released my shoulders. "No, it's something else entirely. Something so rare it's a myth. We don't even have books about it, just stories."

Well, it was shocking, but I couldn't help but see it as a blessing, which was probably why it was named so. "How wonderful to be able to save someone's life, Raife. This cannot be a bad thing."

"It's horrible!" he shouted, scaring me. "The blessed have only so many Breaths of Life in them before they give their own life and die. Each time your hair goes white, you've given one away. When the last strand turns, you will *die*."

I stumbled backwards, pulling my hair out in front of my face to see it. He was right, more had turned white since I'd saved the little girl. Way more than when I'd saved Raife. Maybe the more energy used meant the more hair turned white. The more of my life I just gave away.

"If you'd been around when I was fourteen... my

family would still be alive." He was angry, I could feel it. He was mad at me for having this gift.

"If I had been around, I would have saved them, you know that," I pleaded.

His jaw set. "I know that, but if word gets around, you will be hunted. People will force you to heal family members, loved ones. The Nightfall queen herself could kidnap you in an effort to become immortal."

My hands trembled. "I... I wouldn't do that for her!" I snapped.

Raife shook his head. "Not even if she held a knife to your aunt's throat? Or an innocent child's?"

My stomach dropped. I... I would do anything for my aunt or an innocent.

"You should have told me," I said frustratedly.

"I wasn't sure," he muttered. "I was half conscious last time, and like I said, they were only stories I'd heard as a child. I thought your one strand of hair was from stress." Reaching out, he fingered the lock of my new white hair. "Now I see it's not."

Hades. Being confronted with my own mortality at nineteen years old made me feel a little sick. Still, I didn't regret it.

"I'm not sorry I saved the little girl," I said, and held my chin high.

Raife hooked his palms together and gripped the

back of his neck. "Go back to the castle and dye your hair, Lani. We cannot let this get out."

I frowned. "But I thought we were going out tonight? I brought dinner—"

"I've lost my appetite, Kailani," he snapped, releasing his hands and walking across the room. He pulled his cloak off a hook on the wall and walked over to me, wrapping it around my shoulders. He then pulled the cloak up and started angrily shoving my hair into it.

I was stunned by his anger until I reached up to brush his hand and felt a fierce protectiveness. It was like a rabid animal standing over a fresh kill. Wild, unrestrained feral possessiveness bubbled through Raife and it was all over me. The protectiveness was in fear of my safety. He would kill for me, die for me, do anything to keep me safe.

I grasped his hand and he stilled.

"I'll be okay," I told him.

He yanked his hand from mine. "Whatever," was all he said, and then he tore from the room.

I tried and failed to keep the tears from flowing down my cheeks. Raife Lightstone sure had an interesting way of caring for someone. It was all too confusing for me to bear. Keeping my hood up, I left the room and passed the front desk, not even grabbing the dinner basket I had made. For all I knew the nurse had poisoned it. This was my life now, living in fear at every corner, all because of the Nightfall queen and her psychotic vision to rid the realm of magic.

My stomach grumbled. That chicken and boiled eggs I'd made sounded pretty damn good right now.

I wasn't sure who wanted to kill the queen more right now, me or Raife.

AFTER TELLING Mrs. Tirth I had some early graying hair I wanted to cover, she ran out and purchased some brown hair dye for me. I spent the entire night dying my hair, twice to cover the bright silver strands, and then made a second dinner because I was starved.

I took a long bath, and then got into my nightgown and tucked into my book. The character was having a hard time coming to terms with her new reality of being able to see the spirit realm. It sounded familiar. I'd like a vacation from my reality right about now.

There was a knock at the door. I threw a robe over my silk gown. "Yes?" I said through the wood.

"It's Raife," a slightly slurred voice called from the other side.

I tore the door open, and all thoughts of our earlier fight were forgotten when I looked at his sleepy eyes and the way he swayed in the doorway. His long blond hair was pulled into a sexy messy bun at his nape, and he put one hand on his hip.

"You're drunk!" I said accusingly. I didn't know why this made me happy but it did.

"I may be slightly ib-riniated. Inebretatid." He frowned, unable to say the word, and I couldn't help but bark out in laughter.

"Oh, Raife, this made my night, thank you." I beamed, then a thought struck me. "Who tasted the beer for you?"

"Mybowmen." He rushed the words together and then stepped closer to me, so close in fact that I had to step backwards into my room.

"I've been thinking." His gaze fell to my lips. "If we are to kiss only on our wedding day in front of thousands, it won't look real."

My stomach bottomed out and I licked my lips in anticipation. Gone was the angry Raife from the infirmary. He didn't even look at my hair or say anything about my being blessed.

"What did you have in mind?" I asked. If he wanted to forget my saving the little girl tonight, I was totally okay with that.

All this talk of kissing seemed to have instantly sobered him a little. He stopped swaying, his eyes looking more alert as his gaze fell to my nightgown. I glanced down, following his gaze.

Oops. My cloak had opened, so I covered myself up again.

"I was thinking in order to make it look natural, we should practice. One kiss a day," he stated.

Now I was the one swaying. A heady rush consumed me and my heart pounded madly in my chest.

Kiss Raife? Like a *real* kiss in order to make our fake kissing look real? I didn't know what was what anymore, but if I was being honest I'd thought about kissing this guy a lot since the first day I met him. Most women might care that he was drunk. I did not. Whatever it took to get him to open up about his desire to kiss me was okay with me. Raife lived a lot of the time in his head. He needed to drop into his heart once in a while.

I shrugged casually. "I suppose that would be okay. Especially if you're no good at it. Then I'll have to coach you."

My words had their intended effect. Shock and anger slashed across his face, and then stone-cold determination. One second he was standing before me and then next he rushed forward. One hand grasped my lower back and pulled my body against his, and the other cupped my jaw. He used his thumb to force my chin higher, in line with his. When he breathed, the scent of pumpkin mead washed over me and I inhaled in anticipation.

But he didn't do anything. He just looked down at me as if drinking in my eagerness.

Do it! I wanted to scream.

He grinned then and my knees went weak. Leaning in, he brushed his lips across mine. It was so delicate it almost tickled. Everything in my body went numb and hot all at once. Just when I thought that might be it, he went for the kill.

Pressing his lips to mine with urgency, I whimpered in relief, opening my mouth as his tongue brushed along my own. His fingers dug into my back in a way that felt good, and I pressed my pelvis harder into his.

Our tongues were doing a dance that felt coordinated, and yet I could barely think.

This is the best kiss of my life.

I decided in this moment that every single kiss before it was pathetic and should be forgotten. I would have to burn my journal entries about them because they didn't hold a candle to this kiss.

I felt giddy and slightly intoxicated as Raife's emotions began to bleed into mine. He liked the kiss too, more than liked, but there was a sadness there too, always underlying his happy moments. I wished I could take his pain, forever, not just in these moments.

He pulled away from me then, panting.

I grinned. "I look forward to practicing that again tomorrow."

The halfcocked smile he gave me caused my stomach to flip over. "As do I, Lani, as do I."

Turning around, he left and shut the door, leaving me wondering if I was in fact dating my betrothed.

I slept better that night than I had all week.

The next morning I was eager to see Raife. I couldn't get last night's kiss out of my mind. How real it felt, what it all meant. After frying up some eggs and elkin meat, I stepped into the dining room.

Raife was there hunched over some parchments and maps.

"Morning." I smiled, setting the food before him.

"I've got to leave town for a few weeks," he said without looking up at me.

I tried to keep the disappointment from my voice. "Oh?"

"The king of Embergate's wife is with child. I'm going to draw the Nightfall queen into a skirmish at our eastern border to pull her attention away from him and his new wife."

"That's nice of you." I wondered why he would do that, risk his own men's lives.

Raife shoved some of the fried egg into his mouth and chewed. "He's a childhood friend, and he's agreed to join my alliance in a war against the queen."

I nodded, slowly eating my food while I watched him wolf his down. He still hadn't looked at me. I'd worn a pretty green dress and I was hoping he'd notice.

"Oh, and sorry about last night. I was drunk and barely remember anything," he said as he took the last bite of his food.

I'd heard the term *broken hearted*, but never really understood it until now. The center of my chest indeed cracked open at his flippant comment about the amazing kiss we'd shared.

"You didn't seem *that* drunk," I said, placing my fork on the plate and suddenly losing my appetite.

"Alright." He stood, still not meeting my gaze. "I'm off to the eastern wall with the Bow Men. Cancel my meetings for the next two weeks and take notes for me on anything urgent that comes up. You can brief me when I get back."

I nodded, trying not to physically shrink in on myself. "Who will feed you? Taste for you?"

Raife rested a hand on his bow, which hung on his belt, and finally met my gaze. There was pain there. I didn't know how or why but he looked like he was suffering. "I'm an expert hunter. I'll eat fresh game or the Bow Men will taste for me."

I swallowed hard, trying not to feel unwanted. "Be safe," was all I could mutter, now unable to look at him either. I felt like a discarded piece of trash. He wasn't that drunk. I'd felt the giddiness of being tipsy. But he remembered—I knew he remembered that kiss.

Bastard.

There was a motion to my left but I kept my head down to my plate. Warm lips brushed against my cheek and then he was gone.

TWO WEEKS of planning a fake wedding for a man that you were pretty sure you'd really fallen for, who had rejected you, sucked. Flowers, silk tapestries, cake tasting, it was all overshadowed by the supposedly forgotten kiss. Chef Brulier was back. His mother had unfortunately passed, and the grieving period was over. We'd come up with a vanilla lavender custard cake that was truly incredible, but no matter how many slices I ate I still felt like crap.

That kiss. Why did the bastard kiss me like that if he was planning on leaving? And fake forgetting the kiss and the pact to practice daily...?

"Aargh!" I screamed as I threw my axe at the tree. With no more daily meetings scheduled I'd taken to coming out to the woods and throwing things. It was doing wonders for my mood.

A twig snapped to my left and I spun. It took me a second to figure out what I was seeing.

"Autumn?" I gasped, my brain unable to place why my neighbor from Nightfall was in Archmere. She was covered in mud and twigs and I could smell her from here. She reeked of burned wood and was covered in soot.

She looked relieved to see me. "Lani." She rushed forward, and despite the mud and soot all over her, I pulled her in for a hug.

"What happened? Why are you here?" I asked her.

She was two years older than me and studying to be a mechanical engineer at Nightfall University. "Your aunt has been worried sick about you for weeks. I offered to travel here and enquire about your whereabouts. Then I was nearly killed at the border trying to cross over. Apparently, a small battle has broken out there and I was caught in the middle."

Oh no, Raife's skirmish. No wonder she'd looked like she'd been dragged through the mud and fire. She probably had.

Literally.

Autumn's sister, a human, was married to an elf. I'd forgotten that until just now. She often traveled here in secret to visit her nieces and nephews, so she knew the land well. If she was caught, the queen would kill her.

"So you're... part elf?" She looked at me closer, her eyes going right to my rounded ears. "I heard the debtors sold you into slavery, and then your aunt told me about your lineage. She's hoping the king would be lenient with one of his own. The whole neighborhood has been worried sick about you, Lani."

I opened my mouth to speak and she took in my silk cream colored dress with light blue ribbon detail, then her gaze fell to the ring on my marriage finger and she gasped. "But I guess you're more than okay. Lani, what's going on?"

I wasn't prepared to be confronted with my past, and Autumn was the closest thing to a best friend I had.

I exhaled, running my fingers through my hair. "I was captured, sold as a slave to the elf king, and then somehow I became his personal assistant and now we're engaged." I gave a nervous laugh.

Her mouth dropped open. "I'm sorry. Did you just say you were engaged to the *elf king*?"

I trusted Autumn, but if she was ever interrogated about me I didn't want her to have to keep any secrets, so I decided not to tell her it was a fake marriage. In doing that, I'd have to tell her about the king's war with the queen, and I didn't want to do that and jeopardize his plans.

"Holy Hades, Kailani!" she finally shrieked, grinning. "You're going to become the queen of the elves?"

I swallowed hard. "Yeah."

She was grinning ear to ear and I couldn't help but smile back. "Your aunt is going to flip when I tell her." She pulled a note from her pocket and handed it to me.

"How is she? The seizures?" I looked for signs of worry on her face, but she nodded.

"She's great. The medicine is working, she's been seizure free and back at work."

That was good, but the medicine would run out soon, so the king would have to make good on his promise to get her out of there right after the wedding.

"Hey, Autumn, do you think you could draw me a map of the secret route you use to sneak into Nightfall? In case I want to see my aunt?"

She instantly bristled. "Are you asking as my friend, Lani, or the future queen of Archmere?"

Hades. Autumn wasn't a loyal Nightfall human

who hated magic ones, but she also couldn't be keen on bringing war to her people.

I rolled my eyes. "I'm asking as Lani, your childhood friend who wants to make sure my aunt is safe." That was the truth.

She smiled. "I might be persuaded over dinner, maybe with some of that famous chocolate elf wine I hear so much about?" She eyed the palace, clearly wanting me to invite her in.

I wasn't sure what the king or his council would think of my having a human friend over for lunch. It wasn't like in Nightfall, where all other races were outlawed, but humans were looked down upon here because of their association with our mortal enemy.

"Perfect, I'll go get a picnic basket and we can eat in the garden! Just wait here. I'll be right back." I gestured to the rose bushes and a perfect green meadow for the blanket.

She nodded, taking the hint, and moved to go wait in the garden.

"I'll bring you fresh clothes too," I told her.

She waved me off. "Don't bother. I have tons at my sister's place. I'm going there next."

"Alright, then. I'll be right back."

Running into the kitchen, I grabbed layered pastries, smoked meats, boiled eggs, spicy tomato jam, and fresh fruits, shoving them all in a wicker basket, and then ran back out to my friend. I also grabbed one of Raife's bottles of chocolate elf wine. He had hundreds of them and only seemed to open them for guests. I'd actually never tasted the famous wine in all my time here and was excited to do so.

THREE HOURS later I was drunk and cackling under the night sky with my oldest friend.

Autumn grinned. "Remember when Robbie Pantum tried to touch my boobs in exercise class and you broke his nose?"

I laughed hysterically, feeling the heady rush of the buzz the three glasses of wine had given me. Not only was it the tastiest wine I'd ever had, it was *strong*.

"He was a jerk." I lifted my empty glass and Autumn clinked it with hers. We'd finished the bottle an hour ago and just kept clinking empty glasses.

"Is the elf king dreamy? How did you fall in love? Tell me about him?" Autumn flipped on her belly and looked down at me with puppy dog eyes.

I sighed. "His lips are like pillows and he gets grumpy a lot."

Autumn burst into laughter, which caused me to cackle. Then a shadow cast overhead, blocking out the setting sun.

I peered up to find Raife Lightstone hovering over us with his head cocked to the side, looking down at Autumn and I with intrigue.

Autumn stared at me wide-eyed. "Mr. Pillow Lips?"

I nodded, fear chasing some of my drunkenness away, but not enough. Would he be mad I was drinking with a girlfriend in his garden? Was he back from the war for good? Was he hurt? Did he hear me call him grumpy? So many questions swirled in my head.

"I don't believe we've met?" The king looked down at Autumn, his gaze falling to her short-tipped ears just as my gaze fell to the half-dozen Bow Men behind him.

I sat up quickly, immediately regretting it, and swayed as the wine hit me full force. Why was being drunk while lying down so much easier? The moment you had to walk, the challenges set in.

"My love, I'm so glad you're home!" I stood and swayed, widening my stance to keep from falling.

Raife caught me, placing a hand on either side of my hips and pulling me close to his chest. I leaned forward and planted a light kiss to his lips. Then I looked at Autumn. "This is my dear childhood friend, Autumn. Her sister lives in town, married to an elf."

I felt the king relax under me, as if he suspected me of plotting his assassination with her or something. "Hello, Autumn, it's a pleasure. Would you like one of my Bow Men to escort you to your sister's?"

Autumn stood, stumbled a little, and then snickered before saluting Raife. "Yes sir, Mr. Pillow Lips."

I had to bite my cheeks to keep from laughing.

"Get her to her sister's safely and report to me when it's done," Raife told one of his Bow Men.

"Yes, my king," he said, and then the rest of them dispersed.

Now that we were alone, Raife gazed down at me, still holding me in his arms. Leaning forward, he smelled my lips. "Chocolate elf wine?"

I nodded. "I've never had it." Now that he was this close, I didn't want him to let me go. I missed him; it took me until now, in his arms, to realize how much. Tracing my fingers down his neck, I sighed. "You're not injured. I was worried."

His breathing came out ragged and then his gaze flicked to the picnic blanket. "What's that?" His voice could cut glass.

I turned my head and peered at what he was talking about.

He was staring at the map Autumn had drawn for me.

I looked up at him and grinned. "I want something in return for telling you what that is."

His eyes grew even more suspicious. "Like what? Money?"

I snort-laughed, and then fought for composure. Leaning in, I brushed my lips to his ear. "A kiss."

His whole body coiled tight like a snake. "What is it, Kailani?" he growled.

I could tell by his tone he thought it some nefarious thing. He clearly recognized his land in the map, and it hurt that he didn't trust me.

Pulling back to look into his eyes, I brushed my fingers over his lips. "It's an exact route from here to my aunt's house in Nightfall City. A secret route that Autumn has taken dozens of times without getting caught. I thought we could use it to extract my aunt, but also to win your war when it's time."

His sharp intake of breath indicated his shock, and then before I knew it his lips were on mine. A moan of pleasure ripped from my throat and I threaded my fingers through his hair. Our tongues searched for each other with a hungry need, stroking softly and then hard. These few weeks apart, after that last kiss in my apartment, had been hell. It was all I'd thought about. I pressed my body to his and he placed his hand on my lower back, dipping me backwards as he laid me down on the blanket.

I allowed him to, and lay backwards as he lowered himself on top of me. I had about two seconds to care if someone saw us and thought it improper—and then realized I simply didn't care. I was a soon-to-be queen making out with her betrothed. Nothing to see here. Move along.

Raife's hand slipped under my dress, first near my ankle, and then slowly trailed up my shin, over my knee to the outer thigh. For a wild second, all I could think about was when the last time I'd shaved was, and then he grasped my hip, moaning deeply into my open mouth. I swallowed the sound, feeling the heady dizziness of elf wine combine with lustful thoughts of consuming each other.

He pulled back and looked down at me sadly. "You're drunk," he said almost disappointedly.

I shook my head, opening my eyes really wide in an effort to appear sober. "I'm super clearheaded."

He chuckled, running a finger down my chest. "You know what elf wine does to humans?"

Who cares, just take me. Right here under the moonlight, I wanted to say.

"Huh?" I traced his sharp jawline, imagining running my tongue along it.

He sighed, pulling his hand from under my dress and then creasing the fabric down flat. "It robs them of their memories while drunk. You and your friend Autumn won't remember any of this tomorrow."

Dread settled in my gut. Not remember this

amazing kiss? That was criminal. "I'm only *half* human," I reminded him, dizziness washing over me as I closed one eye in an effort to see Raife's face better.

He shook his head, smiling. "Let's get you to bed."

One second I was lying flat on my back and the next I was being hauled up into his arms.

"The map!" I turned to look at the blanket.

"In my pocket," he told me.

I relaxed, resting my head against his chest, listening to the *boom boom* of his heart. Being this close to him I could feel what he was feeling. *Adoration, fear, loyalty*.

"What are you afraid of?" I asked sleepily as the elf wine tried to pull me under.

He bristled, saying nothing as he navigated the halls of the castle. When he got to my room, he opened the door and set me on my bed, pulling off my shoes and covering me with my blanket.

Leaning into my ear, he whispered, "You. I'm afraid of you. You're the kind of woman I could lose myself in."

I could feel my eyebrows knit together in the center of my forehead. Everything was blurry and my words felt like mishmash in my head. I wanted to say something back but couldn't. Footsteps retreated, and then the door shut.

Eh, best to talk about it tomorrow when I was more clearheaded.

THE NEXT MORNING I woke up feeling like I'd fallen off a horse and had then been punched in the face. I opened one eye, saw that I was in my dress from yesterday, and moaned.

What the Hades had happened last night? All I remembered was having a fun picnic with Autumn, then drinking too much elf wine.

Everything was fuzzy after that.

With a sigh, I sat up and went through the motions of getting ready. Not in the mood to dress up, I decided to leave my hair down and wavy, and applied no makeup. I also didn't bother with a fancy dress. The king was out of town anyway; all of his meetings would be canceled. Instead I wore a knee-length blue sundress with no frills.

Grabbing my angel romance book, I shuffled over to the kitchen to see what Chef Brulier had made. When I entered the kitchen, he looked at my hair and outfit, a stark contrast to how I normally dressed, and raised an eyebrow.

"Too much elf wine," I mumbled.

He smiled a little. "Breakfast is already on the table waiting."

"Thanks." I waved him off. It was nice not to have to cook all the meals anymore now that he was back.

Opening my book, I started to read as I pushed open the doors to the king's personal dining hall, and got about halfway into the room before Raife spoke.

"Good morning, Kailani."

I froze, slowly looking up from the book to see him sitting in front of the two plates of food. A small vase of fresh flowers had been set between them.

"You're back." I snapped the book shut and set it on the table, taking my hair into my hands and starting to braid it in an effort to freshen my appearance.

His face fell and he suddenly looked like I'd shot his horse. "Yeah... I got back last night. You don't remember?"

Oh Maker. Did I see him when I was drunk or something?

"Remember what?" I asked, my stomach dropping.

His jaw clenched, and it was like a wall had gone up around him. "Giving me this map?" he said, and laid it on the table.

I glanced at the map, remembering asking Autumn to draw it, but not that she did or that I'd given it to the king.

"I'm sorry, I don't recall that."

He nodded curtly. "Well... that's probably for the best. Hey, you should taste the food before it gets cold. We have a wedding planning meeting with the council."

I swallowed hard, walking over to the table and sat down, wordlessly putting the food in my mouth. I couldn't escape the feeling that I was missing something. I hadn't seen him in weeks and this was the welcome I got? I eyed the king, glad to see he wasn't bleeding or bruised anywhere.

"I'm glad to see you're not injured," I told him.

He nodded. "Your friend gave us a gold mine in drawing this map. Did you know the queen doesn't bolt her storm drains down? I think that's how your friend gets in and out of the castle walls."

He pointed to the drawing of a drain on the map. I leaned forward, but because I hadn't tied off my braid, my hair unfurled and fell in front of his face.

"Sorry." I tucked it over one shoulder.

He looked up at me with searing blue eyes. "I like your hair down," was all he said, and I swallowed hard.

"Time up? I'm starved," he finally said. We'd moved the one-minute wait to three after the queen's last poison had lasted longer.

I glanced at my pocket watch and nodded.

Something felt different between us. I couldn't

explain it, but he felt distant, and I didn't know what to do about it.

Leaning forward, I pressed my lips to his ear and he stiffened.

"I... missed you," I told him, reaching for his hand. I pulled back to look at him expectantly. Two weeks without him had been hard, especially after that amazing kiss we shared when he'd been drunk. I wasn't sure where I stood with him and I didn't like that. I didn't want to be hot and cold.

He glanced up from one of his parchments as if he hadn't heard me, and pulled his hand from mine. "I've gotta go over some war maps and it's going to take up the whole table, so... you mind eating in the kitchen?"

His icy rejection cut me to my core. I had to bite the inside of my cheek to keep from crying as I stood and grabbed my plate. Turning, I booked it for the kitchen.

"Kailani?" he called as I walked away.

I spun. "Yes?" There was hope in my voice, hope that the kiss we shared before he left had meant something to him, drunk or not.

"Don't forget your book." He gestured to where I'd left the book on the table.

Wow.

It was clear I was the only one who enjoyed that kiss, or maybe his lie about not remembering it *wasn't* a lie. Because he certainly wasn't acting like a man who wanted more kisses from me. This was a fake marriage, and I needed to stop caring and treating it as otherwise.

I blasted through the double doors and slammed my plate on the counter. Chef Brulier looked at me but said nothing as I angrily scarfed down my food.

Raife Lightstone would curse the day he rejected me like that.

Our wedding day arrived and I vowed to spend the next five years of our marriage making Raife think of me in every sexual way possible. This bastard was going to beg for it—and then I was going to deny him. Let him feel the crushing rejection as I had two weeks ago to this day.

Was it mature soon-to-be queenly behavior? *No.*

Did I care? *Nope.*

If he wanted to play mind games, I'd throw his head for a spin.

Somehow Raife and I had barely spent any time

together the past two weeks as I was busy planning the wedding and he was working hard at the infirmary and planning his eventual war with the queen. I couldn't believe that in just a few short hours I would be Raife's wife and queen of Archmere. People were traveling from all over the realm to attend the grand event. White silk tents had been erected in the palace gardens, and floral garland draped over every surface of the castle.

It was pretty magical for a fake wedding.

Standing on a podium, I sighed, lost in my thoughts while the seamstress pulled and prodded at my dress. The makeup attendant dusted my cheeks with some reflective shimmer and then brushed a rosy pink lip stain across my lips.

"My lady, you look so beautiful," the makeup attendant said. "Are you excited?"

I looked at her and put on a fake smile. "Best day of my life," I lied.

I couldn't get Raife's dismissal of me out of my head. What was wrong with him? He clearly liked me at one point, right? He'd called me pretty, told me my hair looked better down, complimented my dresses, and even got mad when he was worried about my safety. My mind chewed on what the next five years of my life would be like as we approached closer and closer to the hour of my wedding.

Another hour droned by and the seamstress, and the hair and makeup ladies finally stepped away from me, massaging their hands.

"You're ready," they said in unison.

I steeled myself as they walked me over to a full-length mirror.

When I saw my own reflection, I gasped. I'd never looked this beautiful in my entire life. Whatever she'd done to my eyes, the makeup made them pop and look wider. The shimmer on my cheeks accentuated my heart-shaped face, and my lips looked plump and kissable.

But the dress was the real head turner. I'd sketched out the design but Samarah had really made it come to life. The neck line was a deep V, not deep enough to be improper but enough for Raife to notice the shadow of the top of my cleavage. The sleeves were a dramatic floor-dusting length of white lace, and the dress hugged my waist in white silk before belling out and trailing behind me a good ten feet. The makeup attendant rushed forward with her little shimmer brush and dabbed it on my cleavage, giving me a wink.

I burst into laughter, tears suddenly lining my eyes as I was overcome with emotion.

I knew it was a fake agreement, but for a half second I wished my auntie could be here. Growing up without parents, my aunt was all I had, and even though it wasn't real it might be the only wedding I ever had. No man was going to want me after the king divorced me. Sure, I might find someone to share companionship with, but exes of royalty were never to legally marry again. It was like we needed to be in mourning for the rest of our lives after we were dumped. This might be my only shot walking down the aisle and saying *I do* formally.

"Thank you," I croaked, dabbing at the corner of my eyes.

They all curtsied to me, which was so weird, and then gathered their things. I sat there for another hour, reading, sweating and just generally freaking out, when a knock came at the door.

I figured it was Mrs. Tirth to come and bring me to the ballroom where the wedding would take place, but when I pulled back the door, I stopped breathing when I saw Raife.

He wore a black silk tunic that hung past his knees. It was embroidered with a shiny silver thread in a typical elvin swirl design. His hair was braided into six small braids in front, and then it was all pulled back in a thick ponytail at the nape of his neck. He looked sexier than I'd ever seen him, and I totally forgot how to speak.

I just stared at him, watching him gaze at me. Neither of us spoke.

"Umm, hi." I finally found my words. "Do you... want to come in?"

Why was he here? We'd barely spoken the past two weeks. Was he going to call it off? My heart hammered in my chest.

Raife's gaze ran from my face slowly down my body unabashedly as he fully checked me out. "I... don't think I should. It's bad luck, right?" He also seemed at a loss for words.

I laughed. "It's bad luck to *see* me. Too late for that."

He rubbed his hands together, looking up into my eyes with a depth that gave me chills.

"I just wanted to... thank you. For doing this. I know it can't be easy for you... you're a good friend," he said.

A slice went through my chest. It was like with each mutter of the word "friend" he was surgically removing my heart.

"That's me... a great *friend*," I muttered. This was the worst idea I'd ever had. While he was commending my friendship I was dreaming of ripping that silk tunic off and bedding him.

He rushed forward then, taking me into his arms and pressing me to his chest. He just... held me. It was the deepest, longest hug I'd ever gotten from anyone, and it nearly brought me to tears. There was no passionate kiss, no seductive feelings coming off of him; it was all respect and loyalty, and my heart melted a little. "I'll never forget this. What you've given me. A chance at justice for my family," he whispered in my ear.

I sighed, relishing being in his arms and also hating it. I wanted so much more than he was capable of giving. It made me sad, but I would be lying if I didn't admit that it was an honor to help Raife get the justice he deserved for his family.

"It's my pleasure, Raife," I told him, and when he finally released me he was smiling.

"See ya soon, then." He waved awkwardly and backed out of the room. When he stopped in the doorway, he looked me up and down again. "You're the most beautiful bride I've ever seen," he said, and then left.

Why did he do that? Call me a *friend* one second and then beautiful the next? Didn't he know the torture it caused me?

I shut the door and then dropped my forehead against the hard wood.

Why? Why did I agree to this fake marriage? I was horrible at following directions. I'd clearly gone and fallen for him.

A light knock rapped at the door and I peeled my face away from it, yanking it backwards with hope that he'd come back to kiss me or something. When I saw Mrs. Tirth, my face fell.

"Oh, hi."

The lead housemaid put a hand on her hip. "*Oh, hi?* You look beautiful! Why the long face?"

I swallowed and then gave a nervous laugh. "I'm just anxious. There will be a lot of people there," I told her.

She nodded. "But the king will be there to get you through it. He's used to these big events." She reached out and clasped my hands. "Lean on him. He's your life partner now. You two will need each other."

I hated that I'd agreed to this. A fake marriage. It was starting to feel real. Lines were blurring and people were going to get hurt.

And by people I meant me.

I was going to get hurt and there was nothing I could do about it. Raife was going to go after the queen whether I married him or not. He'd find someone else to appease his council, and then my aunt would be stuck in a war-torn country. I couldn't let that happen. I wouldn't let Raife down. When I'd suggested the fake marriage in the beginning, it had been out of a duty to Raife. As his assistant, I took my job seriously, but I'd never thought he would suggest me for the part.

"Ready?" Mrs. Tirth held her arm out to me and I nodded.

As we traversed the halls, I couldn't help but feel a somber resonance settle into my bones. The dripping flowers everywhere and the magical harp music playing in the garden... I tried to just enjoy the beauty of the day, even if it wasn't unfolding exactly how I wanted it to.

We passed the exit to the garden on our way to the main hall, and I noticed that the silk tents were already full of people.

"Overflow crowd that couldn't fit in the ballroom. You will greet them after, before the reception," Mrs. Tirth told me.

I nodded. I was going to be a *queen* now. Duty came before comfort.

When we reached the closed doors of the ballroom, my stomach clenched. This was it. There was no turning back now. If I did this, I tied my life to Raife's forever. Long after we divorced there would be a stain on my heart. That one time I fake-married the king would be a funny story that turned too real.

"Congratulations," Councilman Haig said behind me and I stiffened, snapping myself from my thoughts.

I swallowed hard and planted a huge smile on my face. "Thank you, sir."

The rest of the council fanned out behind me and my heart jumped into my throat.

This was it. This moment would change everything. Sadness tried to work its way into my chest then, for the war that had yet to be won, for the heart I had not captured. But I pushed it away and nodded to Mrs. Tirth.

Raife needed me, and although he did not care for me in the way that I had grown to care for him, I wouldn't desert him now. He'd been abandoned by his family at a young age, not willingly but abandoned nonetheless. I would not do that to him now. Even if it killed me, even if it left scars on my heart that would never heal, I would not desert Raife Lightstone. I was loyal to him to the end.

THE DOORS OPENED and the magical harp music started. An airy voice trilled throughout the space and I followed the sound to an elvin woman who stood in the corner of the room as she sang a wordless tune. Her lack of lyrics made the song all the more beautiful as I walked down the aisle of people. I recognized a few faces—Bow Men in uniform with their wives and children, castle staff, and the families of the daughters I had considered marrying Raife off to.

It had all come full circle now. Out of my periphery I could see Raife standing at the end of the aisle. I purposely did not meet his gaze; I wasn't ready to do so yet. Smiling at those who had come, I recognized Autumn in the crowd with her sister and gave her a little wave. Before I knew it, I'd reached the end and my moment of truth was here.

You're a good friend.

Those words would haunt me, and yet they were true. I looked up, and the expression on Raife's face, the emotions coming off of him, they stole my breath.

His eyes were slightly hooded as he swallowed hard, and reached for me. Taking both of my hands into his, I was hit with an overwhelming sense of adoration and lust.

Raife Lightstone wanted to bed me just as much as I wanted to bed him. He'd been hiding it before but he couldn't now, not in this moment with all eyes on me and how beautiful he thought I looked. I could feel his emotions leaking into me too strongly, and my stomach heated.

This changed everything.

My plan to be a loyal friend to the end pivoted to a plan to expose that he was hiding his feelings for me. I was going to make him admit it, to see that no matter how scared he was we would get through it together.

The music died down, and as I held his gaze his feelings of lust and romance quickly turned to fear and regret. I bit down on my cheek, hating that I had this gift to feel what others were feeling. His emotions quickly spiraled into panic as the priest began the blessing of our union, and I reached up and stroked the side of his face.

"We got this. Together," I whispered.

It was like I'd doused a fire in water. He instantly relaxed, his stormy emotions subsiding into decisive action. In the entire one-hour union blessing, I did not break away from his gaze. I watched as he waffled between wanting to run out of here and wanting to kiss me, and I held his hands tightly, feeling the same thing.

When the priest finally placed the giant flower garland over the both of us, encircling us together, Raife's hands relaxed in mine.

"King Lightstone, please declare publicly to all of these witnesses your intention to marry and care for your betrothed." The priest's voice was calm and smooth, anything but how I felt.

Raife cleared his throat, and broke my gaze for the first time since I'd entered the room. "I, Raife Lightstone, intend to marry, care for, and devote all of my time and effort into making Kailani Rose Dulane happy, healthy, and prosperous."

Even though it was a canned phrase said for thousands of years among the elvin people who married, tears pricked the edges of my eyes nonetheless.

The priest looked at me and I stared out to the crowd. "I, Kailani Rose Dulane, intend to marry, care for, and devote all of my time and effort into making King Raife Lightstone happy, healthy and..." I paused. "More prosperous?"

The crowd erupted into laughter, and even the edges of Raife's lip curled. I was glad for the comedic moment, because what came next had my stomach tying up into knots. Would it be a small modest peck for the crowd's enjoyment, or an earnest kiss from his heart?

The priest raised his arms. "Do I have the blessing of the elvin council?" he asked.

I looked to the side, where the council sat in high-backed chairs, and one by one they nodded their heads.

"May the Maker bless this union for ages to come," the priest said, and the crowd went wild. "My king, you may kiss your queen."

I faced him, holding my breath, and watched as indecision crossed his features.

I felt it then. Tendrils of sorrow worked its way into his energy and doused us both. He was holding himself back for fear of falling for me. Watching his entire family die left a scar on his soul, one that would not allow him to love another.

Yet.

Leaning forward, he grasped the sides of my face and pressed his lips to mine. The kiss wasn't as brief as I thought it might be, but it was still painfully short.

Knowing how kissing him could be, this felt like an afterthought, and it was hard not to be saddened by it.

The crowd didn't seem to mind, as claps and cheers rang throughout the space. Raife pulled away from me and then slipped his hand into mine, stroking my palm and raising our interlocked fingers into the air.

He looked at the council with a big smile that said, *See I'm married. Now will you approve my war?*

It was a double event: wedding and coronation. The priest then crowned me as queen, something I still couldn't even process. When he set the crown on my head and I took my vow to protect Archmere and prosper it at all costs, the gathered people clapped and screamed so loudly the windows shook.

I felt slightly numb as we walked through the crowds, waving and fake smiling. All the while I just wanted the man next to me to give me something I wasn't sure he was capable of. I clung to Raife as the throngs pressed in on us, and I picked up on all of their elated energy. Despite the overwhelming nature of it, the night was beautiful. We ate a wonderful meal that Mrs. Tirth tasted—the job was no longer mine as a queen couldn't be food tasting for her husband; it wasn't proper. We danced and walked for hours through the throngs of elvin people as they showered us with praise and well wishes, and before I knew it we were being ushered back into Raife's bedroom.

Two Bow Men stood like sentinels on either side of the door. Raife gave them a nod and led me inside. It was near midnight, and I was tired, but I had completely forgotten to talk to Raife about our living arrangements. He'd briefly discussed sharing a bedroom for the first year so that the council didn't get wind of any issues, and then sleeping apart after the war was funded and done. Now that I was confronted with sharing a room, I felt a whole host of emotions rush through me.

The last time I'd glimpsed into this place, there had been a woman streaking across it. My eyes flitted over the large four-poster bed to the left. There was a giant rug and fireplace to the right, and rows and rows of bookshelves. In front of the fireplace was a large sofa and reading chair. I noticed the room didn't have any windows, which I assumed was for safety, but there were plenty of lights so it didn't feel dark. As soon as Raife closed the door, he walked over to a wardrobe on the far wall and pulled a pillow and blanket from it. He brought it over to the sofa and started to make the bed.

Okay... that answered that question.

"It was a nice day. Everyone looked happy," I said, trying to shake off the nerves I was feeling.

He nodded. "The council seems pleased, and the

people feel secure in the future bloodline of the monarchy."

It was a robotic response, one that was very much focused on the duty of the wedding and not the emotions of it all. I understood. This was a business arrangement to him, or had begun as one. I peered at my dressing gown on the bed that Mrs. Tirth must have brought over, and blushed. Looking over my shoulder, I spied the washroom door and scooped up the dressing gown.

There were about twenty bows that tied up the back of my corset, all individually knotted by my dressing maids, and I knew I wouldn't be able to reach them. I walked over to Raife and cleared my throat. When he looked up at me, there was a curiosity in his gaze.

"It took about three people to get me into this dress. I need help with the back," I told him, feeling heat rising in my cheeks.

He nodded and I spun around, giving him my back. When I felt the heat of his body behind me, my eyes fluttered closed. He laid a warm hand on my right shoulder for leverage and then one by one pulled the bows of my corset. With each undoing, my top got looser and I inhaled a deep breath. Pain for beauty was totally a thing I embraced on special occasions, and this was one of them. I was sure to have indentations on my ribs, but this dress was the most beautiful garment I owned, so it was worth it.

With Raife's hand pressed to my shoulder, I could feel his emotions. He wasn't making any effort to hide them. Lust, desire, respect, and fear. Always fear.

When he got halfway down my back, the sleeves slipped off and I made no effort to pull them back up. He removed his right hand, letting the fabric he'd been holding up fall. The front of my dress was suddenly at my waist and I stood topless facing the bookcase. My eyes were still closed, my heart hammering in my chest as I took a shaky breath.

I should cover myself and walk to the washroom. I should make an effort to pull my sleeves up and act shocked at my unexpected nakedness. I didn't. Because instead of turning away, Raife pressed closer to me. His body was suddenly flush against mine, and then his breath was on my neck. Heat bloomed between my legs in anticipation. For an agonizing ten seconds he hovered over my neck just breathing, and I wanted to reach up and grasp his hair, yanking him down to kiss my flesh. But I knew I couldn't rush him. The tumult of emotions rushing through him was something he had to figure out himself.

The underlying emotion was fear. Just when I couldn't take it anymore, his lips kissed my neck and I moaned, tipping my head back into him. His hands came around to cup my breasts and I turned my head, bringing my mouth to his.

The kiss we had that night when he was drunk was nothing compared to the one he gave me now. This kiss was hungry, aching and utterly all-consuming. Our greedy tongues caressed each other, and then all of a sudden he pulled away from me. I whimpered when he flipped me around to fully face him. I panted, out of breath and unsure what to do.

His gaze was savage in that moment. And then I felt it. A cascade of fear washed over me, coming from him.

I stepped closer to him, reaching for him.

"What are you so afraid of?"

He shook his head, placing his hand over my flittering heart, right between my naked breasts. "Falling in love with you. Losing you. Being inside you. *Not* being inside you. Everything about you scares me, Lani." His words were so raw, so full of truth, I couldn't help but respect them.

I stepped closer, cupping both sides of his jaw. "Let me love you." I stared into his eyes, not even sure what that sentence meant, what I was really trying to say. It just tumbled out of me. I pressed myself even closer, slipping my fingers down the front of his trousers. "Let me take care of you." I kissed his neck. "Heal you."

I grabbed his hardness and then pressed my lips to

his cheek, about to speak again, when his arms wrapped around my waist tightly and then I was lifted up into the air. I pulled my hand from his waistband and straddled him as he walked me with purpose to the bed.

When we reached it, he tossed me on the mattress and helped me shimmy out of my dress. Standing over me, he gazed down at me, all of me, and his eyes glittered. "If we consummate this marriage, it will be harder to get out of."

I don't want out, I wanted to say, but kept my mouth shut. "I like a challenge," I said for his benefit. Getting too serious too quickly would only scare him off.

His eyes hooded, and then he lowered himself on top of me, showing me just what it felt like to be bedded by Raife Lightstone. Every bit of it was as mind blowing as I imagined.

Every. Single. Bit.

9

At the wedding, the Bow Men had invited Raife and me to the beaches of Archmere to watch a sailing competition the very next day. The married Bow Men were bringing their wives and there would be beach games and suntanning. It sounded fun. I'd gone ahead to Samarah's this morning and had her sew me a two-piece swimsuit like the ones we wore in Nightfall. I hoped it gave Raife a heart attack. Since bedding on our wedding night last night, Raife had softened. Kisses here and there at breakfast, holding hands, saying sweet things. He was allowing himself to feel his emotions without being afraid of what they would do, and that made me happier than I'd ever been. All I wanted was for us to give this a real chance. Let it be what it could be.

There was a knock at our bedroom door and I opened it to find Raife with his nose shoved in a typography book.

"Ready?" he asked without glancing up.

"Yep," I announced.

He looked up then, and his eyes ran over my sundress. I normally wore the formal floor-length gowns with heavy embellishments, but that would be ridiculous for a beach event and suntanning. Instead I had on a short little sundress that came well above the knee. It was in a thin purple silk, my favorite color, and the neckline dipped low, giving a small peep of my cleavage.

"I can wait while you get dressed," he said jokingly.

I laughed, throaty and sarcastic. "Oh, darling, I am dressed."

His eyes narrowed, going from my cleavage to my bare legs, and I was delighted to feel a little jealousy coming off of him.

"Oops, I almost forgot." I ran over to my wardrobe and grabbed the large wide-brimmed white hat. "Now I'm ready."

Raife took in a deep breath and then exhaled,

holding the door open as I passed. I swear when I brushed up against him, he smelled me. "You kill me," he breathed, and I just grinned.

Mission accomplished.

IT WAS an active horse and carriage ride to the ocean. Our carriage sat six with a table in between. Raife and I sat across from each other and there were two other couples. Raife's top Bow Men, Ares and Cahal, played a card game with him, and I sat next to their wives, Baylie and Naia, talking about fashion.

"We were so sad when you couldn't come to craft night," Baylie said. "I hope you're feeling better?"

I eyed Raife. He'd told them I was sick and they bought it? Raife was the greatest healer in the land. Would they not think he would heal me?

"Much better, thanks," I told her.

Over the course of our carriage ride, I learned that Baylie was the chatty redhead who knitted and Naia was the quieter blonde who liked to sew. Both were extremely welcoming and I was relieved to see that the hem of their dresses was also short. I had no idea about being queen, but dressing appropriate while also sexy was my goal.

"I love that neckline." Naia pointed to the beading I'd asked Samarah to add. It sparkled and drew the eye.

"Thank you," I said.

We talked about the wedding and how divine the cake was and other light topics. All in all I was feeling pretty relaxed by the time we reached the beach. The carriage came to a stop and the boys exited first before reaching out a hand to each of us. When I took Raife's hand, I started to descend and the tip of my sandal caught the lip of the carriage step. One second I was gracefully exiting a royal carriage for a beach date with my new husband the king, and the next I was flailing. A shriek ripped from my lips as I tumbled forward, ready to faceplant. Raife repositioned himself, grasping my hips tightly and lifting me up like I was made of parchment. When he set me back down before him, I reached out and grabbed his shoulders to steady myself.

"Thanks," I mumbled.

How humiliating. Not only were the Bow Men and their wives looking at me, but so was half the beach. The first time the people meet the new queen and I couldn't even exit a carriage properly. I wanted to die.

"Sorry if I embarrassed you," I whispered to Raife.

He leaned forward, brushing his lips along my neck until they were up against my ear. "You could never embarrass me, Lani," he said, and my stomach dropped.

With that, he slipped his hand into mine, stroking my palm with his thumb, and escorted me to the beach.

We passed some market stalls that had been set up and I peered at the items. Some artisans were selling crafts made of seashells, and some of the tents were food stalls. It all reminded me of my father. He'd written about this very place in his journals, where he would sell his wares. If he were alive today, would he be proud to know his daughter was queen of his people, even if it was all for show? I liked to think he would.

Raife had already counseled me that we would not be eating at this event as the risk was too great. Also, any gifts given needed to be taken by a Bow Man or one of their wives to be inspected later. There apparently were liquid poisons that could be painted onto objects to kill you with one touch. I wasn't sure I would ever get used to constantly being on guard for an assassination plot, but it was my new life so I was trying to settle into it.

There was a trio playing the elvin violin, and with them was a hauntingly beautiful singer. She wore a thin cotton ankle-length beach dress, her black hair braided at the sides hanging way past her waist. She belted a sad love song into the sunny air and chills ran the length of my arms.

"Oh, Raife. She must sing at the Winter Ball," I said. Now that I was queen it was no longer appropriate that I taste Raife's food or be his assistant for much longer. I had been told I would be planning all the palace events until I could find the right tutor to help me become the physician I always dreamed of. They'd need to know the human science aspects of healing as well as the elvin ones. Raife said he would find someone for me, but to throw elegant parties in the meantime, starting with the Winter Ball in a few months' time.

Raife looked at the woman as if sizing up her threat to poison him.

"Pleeeease," I begged, hanging on his arm.

Naia grinned. "Your Highness, you'd better give your wife what she wants. Life is easier that way."

Cahal laughed, swinging an arm around his woman. "It's true, my lord."

Raife looked over at me and I popped my bottom lip out, giving him a frown.

"Fine," he chuckled, and I squealed happily.

After talking to the singer and her band, which we learned were called *Mona and the Brigade*, we booked them for the Royal Winter Ball in two months' time. Mona seemed stunned and honored to be asked.

After that, we were ushered into a special cordoned-off area of the beach that was private with an open cabana of sorts. There were some chairs and towels on the sand for lounging.

"Let's sun. I need a tan before winter hits," Baylie announced and began to shed her dress. She wore an adorable bright yellow one-piece suit with ruffles over the butt. Naia then took off her dress and revealed a pale pink suit that looked modest from the front but was missing the entire back.

I started to take off my sundress, pulling it up over my head, and then locked eyes with Raife. When I finally revealed my black two-piece suit, I wasn't sure if Raife was mad or in love. His eyes were hooded, jaw clenched.

"Oh, Kailani your suit is so chic! I've never seen this type of design before," Naia cooed.

"It's missing the middle piece," Raife said dryly, causing Naia to roll her eyes at him. I loved that his friends didn't treat him like a king with delicate feelings.

"I'm going to go home and cut mine in half," Naia announced to everyone.

"Look at you, a trendsetting queen already," Baylie said with a smile.

I grinned, feeling uplifted at their compliments, but I couldn't get that gray-blue gaze off of me. Raife stared at my bathing suit as if willing it to grow back into one piece. I smiled, walking past him, ignoring his icy glare, and settled myself onto the towel next to Baylie and Naia. The men pulled up chairs beside us and I dug my feet into the warm sand as we looked out onto the water, propped up on our elbows. Raife sat next to me and I could almost physically feel his gaze running over my legs as I sat up talking with the girls about the different boats.

There must have been over a hundred of them, all lining up for the race. Some were small sailboats; there was a giant barge that looked like it could hold a hundred men; and a few bigger rowing boats.

"I'd like to own a boat one day," I announced. "Go exploring around the entire realm and stop at Grim Hollow in Embergate. I hear they have wonderful artisan crafts."

Baylie laughed. "Queen Kailani, you *do* own all of these boats now that you've married the king."

I bristled and looked up at Raife. He was still staring at my legs. "All of these boats are yours?"

He nodded. "Ours. Most of them."

Ours. I liked that.

"But there must be a hundred! What do you use them for?" I asked.

"Most are for war, some I rent out to fishermen to

feed the realm, and a few merchant trading vessels are owned by private citizens," he said.

A tall elf holding a golden horn stepped over to the edge of the tent and glanced at Raife. The king nodded, waving and looking out at the people who stood along the beach with a smile.

"Let the race begin!" the elf screamed, and put the horn to his lips. He blew a long, deep note, and the perfect line of boats broke apart as each one sped out into the water.

I noticed a medium-sized sailboat had broken away from the formation and was headed towards us.

"Someone can't steer." Naia laughed.

I smiled, looking at the poor flustered sailboat captain as he floundered about with the steering wheel. He wore a wool knitted cap pulled down over his ears —which was odd considering the sunny warm weather.

"Ahh, your war boat is beating mine!" Cahal said to the king.

Raife grinned, standing now to get a closer look. The ladies stood as well, throwing their sundresses over their suits, and I did the same. We all walked ten paces closer to the water in order to get a better view. I'd never seen a boat race before, and truth be told I was kind of excited. But the stupid sailboat who couldn't steer had finally figured out how to turn to the side and rejoin the race, which meant he was now blocking our view.

"Sorry, lord!" the captain yelled as he was only a mere fifty feet away. Any closer and he'd get stuck in the sand.

Raife reached up and just waved him off, annoyed. We all turned sideways then to try and peer around the stuck sailing vessel so we didn't miss the race, when something moved in my peripheral vision. I spun to follow what had caught my attention in the direction of the nearly moored boat, and the next second the beach was filled with screams.

Five archers had popped up from the boat and loosed arrows. The projectiles whizzed past me and I flinched at the wet sound of them sinking into flesh.

Cahal threw himself over Raife, knocking him to the ground, and by instinct I tackled Naia as we all went down in a pile. More arrows sank into the sand beside me, and Naia let out a blood-curdling scream.

Suddenly the tent that had been set up to shade us from the sun was upended and thrown over us by Raife's Bow Men on duty—tipped on its side to shield us from the archer assassins.

"Kill them!" Raife screamed beside me, and the Bow Men took off running.

What the Hades was happening? It was all too fast for my mind to process.

Naia whimpered beneath me, and now that the tent was covering us I peeled myself off of Naia and looked down at her. I'd fallen on her sideways at a weird angle and wasn't able to fully cover her. There, at the innermost part of her thigh, was lodged an arrow.

"Are you okay?" Raife suddenly swam into view and reached for me. There was blood on his fingers, and I scanned his body wide-eyed, feeling myself go into shock at the gruesome scene.

"You're hit." I looked down at his stomach and he followed my gaze. I saw it the moment the fear flashed across his face.

"I'm fine," he lied. "Are *you* okay, Lani?"

"Naia!" Cahal screamed for his wife, scrambling from where he'd been at the king's side to where his wife now lay.

I nodded to Raife, staring at the arrow sticking out of his gut. He needed healing, but as I was painfully aware, no one could heal the king except those waters at the healing cave several hours away.

Raife kneeled beside Naia, and Cahal seemed to look at his king for the first time.

"My lord, you need a healer!" The Bow Man looked torn between his wife and his duty to the crown.

"I'm fine," Raife growled, and grabbed the hem of

Naia's dress. "I'm going to pull this up and inspect the wound, okay?" he asked her.

She nodded, tears streaming down her face.

When he pulled her dress up, we all winced. The arrow was so deeply embedded it looked to be pointing out the back side of her thigh.

Raife looked at Cahal. "Give her something to bite down on."

Naia's eyes went wide as her husband pulled off his leather belt and shoved it into his wife's mouth. "You're okay, my love. Just think of the garden. Your lavender is blooming," he cooed into her ear.

"Screw my garden, Cahal—ahhhhhh!" she screamed through the leather as the king snapped the arrow in half and then reached behind her leg to pull it out the back end. Once the arrow tip was out, Raife brought it up to his nose and smelled it.

"No detectable poison," he said with relief.

Blood bubbled out of the hole in her leg and the king placed his hands on her thigh. Purple arcs of light spilled out of his fingers and wrapped around her leg. The whimper died in her throat instantly and she sighed in relief.

When Raife pulled his hands back, there was no longer a bleeding gaping hole but a light pink, puckered scar.

"Thank you, my lord," Cahal breathed, resting his head against his wife's neck.

Raife said nothing, hovering over Naia.

"Raife?" I pulled on his shoulder a little so that I could look at his face, and my heart stopped when I saw his purple lips.

"Poison," he said.

The arrow *was* poisoned. And now not only had he taken in her poison, healed her wound, but the arrow inside of him was as well. A double shot of that nasty odorless stuff the queen tried to kill us with before.

"No." Cahal moved to catch the king just as Raife fell backwards.

Naia whimpered, getting to her knees beside the king and bursting into tears. Bailey and Ares were unharmed, and stood in shock at the edge of the tipped-over tent with their backs to it as the king gasped for breath.

No. Not again. Not like this.

A gust of wind kicked up and the tent blew off of us, revealing the king's dire health to the entire beach. People gasped, burst into tears, and some even dropped to their knees in prayer.

It seemed that the Bow Men had taken care of the archers, because no more arrows fell our way, but even with a crowd watching on I couldn't let that deter me.

I *had* to save him, even if it killed me. The world

was a better place with him in it, and I couldn't conceive of a healing gift I wasn't meant to use.

Falling to my knees beside him, I snapped the arrow off like he'd done, a wave of emotions from everyone around me pressing in on me—Naia's horror and guilt that the king would die because of her; Cahal's remorse that he'd been unable to protect Raife; Ares and Bailey's fear that they might see the king die and were helpless to stop it; the onlookers who genuinely loved their king and now were afraid of being without him.

I looked down at Raife as blood pooled on his tunic and his face went blue.

"No," he whispered, knowing what I was about to do. "It... might... be your last..." was all he could get out before his breath fully left him.

Leaning forward, I brushed my lips against his ear. "Then it would have been worth it to save the man I love."

When I pulled back, his eyes were wide, but I felt it in that moment, his complete and utter joy that I'd confessed such a thing.

Leaning forward, I pressed my lips to his and exhaled, calling up whatever healing energy I had left.

The purple breath rushed over his face, and one by one the people around me gasped.

"She's blessed."

"Is that the Breath of Life?"

"Her hair!"

I gazed down at Raife, and although the blue was fading from his face, he still hadn't breathed. After one breath didn't seem to do it, I did another, feeling a weakness throughout my limbs. Finally the color returned to Raife's face, but he still hadn't breathed or spoken, so I prepared to exhale again, a third breath, everything I had, when Raife's hand reached up and clamped around my mouth.

He gasped and sputtered for air as a collective sigh of relief filled the beach and the crowd sobbed and screamed for joy. I smiled down at Raife, and then everything went black as I collapsed right on top of him.

10

When I came to, I blinked rapidly, trying to get a sense of where I was. The last thing I remembered was saving the king's life on the beach.

My fingers brushed the surface beneath me. We were no longer on the sand.

I looked up, my hazy vision clearing as I was able to finally take in my surroundings properly. I was lying in a bed; the window was open and there were birds chirping outside. The walls were plastered in a beautiful floral wall parchment and the hardwood floors were a rich brown. It was a lovely room, but not one I was familiar with.

"You're awake!" A healer I recognized from the infirmary rushed forward.

Magda.

She was Raife's most trusted healer, wearing her white healing smock. She placed two fingers to my pulse. "Strong heartbeat." Then she held a healing wand over me and scanned it up and down my body. "Wonderful readings. How are you feeling?" She looked down at me with a smile, her gaze running quickly over my hair, which I guessed was whiter than before.

I nodded. "Fine. Is Naia okay? The king?"

Her face faltered a bit but she recovered with a smile. "Everyone from the beach attack is alive and well, and the assassins were caught and put to justice."

Her gaze flicked again to my hair and I ran my fingers over it. "Can I see a mirror please?" I sat up and she ran to the chest of drawers, returning a second later with a handheld mirror.

I pulled it up to my face and gasped. My *entire* hair was white. All but one brown streak in front.

Magda reached out and grasped my arm. "What you did for the king... we're all really grateful."

I stared at her hand on mine and then frowned. "Where is my marriage ring?" I noticed immediately that the swirly yellow gold was missing. I peered over at the dresser but there was nothing on top but a hairbrush.

She shifted uncomfortably.

"Magda, where is my ring?" I didn't mean to sound forceful, but my tone came out icy.

She exhaled, her shoulders falling as she looked away from me and a few inches to my right as if she couldn't meet my gaze. "The king is going to tell everyone you died saving him. I have been given the pleasure of being your personal healer and housemaid—"

"What the Hades did you just say!?" I dropped the mirror on the bed and threw the covers off my legs. "Died? Where is Raife?"

My hands shook as I glanced down at my body to see that I was in a thin dressing gown. I couldn't exactly storm out of the palace in this, but at this point I didn't care.

"My lady, I have been tasked with informing you—"

"You will address me as *queen*. Now WHERE IS MY HUSBAND?" I roared, tears streaming down my cheeks as my scream gave way to a sob. Why was she calling me *lady*? Did he break up with me? I saved the bastard's life and he dumped me, told people I was dead? I'd kill him. Oh Hades, I'd kill the bastard myself for this.

Magda looked alarmed, holding her hands out in an effort to calm me. "He's back at the palace. You're safe here. I've taken a Vow of No Harm on you. This is the only way to keep you safe my la—my queen."

Shock ripped through my system. He was *back* at the *palace?* "Where am I?"

She shifted nervously. "In a lovely safe cottage, all provided for by the ki—"

I stormed forward, grasping Magda by the shoulders. "Cut the crap right now and tell me what's going on."

She swallowed hard. "The king said he could no longer be married to the most hunted woman in Archmere, that it wouldn't be safe for you. The entire realm is talking about you, wondering if you can bring back their dead family members. They are bringing several-day-old bodies to the castle, asking for you to breathe them back to life."

I deflated then; the fight completely left me.

He was right. Raife had said that if people found out about my gift, they would hunt me down.

"Where am I?" My voice was smaller this time, weak.

Magda softened. "Somewhere at the edge of the Briar

Ridge Woods. The king has forgiven your debt and you will remain here forever in every comfort possible. Food is delivered weekly, the house and land are paid off—"

"Forever?" I snapped out of my melancholy and brushed past her to exit the room. I came out into a hallway and went right, which opened up into a living room with soft white and cream furniture. The wall of windows revealed I was nestled in a dense forest. Walking over to the front door, I threw it wide open and stepped outside. My bare feet touched upon damp moss and I did a full spin.

Thick trees for as far as the eye could see. No homes, no villages, just a mountain miles away.

"I'm a prisoner," I breathed.

"You're safe," Magda said.

I spun on her, eyes wide. "I'm in the middle of nowhere! I'm trapped. How could he do this to me?"

Her lips pursed and she motioned that I go inside. "We will do a lot to keep those we love safe."

Love? This wasn't *love*. He wasn't even here to tell me himself.

Holy Hades. The king dumped me and then made me his prisoner. Never in my wildest nightmares did I think he was capable of this.

FIVE DAYS. Five days living in the woods with Magda was all it took for me to go insane. I was grieving the loss of a relationship I'd barely had, and a man I loved who'd clearly never loved me back. I felt trapped in the woods with no one to talk to but Magda. She wasn't so bad, she was pleasant. *Too pleasant*. She just smiled and said nice things all the time. There was no fire in her.

Me: "I hate it here!"

Her: "I'm sorry, dear."

Me: "I want to speak to the king."

Her: "You can't, dear."

Me: "I'm leaving this place, screw Raife!"

Her: "You don't know where we are, you'll die in the woods. Just lie down and I'll braid your hair and then make us some blueberry muffins."

She was a pleasant captor but a captor nonetheless.

Today my new reality started to set in. The king was going to tell the realm I died, which meant my aunt was still stuck in Nightfall with her medications running low. Raife had thrown me to the dogs and hidden me away like a problem. Well, screw that. I wasn't going to live out in this cottage for the rest of my life.

"Magda, I was wondering if my slave master sent any hair dye with our last shipment for me?" I asked her.

She didn't like me calling Raife my slave master, but that's what he was at this point.

Twice a week, a trusted Bow Man brought in fresh fruits and vegetables on horseback. Yesterday it was Cahal. He didn't meet my gaze as he handed Magda the food. When I asked him to take me back to the castle with him so I could speak to Raife, he simply spurred the horse and rode off.

Bastards. All of them.

Magda sighed. "What do you need hair dye for, my dear?"

Because I want to run away and not get recognized. Having all white hair with one brown chunk as a rumor of a blessed swirled around wasn't ideal.

"I don't like this look. I want to look like myself," I told her, grabbing the ends of my white hair.

She pursed her lips. "Would it make you happy?"

When I got close to her I could feel her desire for me to be genuinely happy. She pitied me and how the king left me here after I'd saved his life. She took her charge as my healer very seriously.

"It would," I informed her. It was half true. I didn't care what my hair looked like but being one step closer to breaking out of here would make me happy.

"Alright, I'll be right back, then." She moved to grab a basket and a knife from the kitchen and I frowned.

"Where are you going?"

"The king didn't send hair dye, but muska root is a deep reddish brown that's as close to your old color as we are going to get out here. I can boil it and make the dye myself. My mother taught me how so we could hide her grays." She winked.

My heart pinched. Leaving her here was going to be hard. Not because I worried for her— she'd be fine, she knew where the heck we were and she had a Bow Man visiting every three days—but she would take my running off hard, as a betrayal and a failure.

Over the next several hours, Magda boiled the root and made a condensed reddish brown hair dye for me. Then she gingerly applied it to my locks while I sat and stewed in my guilt. When she was done I looked in the mirror and genuinely smiled. It looked really good, redder and darker brown than the color I was born with, but good. The part of my hair that had still been brown was much darker now that the dye had been applied over it, and as I peered closer, into the mirror, I saw that the right half of my eyelashes had turned white also. Hopefully, no one would notice, because I didn't want dye to get into my eyes.

I smiled at her. "I love it. Thank you."

She looked pleased with my happiness, and whistled as she cleaned up her work. We settled into our nightly routine then, me reading one of the hundreds of books Raife had sent here, and her knitting by the fire.

When I got up to make our final cup of nightly tea, I almost backed out of putting the valerian root in hers.

The fact that I told Raife I loved him and saved his life and he repaid me by locking me up in the woods, I just couldn't get over that. I *had* to get out of here.

Dropping a large pinch of powdered valerian root into Magda's tea, I added extra sugar and brought it to her. She took a sip and made a face. "Sweet," she told me.

I gave a nervous laugh and sipped my plain tea.

Twenty minutes later she was yawning. "Alright, dear. Let's get you to bed."

I nodded, standing. "Let me just go to the washroom first. My tummy feels upset," I said, and walked down the hallway to the washroom, locking myself inside.

If there was any question to my being a prisoner here, it was erased each night when Magda locked my bedroom door. I was not allowed to leave and that thought terrified me. I knew she was doing her job, at the command of a broken king, but I wasn't meant to be caged.

Not now. Not ever.

I sat in the washroom for five minutes before I

heard Magda come to the door. "It's late," she said, sounding sleepy.

I flushed the toilet and made my voice sound in agony. "Ohh, my stomach is cramping. I think it was those eggs we had. I'll be a while. Why don't you lay on the couch for a bit?"

Silence. And then, "Okay, dear."

I paced the washroom for the next twenty minutes, trying to build up the nerve to go out there and check on her. I knew that if I had to fight her I could overwhelm her easily—but I liked her, I didn't want it to come to that. I also knew she had a raven to get word to the king quickly, and I wanted to have a head start before he started looking for me. *If* he started at all. He might very well just want to be free of me and this would absolve him of any guilt he had to protect me in whatever sick way he thought this was.

After what I assumed was thirty minutes of silence, I reached out and unlocked the door, slowly turning the handle in my sweaty palm.

Please be asleep, I prayed as I crossed the hallway and peered into the living room. There, slumped in her knitting chair, was my slightly snoring captor.

I released a shaky breath and then tiptoed into my room, quickly changing into traveling clothes, then reached under the bed to pull out the stuffed pillowcase I'd been collecting things in all week: dried fruits and meats; a map of the realm I'd hand drawn to the best of my ability; an extra set of clothes and a meat knife; a canteen, and a blanket. Lastly was the angel novel I'd been reading. The king had sent it from the castle. It pissed me off that he'd do such a kind thing. Dump me, lock me up, but send my favorite book?

Idiot.

Hoisting the sack over my shoulder, I walked as light-footed as possible to the back door, the one just off the hallway that was farthest from Magda's earshot. With trembling fingers, I reached for the lock and turned it. The door creaked a little as I opened it and my heart leapt into my throat.

Shhh, calm down, I told myself as the terror rushed through me. Slipping out into the night air, I closed the door as softly as possible and then ran into the woods like I was being chased.

I didn't know if there were Bow Men around, or ravens or what. I just knew that other than sitting on the porch at midday I was not encouraged to go outside. The moon was high in the sky, but it told me nothing about where I was going. I'd have to wait for sun-up to gain my bearings of east and west. Nightfall was east, and I intended to save my aunt myself if the king was going to abandon her.

I DIDN'T WANT to get too far away without knowing what direction I was going, but I also didn't want to be too close to the cottage if Magda had woken and sounded the alarm that I was gone. I ended up walking four hours in one direction until I found a small logging village. There was a giant pile of stripped logs outside the gates. I climbed on top of them to keep away from prowling animals, and then promptly fell asleep out of exhaustion.

Men shouting and the warmth of sunlight on my face woke me in the early morning hours.

"There's a woman up there!" one of them yelled in Old Elvish.

I sat bolt upright, rolling my blanket into a ball and shoving it into my pillowcase. Peering down at the men bleary-eyed, I smiled politely and waved.

The elf men looked at me with shock. "Miss, what are you doing out here?" He spoke Old Elvish too, and I thanked the Maker I knew how to respond in the same tongue.

I cleared my throat. "Traveling to see my aunt. Got a bit lost. Where am I exactly?" I asked as one of the elf men, an older man in his fifties with kind eyes, stepped up onto the logs to reach a hand out and help me down.

"You're in Southport, miss. Where does your aunt live?" I took his hand, keeping my ears covered with my hair and let him pull me up into a standing position.

Elves weren't against hybrid humans or anything, but if the realm thought I was dead or missing, the queen, a human-elf hybrid who could supposedly bring back the dead, I would have trouble on my hands. The odds of some logging elves going to a royal wedding were slim though, so I felt good about chances.

"Buckshot Valley," I lied. Buckshot was the closest bordering city to Nightfall that was still within the Archmere realm.

The man whistled low. "You're a day's ride on horseback to Buckshot. Were you going to walk?" He looked confused as he helped me to the ground.

A day's ride on horseback meant probably three days' walk. Two if I was lucky. That bastard Raife had put me as far from the Nightfall border as possible.

"I ran out of coin or I would have hired a horse," I said and shrugged.

My dress was nice but not as nice as the ones I wore while working in the palace, so I didn't look rich.

He nodded, looking down at me with pity. He glanced over at a younger, lithe elf with long brown, braided hair. The young man held a giant axe over one shoulder.

"Say, isn't your brother Reeves going to Buckshot tomorrow? To pick up those new axe heads?"

The young man nodded. "I can ask him if he'll accompany her."

Relief rushed through me. A day's horse ride away from the Nightfall border was ideal. As long as this guy wasn't creepy or anything, I didn't see a problem with it.

"I would be so grateful," I informed them.

The young man tipped his head into the now-open gates of the quaint logging town. "Knock on the blue door. My brother's wife will feed you, take you in for the night," he said.

I didn't relish staying *another* night, but walking two to three days, possibly in the wrong direction, didn't sound great either.

"Thank you," I told them and shouldered my pillowcase as I walked into town.

As I strolled through the open gates, I noticed the town was without the modern touches of the Archmere castle, and yet I loved it even more. It had all the architectural details of the elvish homes—arched doorways, gold inlay, curling vines—but instead of electricity they seemed to still use kerosene lamps and fires out here. It was as if I'd stepped back into time. Little children ran around a large well in the center of town laughing as they played chase, and a few dogs lazed about in the morning sun. I was worried I wouldn't be able to find the "blue door" but I smiled when I looked at the little row of houses in town. There were no more than fifteen of them all smooshed together in a circle, and each one had a different-colored door. Purple, red, orange, green, gold, black, white, and I smiled when my gaze landed on the blue one. A young elvin woman was out front beating a rug with a broom.

I passed a few people who waved to me and we exchanged friendly smiles. If I didn't need to go and save my aunt, I'd plop down right here in this village and live there forever.

"Hello?" I greeted her in Old Elvish, assuming she would speak it as well.

She turned, looking surprised. "Hi."

"Are you Reeves' wife?" I asked.

She wiped her hand on her bright yellow apron and made a fist. "Yes, I'm Flora."

I'd never done a traditional elvin greeting, but I'd read about them in my father's journal. Not even the king did them. They were old-fashioned and going out of style, but I didn't want her to think me rude so I made a fist and we clacked forearms.

"Well met," I told her, tipping my head in respect. "I'm Ka—Kala." I quickly made up a name.

"Well met." She smiled.

Wow, this place was like a time capsule of old elvin ways and ideals. My father would have loved it. The very thought caused a pang of sadness to flicker in my chest. I missed him and my mother terribly, which reminded me of my aunt and her seizures.

"Reeves' brother said your husband might be able to transport me to Buckshot Valley? I need to see my sick aunt and I got lost last night."

She frowned. "You're traveling at night? Alone?"

Crap.

"Well, normally no, but my sister Magda is heavily pregnant and couldn't go with me. Her husband has to stay and work. I thought I would make camp by nightfall, but then I just... got lost." Wow, I was almost too good at lying.

Compassion flickered over her gaze. "Of course Reeves can take you to Buckshot. Come inside. I'll introduce you. We've got some leftover breakfast, and tea if you'd like. You're welcome to stay the night too."

I relaxed, looking forward to a warm meal and nice bed. "Thank you so much."

She set the broom against the brick wall of her house and then rolled the rug up into her arms. Pushing the door open, she called into the house, "Reeves! We have a guest, darling."

The way she spoke to him, with such sweetness and respect, it made me think of Raife. I'd meant it when I said I loved him. I *had* fallen in love with him. It wasn't a fake relationship for me. I wanted to call him darling and come home to him like this and it killed me what had become of us, how quickly he'd discarded me.

A man stepped out of a back room and into the kitchen. He was bigger than his brother, not only taller but wider too, and handsome.

"Hello," he greeted me with a head bow.

"This is Kala. She's lost and was looking to get to Buckshot," his wife told him.

He was staring at me, his eyes going from my hair down to my face in a look that made me uncomfortable.

"I'm going to Buckshot tomorrow. I can take you," he offered.

"Thank you," I said, worried again about the way he was studying me.

I noticed all of the dried flowers then. They hung upside down in bundles all around the kitchen. "Beautiful flowers. Are they from your garden?"

They both shifted uncomfortably. "We... had a death in the family last month. The flowers are from the mourning," Flora said.

I instantly regretting saying anything about them. "I'm so sorry." I rubbed my hands nervously on my dress.

"Hungry?" Flora seemed eager to change the subject, and I nodded.

Reeves pulled out the chair for me at the table and gestured that I sit down. I did, and he sat across from me, *still* staring at me oddly.

Did he recognize me? He couldn't. This was too small a town.

"You look familiar. I can't place it," he finally said, and my stomach dropped.

Flora looked over her shoulder at us, keen on knowing where her husband might know me from.

"Maybe the festival last week?" Flora offered.

He shook his head, gaze going again to my hair. "Do you have a sister?"

I almost said no, but then remembered my cover story. "Yes," I said with relief.

He relaxed a little. "Was she at the sailing competition last weekend? When the king was attacked?"

My entire body froze and he noticed, stiffening himself.

Flora spun from where she was heating something on the stove. "Were you there too? It gave Reeves such a fright. And then to find out our queen is blessed! The village has been talking about it all week. Oh, how I hope she comes out of her unconsciousness."

No, no, no...

I needed to leave. I was stupid to think I could travel alone. That's what Raife told everyone? That I was unconscious for days on end?

"I wasn't there. Neither was my sister," I said quickly. Too quickly.

Flora didn't seem to notice, but Reeves was

watching me like a cougarin about to pounce on his prey.

"It was pretty incredible to see the queen bring him back from death like that," Reeves said, not looking away from me, not even blinking. "Her hair went white, but for a small chunk right here." He reached for the darker reddish-brown part of my hair and I jumped up, bolting for the door.

Everything happened so fast then, I could barely track it. I was almost to the door when Reeves crashed into my back, bringing me to the ground. Flora screamed, and then he rolled off me, pulling me up by the arms.

"Reeves, what the Hades are you doing!?" Flora yelped at her husband.

When I faced him, I expected to see a menacing snarl, but he was... crying—full-on fat, hot tears streamed down his face. "Can you bring back the dead? Is it true?"

Flora was holding a plate, looking like she was about to whack her husband over the head on my honor. When she saw the state of her husband and processed what he'd said to me, she lowered the plate and stared at me with hope in her eyes. "It's her?"

He nodded. "She's dyed her hair but it's her. I was there. I saw her bring him back from the dead."

"Can you?" Flora asked. "We can pay you, not

much but anything we have is yours if you can bring our baby girl back. We buried her out back last month. The pox took her."

Flora's bottom lip quivered and I shook my head violently. "No, you don't understand. I didn't bring him back from the dead, and I can't do any more healing or I'll die."

Flora's mouth popped open in shock, but Reeves fingers squeezed my shoulders. "She's lying! I saw her breathe life into the king!" he shouted, and the tears stopped flowing. Now the menace was there.

Fear sank into my gut. What would these people do to me? Did they really think I could bring back the dead? A month-old decaying body? The Maker created us, and when we died we joined him again. We didn't come back.

Right?

Flora must have seen the falter in my eyes. She pointed to the flowers. "The village brought me flowers, but why would I want to watch them die too? I want my little girl back. Can you at least try?"

Reeves wasn't letting go, and I was stuck between my desire to actually attempt to help this poor couple and my will to live. Raife said I had a death wish, but I didn't. I was just a sucker for people in need.

"Flora, Reeves, I'm going to be honest with you both," I said, and Reeves' grip loosened a little, as if he sensed I was going to help them. "I just got this gift a month or so ago and I've already used most of it up. With every Breath of Life I give, I lose some of my own life. It turns my hair white, which is why I dye it. When all my hair goes white, I will die, having given all my life away."

Flora sank into herself as if understanding my plight. Reeves just narrowed his gaze. "*Almost* used it up, so you don't know how many more breaths you have left?" Reeves asked.

I swallowed hard. "No. And I don't know if I can bring back the dead either. I'm not the Maker. Raife was near death, not dead."

Silence descended onto the room; this family was stuck in the darkest grieving period of their life. They weren't thinking clearly, they saw a way to bring their little girl back, and by the wild look in Reeves' eyes he would do anything to see her again.

Reeves looked at his wife then. "Lock the door and go down to the room and rest."

Oh Hades.

My stomach dropped. I bucked backwards, but his grip dug in like an iron clamp.

Flora's eyes went wide. "What are you going to—?"

"I won't hurt her, you have my word," Reeves told his wife. "Go on now."

"No!" I screamed. "Please, I—"

He spun me, tucking my back against his chest as his hand came around my mouth.

"Reeves!" Flora stepped over to him but he cut her down with a look I couldn't see.

"I'm getting our baby girl back. Stay inside."

That's all it took for Flora to abandon me. Her questions stopped, her footsteps stopped, she gave up. She wanted her daughter back more than she wanted to protect me, and I understood that.

I respected it even, to a degree.

With a deathly grip, Reeves dragged me outside kicking and screaming. I tried to headbutt him, bite his fingers, kick him in the balls. Nothing worked. The man was built like a horse and stronger than one too.

"Maybe the Maker gave you that gift so that you could bring people back. Maybe he sent you to me," Reeves said.

I tried to shake my head vigorously, but he kept his hand so firmly around my lips I could barely move. He pinned my neck in place. It took my eyes a second to adjust to the sunlight of their backyard.

"Stop fighting me. I won't hurt you. I just want my princess back." He was crying again; I could hear it in his voice.

I froze against him, not because of what he said but because my gaze had just landed on the gravestone at the fence line of their small backyard. Small sprouts of grass had poked up through the dirt mound of her burial, a sick reminder that even in death, life goes on. Why someone would want to bury their child in their own backyard, I didn't know. I could never stare at that mound of dirt all day and do anything productive.

It's so small, I thought.

When we neared, my eyes went to the name scrawled across the top.

Molly Rae.

I let out a whimper and Reeves loosened his hold. Maybe he thought he was hurting me. Being this close to him, to Molly's body, it was too much for my empathic gift to take. I'd been pushing against the overwhelming feeling of grief coming off of him, but now it crushed me under its weight. I went limp and he lowered me to my knees as I broke into sobs before the small grave.

"Please. Please bring her back." Reeves let go of me and picked up the shovel that was beside the mound of dirt.

He was insane with grief. Dig up a body that had been dead a month? No one wanted to put life into a half rotten corpse even if it *was* possible.

Reeves stuck the shovel into the ground just as a booming voice ripped through the backyard.

"Stop! On the order of the king." Raife's deep timbre resonated from behind me and Reeves froze, seemingly snapping out of what he was doing. Two Bow Men rushed to either side of him and took the shovel from him, pinning his arms behind his back.

I was still on my knees. The feelings of loss and grief were still freshly running through me. They quickly gave way to anger over Raife. My anger. *Betrayal*. He left me, broke up with me through someone else, and then basically imprisoned me in the woods alone. Why the Hades was he here?

"Arrest him." Raife's voice was closer now, and as much as I didn't want to talk to him or deal with him, I couldn't let them arrest Reeves for this.

"No." I stood, and the Bow Men froze. It was Cahal and Ares, and I knew I'd gained their respect.

I spun, prepared to glare down my fake husband, but when I saw him it was like a punch to the gut.

Here's the thing about falling in love. Once it happens, you can't take it back, you can't slow it down or stop it. It's like a runaway horse with a mind of its own. I'd fallen for Raife, and even though I wanted to kill him right now, I couldn't deny how handsome he looked, how safe he made me feel, and how much his protective blue-eyed gaze affected me.

"He didn't hurt me." I looked into Raife's eyes. "He's grieving. Have a heart." I reached out and touched Raife's chest as if saying, *You, too, remember what this loss is like.*

"He kidnapped the queen of Archmere—"

"Queen?" I placed one hand on my hip. "Is that right?" I held up my ringless hand and Raife's cheeks went pink.

The Bow Men exchanged a look and started to move Reeves inside, giving us the garden alone. Four more Bow Men were perched on the fence, arrows drawn, but they were out of hearing distance.

Raife sighed. "I haven't made a public statement yet about your condition."

It was like he'd reached in and yanked out my heart.

"My condition?" I snapped. "So you're breaking up with me? You'll tell everyone I died or I'm in a coma and never talk to me again?"

I felt stupid, because this was a sham from the beginning.

He actually had the decency to look stricken.

I doubled down. "You didn't even leave a note, Raife. I saved your life and I didn't even get a note!" I snarled, stepping closer to him. "You at least owe me the decency of a goodbye."

The closer I got to him, the more I felt the emotions coming off of him. It was like I'd stepped into a wind-storm of feelings. Shock, adoration, fear, protection, anger, desperation, grief.

He took a step backwards, as if sensing what I was doing.

"It's for your own good, Lani! Everything I do is to protect you. Can't you see that?" Raife said, and then gestured to Molly's grave. "Look at this. Five more minutes and you'd have been wasting your final breath on a rotting corpse. Your *last* breath. You'd be dead."

I swallowed hard. "You don't know that," I said, fingering the darker chunk of my dyed hair. The last chunk I had.

"I didn't ask you to save me, you know," he said, lowering his voice. "I would never want you to die for my expense."

I glowered at him. "Now who has a death wish?"

He reached up, rubbing his temples. "What am I going to do with you?"

I shrugged. "Let me try to bring back their daughter and then you can be rid of me," I said morbidly.

His hands fell away from his temples and he gave me a searing look. "Don't ever say that. They can have more children, Kailani. I can't make more of you."

My heart nearly stopped beating; he sounded like he cared. I was so confused about him, about us, and I hated him for it.

I never should have agreed to this stupid fake marriage in the first place!

Raife turned and peered at Cahal, who was now standing at the back door. Raising his fingers, he gestured the Bow Man over to us.

When Cahal saw me, his cheeks reddened as if he was ashamed to have been a part of hiding me away.

"Take her back to the castle and sneak her into my room. Don't let anyone see her or talk to her. Understood?" Raife asked.

He nodded, bowing deeply. "Yes, my lord."

His room? I opened my mouth to ask what was going on, but I couldn't find the right way to form the question, and by the time I did Raife was halfway across the yard.

"Raife Lightstone!" I yelled after him and he froze, turning to look over his shoulder at me. "Remember what it felt like to lose your siblings before you judge that man in there. He didn't hurt me," I warned him, and his face fell. He looked as though I'd slapped him.

With a nod he moved, slower this time, to the back door of the home, seemingly to dole out judgment on the couple. The other four Bow Men who'd been perched on the fence fell to the ground and followed their leader inside.

Cahal reached into his bag and pulled out a traveling cloak. Handing it to me, I shook it out and pulled it down over my shoulders, and then up over my head.

"Come on, we must go before the other Bow Men notice where I've taken you."

I frowned. "Doesn't he trust his Bow Men?"

Cahal gave me a frightening look. "He trusts no one with you, my queen."

My queen. So I still had some power, that was good to know. I wondered if I ordered him to take me to my aunt if he would have to. He was duty-bound to the Archmere crown. But I knew he'd follow Raife's word above mine.

I frowned, allowing him to quickly lead me away from the backyard and to a waiting horse.

"He trusts you," I told him.

Cahal laughed. "After he threatened to kill my entire family if you were mistreated or taken under my watch."

Geez, he did that? He was so protective over me I didn't know what to make of it. Was it because I could give him information in his fight against the queen? Or was it to protect my gift unless he needed my final breath? Or maybe it was something else entirely. I dared to hope it was that he cherished me. That somewhere deep down inside of him he had allowed himself to fall in love as I had.

217

11

It was a several-hour horseback ride back to the castle. When we reached the stables, Cahal ushered me to a stall in the back.

"Where are we going?" I asked him. This was not the way out of the barn. He put his finger to his lips. Voices could be heard outside the barn and I nodded.

Bending down to the ground, he reached out and began to wipe away hay on the floor. In doing so, he exposed a trapdoor.

"Cool," I whispered, and Cahal winked. Pulling the door back, he gestured that I go first. There were

THE BROKEN ELF KING

wooden steps and a faint orange glow beneath. Sucking up my fear of enclosed spaces, I descended the steps and reached level ground as Cahal shut the trapdoor and then met me. We were in a brick-walled tunnel with torch-lit sconces every twenty feet.

"This is crazy," I told him, no longer whispering.

He nodded. "Every good castle has a secret entrance."

He led the way. We'd walked for quite a while when we reached another set of steps that went up. These led to a door, and I was quite excited to see where it would come out. Cahal pulled out a key and slipped it into the lock, pushing it wide open.

I gasped when we stepped into the king's private bedroom.

"If there is ever an attack, you and the king can be out of the castle and on horseback in minutes," he said.

IT WAS INCREDIBLE, but now that I was alone in the king's bedroom, a place I'd only spent one very memorable night, I wasn't sure what to do.

Cahal bowed deeply to me. "Have a bath, read a book, wait for him to come."

Sit around and wait on someone to come yell at me for running away? Couldn't wait.

I nodded, then Cahal left out the front door of the

bedroom, speaking in hushed tones to the guards outside.

My stomach tightened as I thought of how pissed off Raife was going to be that I'd fled his little cabin prison in the woods. I knew our little conversation at Molly's grave wasn't over, and I wasn't sure what was going to happen now. I took Cahal's advice and had a long bath, relieved to find that my wardrobe closet was still here and stocked full. I slipped into an elegant sleeveless mint green gown and then tied my damp hair into two braids. I grabbed three books off of the shelves and then lay on the couch and began to read. After the first hour passed, I undid my braids and let my hair down, now with a kinky curl that I knew Raife loved. After the second hour, I started to pace the room anxiously, and my stomach grumbled.

When the third hour struck, I started to fear that Raife had killed that poor man and his wife for what they did to me. A knock finally came at the door and I nearly yelped in relief.

"Come in!" I yelled.

The door opened and Mrs. Tirth stepped in, looking over her shoulder to make sure she wasn't followed. "Brought you some soup and a tomato-cheese sandwich," she said. "Tasted it myself."

I was so happy to see her I nearly burst into tears.

Rushing forward, I took the tray from her and set it down. "Thank you."

She nodded, looking anxiously at me.

I chewed my lip. "Is he really mad at me?" I asked her. I didn't know why I cared—he was the one who'd imprisoned me in the woods. But Mrs. Tirth was like a mother figure to Raife and I wanted her opinion.

She pressed her apron flat. "It's been a zoo here, Kailani. He had to fire half the palace staff because he caught them selling information about you. People have been lining up at the doors with their sick and elderly all week."

Hades. It was worse than I thought.

"I didn't mean for people to find out that I'm blessed. But he was dying. What would you have had me do?" Tears lined my eyes and Mrs. Tirth stepped forward to scoop them off my cheek.

"Oh, honey, I would have done the same thing. But that doesn't mean we don't have to live with the consequences of our actions. I've known Raife his entire life. I helped raise him. I haven't seen him this distressed since his parents died. I think the need to protect you from his own people is tearing him apart."

I swallowed hard. And I'd just broken out of the only safe place he'd put me.

"I can't live alone in the woods for the rest of my life. I'd rather die," I told her.

She nodded, looking forlorn. "Well, if the people don't calm down over this, you might just get your wish."

Her bold claim knocked the breath out of me. They would kill me? Was that what she meant? Or force me to use my last healing breath?

"I—"

The door swung open and we both jumped. Raife strode in and cut Mrs. Tirth a look that made her bow and leave without a word.

I was suddenly not so hungry. Staring at the king, at his set jaw, eyes thinned to slits, I was actually kind of scared.

"Did you kill Reeves?" I asked, my voice small.

"No," Raife growled, his voice shaking with anger.

I didn't know what to say, how to make him see that I couldn't live alone in the woods while my aunt died.

"You promised you would save my aunt," I said, the only thing I could think of to reason with him.

"You said I could trust you," he shot back.

My head reared as if he'd slapped me. "You can. I would never hurt you—"

Raife stepped forward, rage coming off of him so strongly it felt murderous. "But you *did* hurt me, Kailani. You bedded me, made me fall for you, and then did something so reckless it ensured that I could *never* love you."

I gasped, my hand going to my chest. "Reckless? Saving your life is reckless?"

He nodded. "You showed the entire beach what you were!" he shouted, his fists clenching. "You painted a target on your back, and now I will have to watch another person I care about die! I can't live through that again. I'll go mad."

He cared about me. At least he was admitting that. It was a huge step for him. "I care about you too." I reached for him and he jerked backwards as if I'd stung him.

"Kailani, I told you not to fall in love with me. *This* is what you get. The walls I built around my heart are too high and too thick to ever love again, and you have proved that. I'm sorry," he snapped, and then turned, tearing out of the room and slamming the door.

I couldn't keep the tears in. They rolled down my cheeks in big fat droplets, making me regret the day I ever met Raife Lightstone.

I ATE my now cold soup and sandwich and then read two more books. Because this room had no windows, I had no idea what time it was. As I started to feel sleepy, Raife returned, looking calmer than he had before.

I folded my book on my lap and then looked up at him. He walked over and sat in the reading chair across from me. Clasping his hands, he exhaled. "I'm sorry I got so angry with you earlier."

I perked up. An apology? I hadn't been expecting that.

Raife ran his fingers through his hair and sighed again. "I'm very protective around you, and now half the kingdom thinks you can bring their lost loved ones from the dead. It's got me..." He shook his head.

"I'm sorry," I told him. "You told me about the repercussions of what would happen if people found out I was blessed and now it's happening." I slipped onto my knees and sat before him, looking up into his eyes. "But, Raife, I would do it all over again if it meant saving you."

He bristled, standing and pacing the room. "You have a big heart. You're a good friend. I'm grateful you saved me, I just wish it hadn't been at the expense of your safety."

A good friend.

I lay back on the carpet like I'd been hit with an arrow, closing my eyes. If he used the F word one more time I was going to scream.

"What are you doing?" he asked, and my eyes snapped open. He was standing over me.

I shrugged. "Wishing I could rewind time and let you die so that you would stop berating me for this mistake."

He smirked. "This isn't berating. I can do that, though, if you like?"

He reached down and I took his hand, allowing him to pull me up. My body slammed flush against his and he stepped backwards a pace, dropping my hand like a hot stone. "If I send you back to the cabin, will you stay there?" he asked seriously.

My eyes bugged. "For the rest of my life? Hades no!"

He pinched the bridge of his nose. "Then I have to keep you near me. It's the only way to keep you safe."

"Awww..." My voice dripped with sarcasm. "You're such a good *friend*, Raife."

His brows drew together in confusion and I growled. Now it was my turn to pace the room.

"You promised me that after we married, you would bring my aunt here and heal her. Now it's time to pay up!"

"Now is the worst possible—"

"Raife. It's time," I deadpanned. "If you don't go and get her with me, I'll go alone."

His jaw unhinged. "You think I'm going to allow

you to go on the mission to retrieve your aunt? Hah. You're insane."

I stomped over to him and poked his chest. "You're insane if you think my aunt would just go into the woods and leave her home and everything she has with some random elves."

He looked offended. "I'm not a random elf. I'm the king."

"She doesn't know that, or the fact that I am your new wife. I haven't gotten word to her. I'm going, and that's final. Besides, you will never know what house is hers. That map Autumn drew just gets you into the castle. You need me to find my auntie's house."

He chewed his bottom lip. "And if you are captured and killed?"

I shrugged. "Then write *Great Friend* on my gravestone."

Again he looked confused. The bastard had no idea.

"Raife, I'm going to see my aunt. End of discussion. I've dyed my hair and I'll wear a hooded cloak. Do you really expect me to live in this bedroom my entire life?"

He thought long and hard about that. "No, which is why I just made it a crime punishable by death to even touch you."

"What!?" I screeched.

He looked down at me coolly. "If you want to live

and travel around at my side, to be my queen, there are going to be rules. One touch and I won't hesitate to kill them. We have to set a precedent or you'll be kidnapped and dragged to every cemetery in the land."

He wasn't serious, was he?

"You won't actually kill them for touching me though, right?"

He raised one eyebrow. "If a king shows weakness, he might as well cut his own throat."

Whoa. Okay. That meant he was serious.

"So I'll never be touched by anyone ever again? Thanks for that!" I snapped, and stormed over to the corner of the room to inspect the bookshelves.

I heard his footsteps retreat, and then he disappeared into the washroom. I stared at the bed where we'd last made love and groaned. All of these hot and cold messages were driving me insane.

Good friend? You didn't threaten to kill someone for merely touching a good friend.

The door to the washroom opened and he stepped out, freshly bathed.

I decided then that for my own sanity I needed to know where he stood. Did he truly just see me as a friend whom he kissed once and accidently bedded? Or was there more? I intended to find out right now.

I unzipped my dress, letting it fall to the floor,

standing in only my undergarments, which were comprised of a white lace bralette and white panties.

Raife froze, eyes raking over my half naked form. "Wh-what are you doing?" His voice dropped two octaves.

"Hmm?" I asked dismissively, as I pranced across the room giving him a view of my backside.

"You're... undressing." He fumbled for words.

I loved the discomfort in his voice. It was layered with something else.

Arousal.

I turned and looked over my shoulder at him. "Yeah, I won't sleep in my gown." I laughed.

His eyes narrowed and his lips pursed into a thin line as I turned back away from him and opened my wardrobe. My nightgowns were folded at the bottom so I bent forward, *slowly*, and grabbed one.

A strangled moan came from behind me and I grinned, pulling the gown out and slipping it over my head.

Gotcha.

"I know what you're doing," Raife said accusatorily.

I spun, making my way back to the bed. "I don't know what you mean." I shrugged innocently, pulling the hem of my short nightgown.

His eyes thinned to slits. He reached down to the

hem of his crisp sleep tunic and pulled it up over his head in one swift move.

Sweet Maker.

I stood there, stunned into silence as he pulled the drawstring of his trousers.

My throat went dry and I had to actively force myself to drag my eyes away from him and keep walking over to the bed. He was trying to play my own game, to seduce me into making a move on him just so he could reject me like before.

Well, screw that.

I slipped into bed, with a grumpy huff, and threw the covers over my face.

Married life sucks.

The next morning we ate breakfast together in the small private dining room I was used to being with him in.

"Can I be your assistant again? Being a party planner is boring," I asked, taking a piece of egg into my mouth and chewing. It was weird not being the food taster anymore. Somehow there was a more heightened sense of anxiety. Did the new taster really eat a piece of every food? Had they waited the full three minutes? Could they be trusted?

I almost wanted to go back to cooking for Raife and having him do the dishes. It was a simpler time then.

He snort-laughed at my question. "No, you're my queen. Being my assistant would be inappropriate."

I chewed on my lip. "Well, I'm bored. Can I help at the infirmary or with planning the war?"

He set down his fork and looked over at me. "I have to go speak to an old friend. It might go better if you were with me."

I perked up. "A trip? Ohh, sounds fun."

"Don't get too excited. This is a trip to see the fae king of Thorngate."

My eyes bugged. "You want to willingly go see the winter king?"

He laughed, as if he enjoyed my assessment of his "old friend."

"I need his help in the war," was all he said.

I nodded. "Okay, and on the way back we can pick up my aunt?"

Raife gave me a stern look. "You're pushing it."

"Those are my terms. You have the map Autumn gave me, and we are married now, so I think the council will approve it." I popped a gooseberry into my mouth and he set his forehead against the table with a thunk.

"Fine," he grumbled, and I smiled, standing and walking over to him. I brushed my fingers along the back of his neck as I passed.

"See you later, darling," I trilled.

Maybe being queen wasn't half bad if I got my way some of the time.

———

I WOULD BE LYING if I didn't admit that I was terrified to meet King Thorne. Lucien Thorne had a reputation for being an unforgiving prick. Steal from him, he'd cut off your hand. Lie to him, lose your tongue. Of the four fae courts, he was always chosen as king year after year because this ruthlessness meant he was feared. Those who were feared did not get taken advantage of. There was even a rumor that the Night-fall queen considered Lucien a worthy adversary and didn't bother him as much as the other royals.

I tried to probe the depth of Raife and Lucien's relationship as we traveled in the carriage. "So you and Lucien were friends growing up?"

Raife was dressed in a Bow Men warrior uniform, and even kept his bow and arrows nearby as if he expected an attack. "Were," was all Raife said.

I frowned. "Why did you stop?"

Raife's eyes flicked to the bust of my cream chiffon gown. I was a queen now, and going to meet with another royal. I had to play the part, and dress to impress. The cut of my neckline was completely proper, and yet Raife still snuck glances as if hoping to catch a glimpse of my cleavage. I wasn't sure if this made me happy at this point or pissed me off. He needed to figure out what he wanted.

Raife sighed. "I went to a really dark place after my parents died and I was crowned king," he said.

I reached out and grasped his hand, and he startled a little, as if he didn't expect the act of kindness. He squeezed it and then let it drop.

"What happened?" Now I really wanted to know, *needed* to know.

Raife winced. "Lucien wasn't able to help me in my fight against the queen as he was only a prince then, but he came and visited often. No matter how many times I tried to throw him out, he came back every weekend."

My heart melted in that moment. Was this the same Lucien Thorne I'd heard about?

"Well, why aren't you friends anymore?"

I felt it then, shame. It burned through Raife fast and hot and over to me.

"When we were seventeen, Lucien asked me to visit him so that I could meet his girlfriend. He was head over heels in love with her, said he was going to marry her. I caught her flirting with my Bow Men and I didn't trust her. I told Lucien to dump her, that she would be bad for him."

Dread sank like a stone in my gut. I swallowed hard.

Raife's energy descended into depression then. "The next night she brought a friend... we all drank elf wine and... Lucien caught me in bed with the love of his life."

I gasped and then smacked his leg. "Raife!"

"I know, okay? I know. I was drunk and I wanted to prove she wasn't loyal to him." Raife hung his head in shame and I sighed.

Standing, I shimmied to where I could sit next to him and placed my hand on his thigh. "We all make mistakes. It sounds like you did indeed save him from a horrible marriage."

Raife cast me a long side look. "I haven't seen him since. He said if I ever showed my face in Thorngate, he would kill me."

I grinned, understanding now why he was dressed for war. "Well, then, going to see him was a great idea."

Raife smirked, chuckling a little. "I'm hoping he won't kill me in front of you. I really need his help with the Nightfall queen. His Winter soldiers are arguably the most powerful in the land."

I chewed the inside of my cheek, now wondering if coming along was a good idea. He wouldn't really kill Raife, would he? That was years ago. It would start a war, and they used to be friends. Surely he would remember that.

"Approaching the entrance of Thorngate, sir," one of Raife's Bow Men said from the window of our carriage.

Raife swallowed hard and nodded.

As we slowed, I heard the fae guards ask what we were doing.

"I have King Raife Lightstone and his new wife, Kailani Dulane, to see King Lucien Thorne," the Bow Men said formally.

"Wait here. I'll send a messenger," was the curt reply.

We waited. And waited. And waited. Over two hours we waited, snacking and getting out to stretch our feet, when finally a fae on horseback rode up to the wrought iron gates.

The guard at the gate spoke to him briefly and then nodded to the lead Bow Men. "Your king and his wife may enter. You may not," he told the Bow Men.

They all growled, staring at Raife for instruction, and I wasn't prepared for it when he looked to me. As if asking my opinion. Go into possible enemy territory without a royal guard? But why would we bring an armed guard unless we didn't trust Lucien? We needed to extend the first hand of peace.

I nodded once to Raife, telling him I was okay with it.

"Grab your cloak. It gets cold," was all Raife said to me.

I dug into the carriage and pulled out my white fur cloak, fastening it to my shoulders. After being helped up onto Raife's horse, I rode sidesaddle as I clung to him and we passed through the entrance of Thorngate.

I'd never been into the fae territory. All I knew was that it was split up into four regions. Summer, Spring, Fall, and Winter. Each region had a prince or princess, but the winter king ruled over them all with an iron first. By the looks of the orange- and yellow-leafed trees and the gust of wind blowing through the fields, I would have guessed we'd just ridden into Fall lands. The king's messenger rode alongside us, watching us carefully. I noticed he didn't have a weapon on him, and wondered if that meant he had a magical power that was more harmful than a sword. He wore the steely black uniform of winter, and thick gray fur boots.

Over the next hour we passed two small towns and a palace trimmed in red brick, but were told to keep going. A visit with the royalty of Fall was not on our agenda.

As we came up and over a small hill, I gasped at the stark difference in the two lands. Thick snow demarcated a line between the two courts. Mountains and trees were covered in the white fluff, and I quickly pulled my fur hood up, clinging to Raife tighter as he plunged us into Winter.

The path had been almost magically cleared of any snow or ice, the cobblestones completely dry. It was eerie, unnatural. I peered all around, taking in the wonderous sight. Every tree, every rooftop, every mountain, was coated in white. But it was magical, cold, and yet one of the most beautiful things I'd ever seen.

The houses had gardens where the snow had melted off, giving way to a small pumpkin patch or squash vines. I wondered if they could control where the snow fell and where it didn't, and was instantly fascinated.

I looked at the messenger and noticed his uniform was quite thin and yet he didn't look the slightest bit cold. The deeper into the realm we went, the colder it got. By the time we peered over the ridge and at the white castle of Winter, my lungs felt frozen in my chest.

"It's beautiful," I said through chattering teeth.

Raife growled. "And not normally *this* cold. He's doing this to make us uncomfortable."

The winter king? He could do that? So quickly? That was simultaneously scary and fascinating all at once. The white stone castle was topped with several inches of snow, making it look magical against the backdrop of the large mountains flanking it.

Half a dozen guards glared us down at the entrance of the gates, and when we passed the people they kept their heads down, not making eye contact.

The market shops were all painted a pale ice-blue and topped with snow, which just made them look almost unreal, like out of a picture. I peered through the glass to what they held inside and noticed beautiful jewelry, pottery, and clothing.

Oh, how I would love to stop for shopping. Maybe another time, when we had made sure that Lucien wasn't going to kill my fake-maybe-not-so-fake-husband.

Raife pulled the horse right up to the castle gates, where a large warrior stood tall and erect. Fae were not known for their bulkiness, so this man was quite the sight among the others.

Raife dismounted and helped me down, and I instantly regretted my shoe choice. Cold snow bit into my ankles as Raife slipped his hand into mine, that light palm stroke making my heart pinch a little. We were led up the grand exterior stairs and into a set of double doors. The inside was completely stark white and gray. White stone tile lined the walls and floors, and we were led to a large drawing room. The castle was warmer but not by much. The fireplace on the far wall was dead, with no logs in it.

"Clearly not wanting us to feel welcome," Raife grumbled.

"Clearly not," a voice came from behind us, and we both jumped a little.

Turning, I took in Lucien Thorne as he stood in the doorway.

He was the opposite of Raife in every way possible: black hair, sharper-pointed ears, gray stern eyes. Where Raife was lightness and healing, this man was cold and unforgiving. Still, I could not deny that he was handsome. His sharp jawline and cocky smile would win many hearts.

"You found someone to marry you?" Lucien said, sounding surprised. "A looker too. Well done."

Raife's hand clamped down on mine and I stroked his with my thumb, hoping to express to him that he needed to not get baited into an argument. Lucien was clearly still hurt about Raife sleeping with his girlfriend.

I dropped Raife's hand and stepped closer to Lucien, extending mine. "Hello, Your Highness, it's nice to finally meet you. I'm Kailani."

Lucien's smile grew wider. It only made him more handsome. "*And* she has manners."

He took my hand and slowly leaned forward,

kissing the top of my fingers for longer than was appropriate.

"I came to talk about official matters," Raife said as I pulled my hand back.

Lucien's smile fell then and his eyes grew stony. "And I told you that if you ever showed your face here again, I would kill you." Reaching up into the air, Lucien made a fist. It was an odd thing to do, so I just stared at him, wondering what was going on, until I heard Raife choking behind me.

I spun, seeing Raife's face go blue. Icicles formed on his lips, and his breath came out in cold puffs of white.

"Stop it!" I screamed at Lucien, but he showed no interest in stopping.

I stormed over to the king of Winter, and without thinking I grabbed his manhood tightly in my hand. He flinched, looking surprised, but didn't let Raife go.

"Kill him and I'll rip your prick right off," I growled with his meat in my hands.

He turned, meeting my gaze, and grinned at me. I felt him stiffen and grow hard beneath my fingers. With a gasp, I yanked my hand away and he dropped Raife, laughing deeply.

Raife gasped for air as Lucien continued his amused snickering. "Oh, Raife, she is a treasure. You have married well, I'll give you that. Now get the Hades out of my realm and *don't* come back."

I was so relieved he'd stopped choking Raife, but still in shock by the fact that he'd just... it was too inappropriate to even think of! This man really did live up to his bad boy reputation.

Raife stood, still panting, and glared at Lucien, a murderous gleam in his eyes. "I said I was sorry for Lorna, but you never would have been happy with her! I proved her unfaithfulness," Raife said, cutting to the very heart of the issue at hand.

One second Lucien was standing there, and the next he was screaming as he ran at Raife, fists raised.

I winced as his fist cracked down on Raife's face, the sound of his bone cracking. Raife reached up and gave Lucien an uppercut to the chin. Then they both went at each other like wild dogs.

I stepped back a few feet, watching as they worked through their issues. A fistfight I could handle. My old house in Nightfall was across from a tavern, so I saw many fistfights on a daily basis. This one, however, was the most passion-filled. Lucien was screaming something about bedding Lorna while Raife suddenly stopped fighting, allowing Lucien to pound into him, hit after hit.

"Stop!" I screamed.

Lucien picked up Raife then and threw him into

the wall and I shrieked. They were going to kill each other if I didn't break this up.

"That's enough!" I shouted.

Raife got up quickly, brushing the blow off, and then stood facing Lucien without even lifting his arms.

"Fight back, you bastard!" Lucien raised his fist and an icicle formed inside his palm.

My sharp intake of breath echoed throughout the room. I went to move forward to stop him, but when I looked down my feet were frozen to the spot, literally. He'd immobilized me.

Fear tightened in my gut as I watched the scene unfold before me.

"I'm sorry," Raife said in the most earnest way possible. "I'm sorry, Lucien. You were like a brother to me, and I'm... so sorry."

The fae king's chest heaved as he held the icicle to Raife's throat. Raife tipped his chin high, as if asking him to do it. I yanked my foot from my frozen shoe and prepared to jump on the winter king's back or something crazy to get him to stop.

But the fae dropped his hand and the icicle crashed to the ground. "Go away, and don't come back." He sounded resigned.

I nearly melted in relief that he wasn't going to kill Raife. Slipping my foot back into my shoe, I looked down at the ice blocks; they were now powdered snow.

If I weren't so terrified I might actually process how cool that was.

Raife looked at me and crossed the room. Lucien stayed where he was, keeping his back to us.

Raife slipped his hand into mine and then stared at Lucien's back. "Drae has agreed to march on the Nightfall queen. We're going to stop her reign of terror, and I'd really like if you'd joined us."

Lucien laughed, a cold and biting sound. "The dragon king has agreed to take on the Nightfall queen with you?"

"Yes," Raife growled.

Lucien spun, his eyes flashing silver for a wild moment. "I'll believe that when I hear it from Drae's mouth. Now get the Hades off my land!" A flurry of snow came out of nowhere and flew at us. Raife scooped me up as if I were made of air and tucked me into his chest, carrying me out of the castle at a brisk walk.

The snow danced around us like a wind tunnel until we reached our horse, then it dropped to the ground.

I looked up at Raife for the first time, trying to conceal my terror. "That went awful," I said as he let me down, my body sliding slowly down his.

Raife's lip was split and bleeding; his cheek was swollen and red. But he was... grinning, and I couldn't for the life of me understand what would make him smile.

"I just need to bring Drae back and Lucien will believe him. You heard him."

I frowned. "That doesn't mean he will fight with you. Sending his people to war is a big deal, Raife."

Raife nodded. "He could have killed me and he didn't. That means somewhere in there, he's still my old dear friend. And an old dear friend will help me avenge my family."

My heart pinched at his words as he helped me mount the horse. "You really won't stop until you take out Zaphira, will you?"

He swung his leg over the horse and stared back at me with a fierceness I wasn't prepared for.

"Since the day my family died, writhing on the floor and foaming at the mouth, I've been planning this war. I will not stop until I get what I want."

Chills broke out on my arms. The elves might be healers and therefore seen as "weak" among other races, but what elves lacked in brute force, they made up for in archery, marksmanship and cunning. Raife had planned this war for nearly ten years. I knew he would allow nothing to get in his way.

Not even me.

It all made sense now, the way he pushed me away when I got too close. I was sure he was afraid to care for someone again and lose them like his family, but I also thought he didn't want anything to distract him from the justice he sought for them. From his war. Hades, after that bitch poisoned me in an effort to get to him, I couldn't wait to see her head on a spike. But also for his family, for every magical creature she'd killed merely for being born with magic. A blessed gift from the Maker.

She was sickening, evil, and I just didn't talk about it much because it was engrained in me not to. Growing up in Nightfall meant we didn't utter a bad word about Queen Zaphira for fear of being hanged for treason. Maybe Raife didn't know how much I supported him and this war, this quest for revenge. Maybe he needed to.

"Raife, I just want you to know that whatever part, big or small, that I can play in helping you get justice for your family, I will."

His eyes softened, and I knew that my commitment meant a lot.

"Zaphira is absolute evil," I told him. "She must be stopped. I just don't say that out loud much because I'm used to not being able to talk bad about her for fear of retribution."

His features softened even more. "I wasn't sure how you really felt about my quest to remove her from power and kill her slowly."

"Full support. The bitch needs to die," I confirmed.

His entire body relaxed, as if he realized in that moment he didn't have to carry this weight alone. "Really?"

I nodded. "I think after we get my aunt, you should go to the dragon king, get him to visit Lucien with you, and convince Lucien to pledge his efforts to the war. The winter king not only borders the queen's land, but her palace is nearest his. She would never suspect an attack from the fae. It's a known thing that she considers the winter king a worthy adversary and would save him for last. This could be the home base of the war against her," I informed him in a rush of excitement.

His eyes glittered, as if he too were eager about the idea. "I have to get Lucien to say yes first."

I nodded. "You will. Like you said, he didn't kill you. That's a plus."

A halfcocked smile graced Raife's lips. I could feel his confidence in his plan returning. "Let's go get your aunt," he said.

13

As we set off on horseback with our trusty escort, I snuggled into Raife's back, feeling more at ease with our relationship than I had in a long time. We had somehow made amends, and now we were a team again. Even if it were just as friends which was not ideal, it was a step forward. Because a true friend wanted the other person's dreams to come true, even if it crushed their own. I realized then that Raife was probably incapable of love at this point in his life and I'd been living a fairy tale thinking a few kisses or one night together would suddenly make him fall wildly in love with me.

This was a five-year business arrangement, and Raife deserved that after everything he'd lost.

Heading out of Thorngate and to the portion of the eastern woods that Autumn had marked on the map took only a half day's ride. But that half day put us in the dead of night at the Nightfall border. Autumn had sketched a farm on the map with a bright yellow barn, and then had drawn a broken fence. From there she'd shown certain landmarks through the woods that led to the gates of Nightfall City.

The map showed that when we finally got to the gates, there was a picture of a tree split in two, like lightning had struck it, and then an arrow showing that you went under the gate. I had no idea of the landmark, as I didn't make an effort to memorize trees, but I hoped we'd figure it out once we got there.

We found the farm with the yellow barn and Raife had our group stop.

"Kailani and I will go on alone from here," Raife said to his lead Bow Men.

Both Cahal's and my eyes widened at his statement.

"What?" we said in unison.

Raife pointed to the map and the words *Three people only* written on the bottom.

"I assume this means more than three people would be seen, or not fit or whatever the instructions are," Raife says. "Once we get Kailani's aunt, we will be three."

"My lord, you're the king, you cannot go into Nightfall territory alone," Cahal said, and I nodded in agreement.

"I have to go or my aunt will not leave with you," I said. "But I can go with any of your Bow Men," I told Raife.

Cahal bowed deeply. "I would be honored—"

"No. She's my wife, *I* will keep her safe," Raife snapped.

My wife. I hadn't heard him say that enough, and even though it was all for show I would never tire of it.

Raife was good at loving people while not *truly* loving them. He was fiercely protective but undeniably cold. I wondered in that moment if I could do this for five whole years. To hear him say romantic things like "She's my wife. I will keep her safe," and have my heart beat out of my chest as I stared at his soft lips.

Cahal looked unnerved. "My lord, I would never question your authority, but the Nightfall queen could capture you, she could kill you and Kailani, and then we'd be left with no one."

Raife shook his head. "You'd have the council. They'd form a quorum. Besides, if Drae Valdren can sneak into Nightfall and kill the queen's oldest son, I can sneak in and steal Lani's feeble aunt." There was determination in his gaze.

Cahal and I shared a knowing look. Was that what this was about? He wanted to prove that he could also one-up the queen?

I placed a hand on Cahal's shoulder. "My friend, Autumn, does this every moon to visit her sister and nephew in Archmere. The fewer of us that go, the less likely we are to be seen."

He looked stricken, like he couldn't possibly think of letting his king go into enemy territory alone.

"Stay here. That's an order," Raife commanded, and ended the argument before it could begin.

"Yes, lord." Cahal lowered his head.

With that, Raife and I dismounted the horse and went back into the carriage to grab some supplies. We took a small pack with water, and dried fruits, in case we were delayed, but intended to be back by morning light. There would be no sleep and lots of walking, but getting my aunt to safety before the war started was important to me. Healing her seizures was important. The Nightfall doctors said with each one her brain could be damaged. I knew Raife was risking a lot on this mission, but I didn't see any other way.

As we cut across the farm, peering at the back

fence for a break in the wood, I reached out and squeezed Raife's hand.

"Thank you for doing this." I held his hand, hoping to get across to him how much I appreciated him, but he just gave me a curt nod and dropped my fingers.

The familiar pain of his icy cold rejection wormed into my heart but I brushed it aside. This was just what we were now. It was a good thing I was the empath and not him. I wouldn't want him to know how much I'd wrapped my happiness up in him and how badly he hurt me with small actions such as dropping my hand.

Suck it up, Kailani.

"There it is!" Raife said as we tiptoed across the field and over to a corner of the fence. These sleeping farmers had no idea their king and queen were traipsing through their pasture at odd hours of the night. Sure enough, there was a gap in the fence big enough for a person to slip through if they went sideways. Every inch of the Nightfall border was walled off, from Fallenmoore to Necromere. It was stone and at least ten feet high. The queen made every citizen take a rotating "civil duty" weekend to build it about twenty years ago. *Keep the pests out*, she would tell us. On top of the wall were guard posts every few miles. This was right in between two of them. About four of the large stones were missing, allowing a person to squeeze through if they crouched.

Raife stared at the breach in the wall and rubbed his chin. "I'm torn between wanting to close this off after tonight to keep Nightfall soldiers out of Archmere, or leave it open so that we can sneak in at a future date."

Always thinking like a king.

"My vote is to leave it open. If Nightfall really wanted in, they would just climb the fence and jump over." Which we could have done as well, but it increased the risk of being seen by the guards up top.

He nodded. "I think you're right."

I'd read a war theory book in his bedroom yesterday while I was stuck there for several hours. So I knew a little about what he might be thinking.

Raife ducked down, going through the hole in the fence first, and I held my breath, waiting to see if it was safe to follow.

"Come on," he whispered.

I crouched down and looked through just as he held out a hand for me. Taking his offered assistance, I allowed him to pull me through, and stood before him, brushing off my dress. He didn't back up to give me space, so I stood right up against his chest with the wall at my back.

With our bodies this close together, my heart ratcheted in my chest so loudly I was certain he heard it.

"If things get dangerous, I want you to come back

here and wait for me, okay?" His voice was deep, and the protective vibes coming off of him were so strong I could feel my jaw tighten.

I laughed nervously. "You're the king. If things get dangerous, *you* need to come back here and I'll press on."

"No," he growled, holding my gaze. "I've had enough of your heroic efforts to last me a lifetime. If I tell you to run, you run. Got it?"

I hadn't really known what my empathic gift was. All my life I'd just sort of kept to myself because people overwhelmed me. Now that I knew what it was and that the feelings weren't mine, they were his, it still confused me. Because in this moment, underneath all of that protectiveness, was a deep love. Or at least what felt like love. Was that my love for him? It felt different, like a raw love mixed with so much fear. Because I wasn't afraid to love; I welcomed the feeling.

"Okay, Raife." I reached up and trailed my fingers down his jaw.

His eyelids fluttered, but then that fear surged up so strongly that it drowned out all the adoration left in him and he stepped back.

He's at war already, I thought. *A war with himself.*

And there was nothing I could do about it.

"Stay behind me," he muttered, and then took off into the woods.

With a sigh I followed him and shoved down all of the tumultuous feelings I was having.

We trudged through the woods, following the map. Raife kept his hood pulled up over his elvin ears and an arrow nocked into his bow. I was a foot behind him the entire way as we wound through the path that Autumn had left us on the map. There were little clues letting us know we were going the right way. A flat stack of rocks, a ribbon tied to a tree. I assumed this path kept one out of sight of any of the woodland guards, and I was right, because when the giant Nightfall castle loomed in the distance I nearly cried out in relief.

It was my home—filled with bittersweet memories, but my home nonetheless.

Raife stopped abruptly and I slammed into his back.

"What's wrong?" I asked.

He shook his head. "Nothing. It's just... bigger than I thought."

I nodded. The Nightfall queen was a visionary, an inventor, a builder. Everything was big, strong, made of steel or stone. Made to last and made from the blood, sweat, and tears of the Nightfall population. What the humans lacked in magic, they made up for in good old-fashioned hard work.

We were still hidden in the tree line and I watched his face as he stared up at the looming fifty-foot stone wall erected around the city. His gaze flicked to the dozens of archers patrolling the top wall, and the river moat that ran around the entire city. His eyes held wonder, disappointment, and determination. Or maybe that's what I felt from him.

"It's nearly impenetrable," he breathed. "For a large army to breach that will take..." I let him trail off, knowing his mind was working out the kinks of his eventual war plan. While he stared, working through all the different ways of attack, I turned around every few seconds and scanned the tree line for Nightfall warriors. I had thought up a cover story if we were caught by soldiers, but I was hoping that didn't happen, because I wasn't sure if Raife would go for it. Humans couldn't smell supernaturals. So long as Raife didn't show his ears we should be okay. I'd made him take off any insignia of Archmere before we left. The queen did employ a few sniffers, but they were rare. Not many fae wanted to betray their own kind for gold coin.

"We should move." I finally dragged Raife away from his gawking and towards the two sharp rocks that matched the ones on the map that Autumn had drawn. She'd sketched a log and then a plus sign and then a boat. I wasn't sure what it meant, but I was hoping it would make sense when we reached the two sharp rocks.

Raife followed my lead, and I quietly celebrated when I noticed the two rocks jutting out of the ground just a few paces to our right. The rocks were at the edge of the river moat, and when we reached them I looked down at the hollowed-out log on shore and grinned.

The log was a boat. Log, plus sign, boat. And it looked like it wouldn't fit more than three grown men, hence why this route was only enough for three.

Bless you, Autumn.

She had no idea that she was saving my aunt right now. I'd have to eventually get word to her as well, and get her out of the city before an attack. But there was a slight chance she would spread word to others and then the queen would find out, so I'd have to figure out a way to just take her and keep her locked down until after the attack. Though it seemed we were months away from that, so all I really needed to focus on now was my aunt and healing her of her seizures.

Raife reached down and grasped the edge of the hollowed-out log, using the rock to steady himself as he set his bow inside and then stepped down. The two sharp rocks were large, and we were positioned between them, so unless you were standing on the high castle wall directly in front of us, you couldn't see us. Raife stretched out a hand for me and I grabbed it, aiming one foot for the boat, and then pushed off the ground. The small log canoe wobbled and I had to suppress a shriek as I fell forward. Raife caught me by the hips, falling backwards with my weight, and then I was suddenly on top of him. Heat bloomed to life between us and I felt his entire body stiffen beneath me.

I swallowed hard, trying not to think about how much I loved him underneath me. How much I missed his body pressed against mine. How much I thought about the one time we'd laid together.

With little effort, he hoisted me up into a sitting position, but not before glancing quickly down at my lips.

It felt like a small triumph that he was still thinking about my lips, but before I could dwell on it Raife grabbed a rope and got into position to pull us across. It was a pulley system, I realized. The boat pulled back and forth, so no matter what side you were on you could pull it back over. I wondered if Autumn had made it or someone before her. The river wasn't terribly wide, but there were all kinds of rumors about the queen poisoning the water so that if you went in you would die. This forced the residents to use the front gates, which were monitored. I saw some leather gloves in the bottom of the boat and handed them to him.

"Don't touch the water. Rumor says it's poisoned," I told him, keeping my voice low.

He scowled at the murky water and then took the gloves, putting them on. "Of course it is."

Looking up at the high wall and the guards patrolling it, Raife waited for his chance to cross, eyeing the tall reeds on the other side of the river. The grasses were high, maybe three feet, and we could easily lie flat and inch across to avoid being seen. When he felt it was a good time to go, he pushed us off the edge of the river and then pulled the rope quickly but silently. I crouched down as far as I could go as we were directly exposed in the middle of the river. Raife grunted and puffed as he heaved forward with each pull, sweat beading his brow. His muscles strained against his tunic as he hauled us across the water at breakneck speed. Before I knew it, we were across and I reached out and held on to the tall reeds, hiding us in them as we waited for the alarm that we might have been seen. Raife ducked as well, laying his head against my shoulder and fiddling with the land anchor. A minute passed, and then two. No arrows flew, no horn sounded. We were clear.

Raife pulled out the map and we consulted it under the moonlight. There was a big black circle about ten feet from the river's edge. It was at the base of the tree split in two, and it was marked with one word: hole. That's where the map ended.

Hole.

He looked at me pleadingly. This was my home-town after all. But the thing about growing up in Nightfall was that our queen was constantly paranoid of assassination. We had curfews, and if we wanted to travel we had to register. We didn't just frolic along the palace walls staring at trees. I shrugged, looking at a few trees ten or twenty paces away.

Autumn was drunk on elf wine when she made this. The word *hole* was barely legible, and the split tree, if you looked closely, wasn't really split in two so much as it could have just been a bad drawing of a tree from a drunken girl.

Tipping my head in the direction of the trees, I hiked up my dress and began to crawl on all fours through the tall grass.

"You should have worn trousers," Raife muttered behind me.

I scoffed. "Nonsense, I want to look pretty while pulling off a rescue," I joked.

Trousers would have been smart, but I hadn't even thought about it until now. The poor silk of my dress was already getting stained.

Rest in peace, beautiful dress.

We reached a cluster of four trees and I sat in front

of them, still hidden in the tall grass. Raife seated himself next to me, looking down at the map. "None of them are split in half, and what does hole mean?"

I sighed. "Listen, Autumn would never intentionally lead me astray, but we were really drunk that night."

Raife's eyes danced with something I couldn't place. "Yes. I remember."

My belly warmed at the way he said it, and I wondered if we'd done something I wished I remembered.

"So maybe her drawing just wasn't good. It has to be one of these trees." I pointed to the four of them before us.

Raife nodded, looking perplexed. "Okay, and the word 'hole?' Once inside the city, it shows us coming up a storm drain. Is storm drain 'hole' in Autumn's drunken language?"

This was absolutely *not* the time to giggle but I couldn't help it. "I think it might be," I told him, and then chewed my lip. Was there a hole in the tree with a key to the storm drain? Had she meant to finish the map but we got drunk and it slipped her mind? I wished I remembered everything from that night so that I would know. Getting on my hands and knees again, I crawled to the base of the first tree, inspecting it.

I went to the second tree but found nothing. It was as I was crawling over to the third that my hand suddenly came down to the ground and fell into a—

"Hole!" I whisper-screamed, losing balance. I threw myself to the side so I wouldn't fall into the giant gaping hole in the ground. It was impossible to see with the tall grass surrounding it unless you were close to it, and it looked wide enough for a very large man to crawl down.

Raife crawled up beside me and we stared down into the hole. It was completely black, which was actually terrifying.

"Are we supposed to go down there?" I asked him. "Do you think this is the storm drain that leads into the city?"

Raife frowned. "I hope it's a secret tunnel to the queen's bedroom. I'll slit her throat in her sleep and end this war before it starts."

I knew he was dead serious, so I didn't laugh.

"I highly doubt that the queen would have a secret access unguarded like this." I felt around the outside of the hole and my fingers caught the edge of cold steel. I gasped. "It *is* a storm drain!"

He looked impressed for a moment, and then stuck his head into the hole before coming back up. "I hear slow trickling water," he confirmed.

It was dry season, so hopefully that meant we weren't about to go swimming.

"Do you mind jumping into the dark scary hole first?" I asked with a nervous laugh.

Raife gave me a winning smile that made my stomach flip over. "Always," he said, and there was something about that word and the way he said it that melted my heart.

With a fearless wink, he leapt into the dark abyss and I immediately heard the splashing of water as he landed. "Jump down, I'll catch you!"

I swallowed hard, closing my eyes, and then jumped up into the air, and down. His arms came around me, hooking under my knees and back, holding me to his chest. I was plunged into complete darkness, only the beating of Raife's heart and his strong arms to keep me sane. A purple light then illuminated the space and I looked up to see that it was coming from him. He was staring down at me with a serious look on his face.

"Being close to you like this... it's the best feeling in the world," he breathed.

I forgot where we were then. Who I was. What was up or down. I was just lost in his eyes, which were glowing light purple with elvin magic. What was he talking about? It came out of nowhere but I didn't care. I just smiled.

"You take the pain away. I forget what it's like not to be consumed by grief and revenge all the time," he clarified, and it was like I'd been plunged into ice cold water.

Oh.

He wanted to be close to me because I was an empath, not because I was... me.

"Glad to help," I said with a wan smile. Was this what it was like for his mother too? Always having people want her for her power? I wished she were still alive so that I could ask. It would be nice to know another empath.

I noticed a metal ladder behind him. "Ladder for the way back," I pointed out, hoping to cut this tension. In this moment, I wasn't sure I could stay fake-married to him for the next five years. It would be painful for me.

He started to walk to the castle and I tapped his chest. "You can put me down now."

He shook his head. "You'll ruin your dress. And your shoes aren't right for this."

I wasn't going to argue with that, so I allowed him to carry me the next hundred or so feet under the castle wall, all the while absorbing the emotions coming off of him as if it were second nature.

Guilt. Sadness. Fear. Lust.

I used to think that the lust was for me, but now I

wondered if he was just thinking of one of the previous girls he'd bedded. This whole empath thing was new, and picking up on emotions in real time was hard to discern.

I sighed, wishing someone would come along and take away my heartache and rejection as easily as I could take his.

Raife stopped beneath a big metal storm drain with another ladder hanging from it and looked down at me. "You think this is it?"

I nodded; I'd been tracking how deep in we'd gone. "One of many, but this is closer to the west wall, which is where I lived. It's pretty quiet at night since it's full of neighborhoods."

Raife heaved me onto the ladder. I clung to it as he then reached up and pushed the steel drain up and over with a grunt.

"Shhh," I told him.

He paused, and then pushed again. It wasn't scraping, so I was guessing this was in the grasses by the community garden. I didn't know where every storm drain was, but I knew generally where we were, and that was the only grassy area near the west wall. When the drain cap was completely off, I climbed up the ladder and peeked my head out a few inches.

I didn't expect my heart to ache when I looked upon the sleepy street of my old neighborhood, but it did. We were in the gardens, one of my favorite places, and I could see the university off in the distance, and the queen's palace. Autumn's cottage was within stone's throw, and so was my aunt's. Tears welled in my eyes. I wasn't prepared for the emotions of it all.

"All clear?" Raife asked below.

I wiped at my eyes and nodded, hoisting myself up out of the drain. I stood and Raife popped up out of the hole in the ground too and stood beside me, looking around wildly with his bow drawn.

"Put that in your cloak," I told him. "They will assume you are human if you are if you are with me."

He obliged and tucked it into his waistbelt, under his cloak with the hood pulled up. I watched as his eyes darted around in fascination. Grabbing his hand, I pulled him onto the cobblestone walkway and past the rows of houses. My street was three more over, and we'd have to pass McFee's Tavern to get there. Technically, it was after curfew, but the guards let us drink at the tavern and go right home if we didn't get in fights or vandalize property. I wondered if any of my friends from the university were inside right now.

Penelope? Matt? Did they all think I was a slave sold off to some horrible master who whipped me daily? As we approached the tavern, a figure walked up out of one of the alleys.

I recognized his guard's uniform immediately.

Wasting no time, I pushed Raife into the wall of Mrs. Honeycutt's house and then pressed my lips to his. He froze, seemingly in shock at my sudden kiss, but then the guard's voice made its way to us.

"Hey, you're out after curfew," he snapped.

Raife's lips parted then, his tongue stroking mine; his hand came around to grasp my butt. I moaned in surprise, not even caring if this was all for show, and heat flared to life between us. The guard's voice was closer this time.

"Lovebirds... time to go home or I'll have to take you in."

We broke away panting, locking eyes for a moment, and I forgot about the guard or the fact that we were doing a high-stakes rescue mission. It was just Raife and I in this moment.

"Get your lady home." The guard looked at Raife and Raife nodded, threading his fingers through mine, stroking my palm and then pulling me away from the guard and towards the tavern.

My legs felt weak from that kiss, but I knew Raife had only played along for the guard. "See, top marks in theatre," I told him.

Raife gave me a side glance, and I was surprised to see hurt there.

"This is my street," I said before he could speak, and pointed to our lane just beyond the tavern. Music blared from the open windows of the neighborhood pub, and I wondered who was playing tonight. *Moxie and the Heartbreakers? The Radical Six?*

Raife screwed up his face. "What is that awful music?"

I laughed. "Rock."

The drums were loud and nothing like they had in Archmere. It probably just sounded like a bunch of noise.

Grasping his hand, I broke into a run down my street and towards the little brown cottage with the bird feeder outside. I hadn't seen my aunt in over a month. Not since they were yanking me away as a slave.

Autumn promised to bring her news that I was alive and well in Archmere, but I knew she wouldn't believe it until she saw it. She was very protective over me, much like Raife.

Raife kept scanning the street, left and right, until we reached my door.

The little sign I helped my auntie paint when I was four years old hung above the doorway. "Love grows here," it read. The pink and purple flowers were chipping off, but the black lettering was still legible. We'd painted it after I moved in with her, after my parents died and she assured me this would always be a home where I felt safe and loved. I bent down and pulled up the pot near the door, grinning when I saw the key was still there.

Slipping the key into the lock, Raife and I stepped inside and I closed the door quickly behind us. The house was dark and quiet, and I knew she would be sleeping at this hour. I didn't want to scare her by looming over her bed, so I called out loudly into the house, "Auntie!"

We passed the little sitting room and I called out again, "Auntie, it's me!"

There was a rustling in the back of the house, near her room, and then I heard her, "Lani?"

I broke into a run then, going left at the kitchen and then down the hall to her open door. She was sitting on the edge of her bed with the light turned on. Her blankets were at her waist; she was wearing one of her floral nightgowns. I looked at her with tears in my eyes. I didn't even give her a chance to speak, I just crashed into her with the biggest hug, pushing her backwards on the bed. Her throaty laughter filled the room and it was the best sound, the sound of my childhood, of happiness and better days.

I pulled back to look at her, and the second she saw me she broke into a huge grin. But what I saw stopped me dead in my tracks.

Half of her face wasn't moving. She seemed to notice my reaction and touched the slack side of her face. "I had another seizure yesterday, a bad one. The medicine doesn't work anymore."

"Raife!" I called, but he was right there, swooping in front of me. He pulled back his hood.

"Hello..." He knelt before her and extended his hand. "I'm Kailani's husband, the king of the elves."

My aunt looked like she was in shock, which was understandable. "So it's true." She reached out and took his hand. "You shouldn't be here," she told him. "The queen hates you."

Raife gave her a dazzling smile. "Well, the feeling is mutual."

"Raife is the greatest healer in the realm, Auntie. He's going to fix you," I told her.

Raife held a hand over her head and squinted as if he were reading a complicated text. He frowned, and then nodded as if understanding something.

"What is it?" I asked.

Raife looked at my aunt instead of me. "Your seizures are caused by a growth in your brain. As the growth gets bigger, it damages the surrounding tissue."

My heart felt like it had stopped beating. In all our tests and all of our machines here in Nightfall, we hadn't figured that out. "A mystery illness" they called it. Seizure disorder of "unknown cause," they'd said. They drugged her instead of finding the root cause, and now in ten seconds Raife had figured it all out.

"Please tell me you can fix it." I knelt beside him and took her hand.

Raife gazed at me with a smile, and then at my aunt. "I can. It will take a few sessions at the infirmary in Archmere. The goal is to slowly shrink the mass. If we do it too quickly, it can disturb things and cause another seizure. With the mass gone, you should get full facial movement back immediately."

I'd been watching my aunt this entire time, stony faced, in shock, but at Raife's words she burst into tears and then pulled him in for a hug.

"Bless you, child," she whispered and I smiled.

Watching my auntie call the king of the elves a child brought me great joy. And to my surprise, Raife reached around and returned her hug.

When they pulled back, my aunt looked back at me. "You got married without me?" She picked up my hand and inspected the ring. Raife had given it back to me so that the palace staff didn't ask questions if I was seen without it.

I glanced at Raife and he nodded. I'd told him that I could lie to anyone in the realm but I wouldn't lie to my aunt, so she would be the only person we would tell.

"It's fake. In order for Raife to get what he wanted from his council and to pay off my debt. In five years, we will file for a dissolution," I told her.

She frowned, looking from Raife to me. "Oh," was all she said, dropping the ring back down.

"Naturally, no one knows that, so I would appreciate your discretion," Raife added.

My aunt nodded. "As long as you treat her with respect and kindness, I don't care what kind of little arrangement you two have going on."

I squeezed her hand, grateful she was taking this well and knowing one hundred percent that she was lying when she said she didn't care. She wanted me to marry for love—she'd always told me so—but she was trying to be agreeable. Raife sensed the lie too, because he made the face he always did when he knew someone was lying. Like he smelled something distasteful.

"Shall we get out of the place?" I asked my aunt.

She stood, looking around her room. "How long should I pack for?"

Raife and I shared another look. The war on Nightfall was his thing, and I didn't want to spill the beans and jeopardize the mission in any way.

Raife cleared his throat. "It would be my honor if you would come live at the palace with Kailani and I for the foreseeable future."

My heart warmed at the way he'd worded it. My aunt seemed surprised at that, her mouth popping open, and then she looked at me as if needing confirmation.

"Auntie, you can't come back. You can only pack one bag," I told her, hoping she understood I would never ask this if it wasn't important. Life or death.

She swallowed hard, seeming to understand that it would be unsafe to come back, and unsafe meant war.

My aunt nodded. "Doesn't matter. Stuff doesn't make a home. Family does."

My heart pinched at that.

Over the next ten minutes she packed her bag, bringing items that surprised me. All of her silver, which made sense, but not a single piece of clothing, I guessed because she could make more; she was an expert seamstress. She brought her favorite tea mug, a bunch of my baby pictures, and pictures with my mom and her growing up, all of her jewelry, and a bag of her favorite cookies.

"Ready." She beamed, always in a chipper mood, and I tried not to react to the fact that half of her face wasn't moving. Raife gave me a sweet smile, letting me know he would heal her and all would be well, and then we moved to the front door. I gave my aunt a quick rundown of the escape route, knowing that lowering her down the ladder and into the tunnel would take the longest time and we'd be the most exposed.

"The guards patrol right in front of the tavern. It's a bit longer route but we should pass the industrial complex instead," my aunt offered after I told her we were confronted with a guard on our way here.

Raife looked to me to take the lead and I nodded. It was a good idea. The industrial complex was only busy in the daytime, and rarely had but one guard at night. I used to sneak over there as a teen and shoot at glass bottle targets with friends with our rock launchers we made in school.

"Let's do it," I agreed.

Raife held out a hand. "I'll let you ladies take the lead."

My aunt gave me a knowing look, a look that said she liked him, and I tried not to blush. Opening the front door, I looked left and right, making sure it was clear. It was. We all stepped out onto the street and I palmed the key in my hand, seeing no use to lock up or put it back. I wanted to keep it as a memento. My aunt started to walk left, away from the tavern and down the back of the road that would lead to the industrial complex, but then I got an idea.

"Be right back," I told them, and turned. Lifting up on my tiptoes, I grabbed the "love grows here" sign, having to wiggle it back and forth to loosen the nail that held it in place. When I finally got it off, my aunt was waiting behind me with her small suitcase open.

I grinned, placing it on top of all of her beloved possessions, and then we were ready to go.

We made quick work of the longer route, but as we neared the industrial building I noticed the lights were on in one of them. This was where all of the queen's machines were made and tested and replicated en masse. A lot of the citizens worked machine factory jobs, but they were usually only working during the daylight hours.

There were shadows moving behind the frosted glass windows and we walked faster, hoping to pass before anyone saw us. Just as we neared the closest window with a light on, a blood-curdling scream ripped through the air and the hair on my arms stood up.

Raife stopped and I did as well, sharing a look with him.

My aunt chewed her lip, eyeing the window, then the scream came again. It was female, and it was clear she was in pain or being tortured.

"Not sure I can sleep at night if we pass by and don't try to help." My aunt was always direct and to the point, which was a big thing I loved about her.

"Same," I agreed.

Raife sighed, pulling out his small dagger, and handed it to me. "You know how to use one, I assume?" He'd seen me fight the slaver the first day, and although

I didn't relish violence I would use it when needed, without hesitation.

I nodded and he pulled out his bow. Turning to my aunt, he held her gaze. "Meet us at the garden storm drain. If a guard stops you on the way, tell him you're leaving your husband, that you caught him cheating. Make a big scene and make the guard feel uncomfortable."

My aunt nodded. "Won't be too far from the truth."

I winced; her husband really had cheated on her, but it was he who left for the other woman. Raife looked stricken, but my aunt smiled her crooked smile. "His loss. See you soon. Save that girl, or at least put her out of her misery."

We nodded, but the thought of killing the girl hadn't crossed my mind, and now I felt sick.

We slipped through the open unguarded gate of the industrial machine park and then approached the building. The windows at street level were frosted with an acid wash on the lower half to give privacy, but the upper half of the window was crystal clear. There were two windows with the lights on, and one of them was cracked open for fresh air. If we could just climb on top of something and peek over the frosted bit, we could get a better view of what the Hades was going on.

The screaming had stopped and that worried me.

Did they kill her? Who was she and what had she done to deserve such treatment?

"Here," Raife whispered, and I peered over to see him lifting a big wooden crate that once held one of the queen's machines. Scurrying over to help him, I hooked my fingers into the slats and carried it over to the base of the window that was closed so there was less chance we would be seen.

If we held absolutely still, we could hear the voices inside.

"Is she dead?" a man said.

"No, just passed out," another male said.

Once the large crate was firmly in place, Raife and I both scrambled quietly on top of it and then looked at each other.

It was as if we were waiting for the other to say this was a horrible idea and we shouldn't look. *We should run to the garden and get back to Archmere and forget we ever heard those screams.* But then, as if we shared one mind, we both slowly raised ourselves up to peer into the clear part of the window. It took a moment for my mind to process what I was seeing. There was a large machine the size and appearance of a giant fan with a hole in the center. In that hole was a glass box the shape of a coffin. In the box was a girl, limp but breathing slowly. The tips of her ears indicated she was either elf or fae. I couldn't tell from here but I felt Raife go rigid beside me, which made me wonder if she was an elf. There were four guards, one at each corner of the room; they held various weapons that would overwhelm the small dagger I had brought.

"Will her ears shrink once the treatment is done?" a bald man wearing a white lab coat asked another male with long reddish hair that was tied back into a bun at his nape.

"No. I already told Queen Zaphira I could build her a machine that strips a magical creature of their power so they *appear* human, but it will not make them one genetically."

Dizziness washed over me at his words. They just... did they somehow strip that girl of her magic? That was possible? Bile rose in my throat, and Raife ever so quietly pulled out his bow. I reached out and stopped his hand, giving him a pleading look. If he sounded the alarm now, we would never get out of here with my aunt.

I could not only see the rage boiling in Raife's expression, I could feel it, his and then mine. I was angry too. I wanted to light this entire place on fire and burn it all to the ground, but I also wanted to live to fight another day. The queen was the brains of all of these inventions. So long as she lived they would still be popping up long after we destroyed one scientist or one machine. She had blueprints of all the machines in her safe, and dozens of engineers and scientists. These people were expendable. I hoped to convey that to Raife with a look.

"She's waking," the redhead said, and both of our heads snapped back in their direction. The girl whimpered as she looked up at the two men.

"Display your power," one of them commanded her.

She lay there shaking like a leaf, sweating, and ignored him.

"Display your magic now or I turn the machine back on!" he snapped, and she flinched, holding up her hand. She held her fingers out like claws and stared at them in shock.

What happened next was too much for me to watch. A gut-wrenching wail ripped through the room and her sorrow slammed into me as if I were right in front of her. I fell backwards, scrambling off the box at the realization that she'd lost her magic, what made her who she was.

"Welcome to Nightfall. You are now human." The man's voice filtered through the window and reached me just as I threw up on the rocks. Her sobs were soul crushing, filtering out into the night. I couldn't imagine what it must be like to be her to find out her magic had been stripped from her. She felt half empty, and my empathic gift was soaking it all up, even from out here. It was too much for me.

I turned, wondering why Raife wasn't behind me, when I saw him standing in front of the now cracked-open window, arrow nocked in his bow.

I wanted to scream for him to stop but it was too late. Before I reached him he'd already loosed three arrows. I'd never seen someone move that fast. His arm was a blur, the arrows hitting their marks, because I could hear grunts of pain and shouts of surprise inside, before bodies thudded to the ground. By the time I reached the window to peer through, every man in that room was on the ground bleeding out. Arrow in neck, in chest, in stomach. It was insane, and I now knew why Raife commanded the army of Bow Men. He was the fastest, most accurate marksmen I'd ever seen.

The girl in the glass coffin sat bolt upright then and stared at Raife.

He pulled his hood back and she wept. "My lord."

I didn't know if he knew her personally or just as any elf would know her king, but she leapt out of the glass case and then sprinted across the room in record time. The feelings coming from Raife were similar to what he felt for me, an intense need to guard this woman and bring her to safety. She was one of his. Jealousy surged up inside of me but I pushed it down. It wasn't right to feel that way. He didn't feel romantically towards her, at least not any feelings that I felt, but still, I couldn't help the envy. Just another sign how far I'd fallen in this one-way marriage.

Raife pushed the window wide open and told her to jump as he held out his arms. She looked to be in her early twenties, and was wearing a thin white medical gown. Without hesitation, she leapt and Raife caught her, setting her to her feet.

"Can you run?" he asked.

She nodded, her eyes bloodshot, lip quivering. She seemed to notice me for the first time and burst into a sob. "My queen..." She reached for me as if she needed a fellow female companion, and even though I knew it was going to be awful, I grasped her hands.

Absolute desolation and darkness enveloped me then and the girl gasped. "Empath," she whispered, looking relieved.

There was no time for this, so I pushed her emotions deep down inside of me so that I could still function, and then dragged her along as Raife directed us to run.

Tears leaked from my eyes and muffled sobs escaped me as I processed the realization that she would never again heal anyone, nor be considered an elf among her own kind. Raife was nervously casting side glances at me as we ran down the road, coming to the edge of the palace before needing to cut back into the neighborhood and avoid the tavern. My aunt would be waiting at the gardens. Probably worried sick by now.

As we passed, Raife stopped, tucking us into the shadows and eyeing the palace in the distance with disdain.

"I could sneak in. Find Zaphira. Kill her. Meet up with you," he breathed against my ear.

I shook my head, pointing to the large columns that decorated the front walk. There were at least twenty of them. "You see those columns?"

He nodded.

"They are hollow. A guard stands inside each one. And there are probably fifty more inside and twenty outside her bedchamber. Raife, you're good but not *that* good."

The hope died in his eyes and I hated that I was the one to do that to him.

"We need the others. We need an army," I told him.

"I want to go home," the girl whimpered, still clutching my hand.

I was torn between my own emotions, the broken girl beside me, and now Raife's bloodthirsty revenge. It was causing my empathic gift to go haywire and overwhelm me.

"My aunt is probably worried, and someone will find those bodies soon," I informed Raife.

He dipped his head, a defeated frown pulling at his lips, then we ran for the gardens.

It was a short run, but I counted the amount of times he looked back at the castle.

Five.

Five times he wrestled with ditching us and going after the woman who murdered his entire family in one night. I didn't blame him. We found my aunt sitting near the open storm drain clutching her bag, and Raife helped all of us down into the tunnel quickly. He joined us inside the ankle-deep water and then covered the grate overhead so we couldn't be followed.

Illuminating our path, we made it to the hollowed-out log boat at the river without incident. Raife had to take my aunt across first, then double back for me and the girl. She told me her name was Natasia, and she wouldn't leave my side, no doubt enjoying the numbness of not having to feel her emotional damage and pain. Because *I* was feeling it all—nausea swam inside my stomach, and my mind was in a dark place. But I kept quiet. This poor girl had just been tortured within an inch of her life and then stripped of her power. I was going to carry that pain as long as I could.

We trudged through the woods, Raife carrying my aunt's suitcase in one hand and guiding her elbow with the other. Watching him tend to her like she was his own family just made my hopelessness deepen.

When we finally reached the hole in the wall, I didn't have much will to live. What was the point? No one would love me now that I had no powers. I couldn't tell my parents I was... magically castrated.

I shook my head, dislodging thoughts that were not my own, and looked down at Natasia, who rested her head on my shoulder.

Raife helped my aunt through the gap in the wall and then reached for Natasia just as the siren sounded behind us at Nightfall Castle.

"Time to ride fast and hard out of here," Raife said, yanking the girl from my clutches and shoving her through the opening in the stone.

I stood there in shock, a shell of self-pity as Raife stepped up to thread his fingers into my hair and cup my face. "Kailani, look at me."

I looked up at him, realizing that I was sobbing uncontrollably.

"Kailani, listen to my voice. My mother had to learn when to let go of other people's emotions. As an empath, you take everything, absorb it like a sponge and process it way too fast. You have to remember who *you* are. You are not her. You are loved, you have a family, you—"

"*You* don't love me," I said between sobs. "And now

that I can't heal, no one will."

Raife looked concerned, his eyes going to my lips. "Kailani, snap out of it! This isn't you." He shook my face a little in his hands, but I tried to pull away from him.

"Just let me go. Let me die!" I screamed, wanting to go back and let them find me, kill me rather than live like this without my healing magic. I was her. She was me. We were one.

Raife pulled me against him, pinning my body to his, and then leaned forward, brushing his lips over mine ever so softly. It reminded me of our first kiss, the one when he was drunk and said he didn't remember. He was toying with me, teasing me. And I loved every second of it.

"Lani, come back to me. *I need you*," he whispered against my mouth. I gasped and the storm cloud of emotions retreated, and I was suddenly myself again. My chest heaved, the sobbing stopped, and I finally felt clearheaded. It was like being intoxicated and then rapidly sobering.

I shook myself, pulling back to look at him. "You remember our first kiss?" I asked him.

He gave me a crooked smile. "A man doesn't forget a kiss like that. I'll remember it as long as I live." He then dropped my face and pulled me towards the hole in the wall as my head swam with what he'd just said.

He *did* remember the kiss and he'd used it again to bring me out of *whatever* that was.

"My lord!" Cahal was on the other side, sounding panicked.

The barking of far-off scent dogs rang throughout the forest, so I allowed Raife to guide me through the opening. Then he came through himself.

When we stood up in the farmlands of Archmere, I nearly collapsed in relief.

We made it! I scanned the space to take in all that was happening. My aunt was consoling poor Natasia as Raife guided me away from her, a clear twenty-foot distance.

"You can't let her be alone," I told him. "Her thoughts are too dark right now."

Frankly, I was afraid she'd tried to end her life. That's how I'd felt only moments ago.

Raife nodded. "I'll have her under round-the-clock surveillance at the infirmary. And I'll start your aunt's first healing tonight," he said. "But I can't let you near her right now. You need to be alone and rest. That always helped my mom."

I threaded my fingers through his and squeezed his hand. "Thank you."

I was slightly embarrassed about my behavior a moment ago, saying he didn't love me and all that other stuff.

Raife squeezed my hand in return and then got me in the carriage. "I'll be right back," he said, and then disappeared. A moment later my aunt was there, climbing in.

She sat across from me, and stared at me in the dim carriage light. I wondered what she would say. We were finally alone, and she'd just been torn from her home in the middle of the night indefinitely. She found out I was fake-married and then had consoled a poor girl who'd been tortured.

She looked me right in the eye and gave me a lopsided smile. "If you're queen, what does that make me? Surely a duchess or something?"

I burst out into laughter, which turned to tears of relief. My aunt's lighthearted personality was another one of my favorite things about her. Stepping over to sit beside her, I lay my head on her shoulder, snuggling next to her as I would when I was a little girl. Her energy was cool as a breeze in winter, and I nearly sighed in relief, taking that into myself and allowing it to relax my frazzled thoughts. Sleep was pulling at my limbs but I tried to keep my eyes open as I heard Raife barking orders to his men. He was calling the Bow Men troops up to defend the wall just in case Zaphira decided to come over. Then he asked Cahal to take the girl to the infirmary.

My aunt sighed, and I could feel her sudden anxiety fill up the entire carriage, which had me alert.

"He's going to bring war to Nightfall, isn't he? That's why you had to get me out?" she asked.

I pulled my head up and looked at her. Her friends were there, and my childhood friends, and war wasn't good for the people—it never was—but the queen had to die. She'd killed his entire family and almost poisoned me.

"Yes. Queen Zaphira will die. I will make sure of it." I surprised myself with how much I'd taken on Raife's duty.

My aunt just nodded, as if she expected as much to eventually happen. With that, we both rested our heads on each other, and then I drifted off to sleep.

When I woke up, it was only for a moment as Raife was slipping me into our bed in his room. Then again, I woke for a second time, in the middle of the night as the bedroom door shut and I saw him sleeping on the chaise lounge. I remember the pang of sadness that sliced through my chest that he wouldn't sleep next to me, but I was too tired to dwell on it.

The next morning I woke late and found that it was already lunchtime. Raife was in the private dining room when I entered, looking at some maps.

"Morning," he said in greeting. "Natasia is doing much better with an emotional healing but is still on watch, and your aunt's mass has shrunk about half the size. She's resting in the infirmary for the next two days just as a precaution. She will be very sleepy."

He'd already done it? I'd wanted to be there, but I suppose time was of the essence. She could have another seizure, and then we would be in trouble with more damage.

"Thank you," I told him.

He nodded, chewing at his lip, and I knew he was dealing with a lot this morning as king.

"Did Nightfall retaliate?" I asked.

He rubbed his face. "Not yet. I was told their scent dogs found the gap in the fence and then they left."

We hadn't talked about the machine yet, the one that could strip us of our power. It felt too dark to speak out loud, but I knew we had to.

"Raife. That machine... you have to stop her." Emotion clogged my throat when I thought of Natasia in the infirmary on twenty-four-hour watch because that machine had taken everything from her. Magic was what made up a magical creature's essence. Now that I had this ability to be empathic, or breathe the Breath of Life into someone, I couldn't imagine it being taken away.

"I know," he said, his voice sounding hollow as if he was warring with something. "I need to go get word to Drae about this machine. His people cannot live without their magic, but I don't trust a messenger. It would cause panic across the entire realm."

I nodded and Raife shook his head. "But I also need to stay and prepare for a possible retaliation. Those arrows I left in the men are elvin-made. The queen will know it was someone from Archmere who assassinated her scientists."

"So what?" I growled, and Raife appeared shocked at my sudden anger, his eyes going wide. "Let that evil witch *try* to retaliate."

Raife looked approvingly over at me. "My queen, I admire your willingness to go to war with Zaphira, but if she were to attack in full force without me here, it would end in disaster."

"If you don't get word to Drae, then she could use that machine on the people of Embergate and kill them. The dragon king would be wholly unprepared."

He leaned forward and placed his face in his hands. I abandoned my lunch and dragged my chair closer to him. When I sat next to him, he looked up at me and I saw all of the responsibility of a king warring in his eyes.

"If you can get Drae to go to Thorngate and tell Lucien of this machine, you might be able to unite all of the races against her. I know how things work in Nightfall, Raife. She'll put all of her engineers into an assembly line, reproducing that one machine, and by month's end she will have a hundred of them. By years end, a thousand."

He audibly choked at my words and I nodded.

"So go. Go get Drae, and if anything happens while you're gone, the council and I can handle it."

His eyes burned into mine as if assessing my ability to do so.

I leaned back and crossed my arms, raising one eyebrow. "I read the entirety of *The Nature of War* in your room the other day. I can handle a skirmish at the border."

He nodded. "Good, because as queen that's exactly what you'll be called to do in my absence."

Anxiety roiled through me at that but I just nodded. Servant becomes queen, and then acting war leader? Sounded like a recipe for disaster.

"I'll give Zaphira one more night to make her move. If she doesn't, I'll ride out to Embergate first thing in the morning. I'll tell Drae about the machine, and ask him to see Lucien with me." He stood then and told me he had meetings to get to.

I inclined my head and finished my lunch in relative silence. I didn't like this laidback queen role. I wanted to be in on the meetings. I missed being his assistant and being busy, but I understood that job was no longer appropriate. At least I didn't need to taste the food anymore. I never liked that.

THE DAY PASSED QUICKLY. I spent the entirety of it at the infirmary with my aunt, and even visited Natasia briefly, keeping a distance from her.

"I should go," I told my aunt, yawning. It was after dinner and I was tired even though I'd slept in.

My aunt nodded, she'd slept half the time I was there and spent the rest of the time listening to me read to her quietly.

When I kissed her cheek she smiled, with all of her facial muscles, and I nearly wept in relief. "Goodnight, Auntie." I stood and crossed the room, reaching for the door.

"Lani..." My aunt's voice was serious, the kind of serious tone she used when I was in trouble or she wanted to convey something with gravity.

I turned and looked at her in concern.

"He loves you. Don't let him tell you any different," she said.

Tears spilled over onto my cheeks at her assessment of Raife. I pulled my hand away from the door and walked back over to the bed.

"I know how a man looks at a woman when he's in love. That man loves you," she said with even more seriousness to her voice.

I thought I had been doing a good job of keeping my heartbreak over Raife silent, but I guessed not.

My stomach tied in knots. I wanted it to be true

with every fiber of my being. "Even if that were true, he's emotionally unavailable," I said.

My aunt peered up at me from her place nestled in the bed. "Maybe you've made it too easy for him."

I frowned. "What do you mean?"

My aunt shrugged innocently. "If it's a fake marriage, then you should both be able to take a secret lover with no issue, right?"

My mouth popped open in shock—but then closed, opened again, and then closed. I didn't *want* to take a lover and I believed she knew that. Was she saying that I should pretend to take one to make him jealous? That just seemed cruel.

"Sometimes men need to be afraid of losing something to realize they want it," she said finally, and then closed her eyes as if that was that.

Her words had thrown my entire being into a frenzy. But she was right. I was being too soft with him, available when he wanted, shutting down when he wanted.

Screw that!

It was time to shit or get off the pot, as they liked to say in Nightfall. If Raife didn't want a sexual relationship with me, then we should take lovers. Did we really both expect to be celibate for the next five years?

I left the infirmary with the two guards that Raife had assigned to me and made it back to the palace in record time. It was well past dinner so I didn't expect to see him in the dining room, and was pleased when I found him standing by the bookshelf in our room, selecting a book to read.

When I walked in, he turned. "Hey, how's your au—?"

I pushed him against the bookshelf and claimed his mouth in a fiery kiss. It was angry, and forceful and... *hot*. It lit the core of my being on fire. But I needed to remain in control here. I had a plan. He growled the second my lips hit his and parted them, stroking his tongue against mine. When he did, I sucked his tongue and caused him to moan so loud I was sure the guards at the door heard it. When I had him right where I wanted him, I pulled back and met his hooded steely gaze.

"Raife, I'm a woman," I breathed against his mouth, "I have *needs*, and I understand if you can't or won't meet them, but they need to be met." I pulled away then, taking two full steps back. "This is all fake anyway, right?"

There was a fire in his eyes, but he stayed silent.

"You clearly have had an arrangement in the past with that woman Dara I saw visit your bedroom. I will make the same type of arrangement. We can live out the next five years of this fake marriage, at least not being totally miserable and sexually frustrated."

He swallowed hard, his chest heaving.

I had zero intention of taking a lover but I wanted to test whether or not we were truly just friends. Was I crazy? Were the feelings of love and adoration coming from him for me? I just didn't know anymore.

"You're unhappy," he said, with more sadness in his voice than I anticipated.

"I'm unsatisfied," I corrected, and stepped closer to him.

Another hard swallow.

"It's up to you how you want to play this, Raife." I kissed his cheek. "Goodnight. Have a safe trip to Embergate," I whispered in his ear, and then brushed past him, walking into the washroom with my heart beating on the floor at his feet.

That was by far the bravest thing I'd ever done. I couldn't stop the frantic beating of my heart throughout my entire bath. So when I finally had the guts to leave the washroom, I prayed he was in our bed, ready to accept what this really was. Ready to make me and my aunt not crazy. Ready to love me.

But when I saw the lights were off and the bed was made, my stomach dropped. On the couch was Raife's slow-breathing form.

I bared my soul to him and he fell asleep.

If that wasn't the most depressing thing in the world, I didn't know what was.

It was a long time before I drifted off.

THE NEXT MORNING I woke up and peered across the room at the couch. The sheets were folded and stacked at the end of the cushion with the pillow on top. Did he leave for Embergate without saying goodbye?

It was then that I noticed the note next to my pillow, on his side of the bed, and my stomach tightened.

LANI,

You are one of the most beautiful women I have ever met. You're incredibly kind and you might even be smarter than me.

I STOPPED READING for a moment and pressed the letter to my chest, grinning up at the ceiling. It was a love letter. A love letter before he left. I would cherish it always. I pulled the parchment from my chest and read the next line, my heart plummeting into my stomach.

· · ·

BUT I CAN'T GIVE *you the life you want, the life you deserve. I won't lie, I do care about you, I am deeply attracted to you, but I told you when we started this not to fall in love with me. I'm dead inside and I can't love you back. It's just another thing Zaphira took from me. I'm paralyzed, afraid to care for anyone too deeply in the fear that I will have to watch them die. Some people have scars on the outside, mine are on the inside. They are invisible, so they are easy for others to forget. So you will have to settle for a deep and respectful friendship with me.*

THE TEARS FELL onto the parchment and my vision blurred, making it impossible to read further. A body-numbing grief spread through my entire being as I realized I had truly and fully fallen in love with him. Now I had to let him go. I blinked rapidly and read the last bit of the letter.

I JUST WANT *you to be happy. Your mere presence makes me happy, and ruling beside you these next five years will be my absolute pleasure. Thank you for doing this for me, for getting the council to approve my war so I can get the revenge my family deserves and heal that part of my soul that feels like it bleeds every day.*

. . .

I HEARD YOU LAST NIGHT. *It killed me but I heard you. If you want to take a lover to satisfy your needs...*

Okay.

-Raife

THE SOBS that ripped from my throat sounded animalistic. Raw agony tore through my chest, and I was afraid to look down for fear that my heart might actually be lying on the bed in a bloody mangled mess. As awful as the letter was, it was everything I needed to hear. I wanted the truth and I got it. He called me beautiful, sweet, and smart. He admitted he cared and was sexually attracted to me. He praised our friendship and told me to do what it took to be happy. It was a sweet and respectful letter and it *killed* me. What Zaphira did to him killed me. She robbed him of true love. She took from him a normal life and scarred up his insides so that he wouldn't even allow himself to love. I hated her for it and I wanted her dead.

I started to think up wild assassination plots then. Poison was impossible because she kept her food so well guarded and had half a dozen tasters. She once didn't eat for four days when she suspected the dragon king might have sent poison in retaliation for killing his betrothed. Instead, he killed her favorite son.

I was fuming mad, tearing across the room to get ready for the day with the grumpiest, most heartbroken feelings slamming around my body. I hoped Raife wasn't still here. If I saw him, I would burst into tears and then hug him. I couldn't be mad at him; he spoke his truth and I accepted that. I accepted being his friend. And I wouldn't take a lover. I never wanted one in the first place. I wanted him.

By the time I dressed and covered my red puffy eyes, it was late morning. The dining hall was empty but for Mrs. Tirth waiting with my food.

"Sorry. I slept in," I told her, and my gaze flicked to Raife's empty chair.

She looked at me compassionately. "He left before the sun even came up. Been gone for several hours."

I nodded, unable to help the tears that lined my eyes. Mrs. Tirth pretended not to notice when I blinked them away, and set my food in front of me. "Thank you," I murmured.

She dipped her chin. "The king requested that you sit in on his meetings for him while he is away and take notes. Here is your schedule for the day." She handed me a parchment and I relaxed a little. I was a busybody, needing something to keep my mind active, and right now I was so heartbroken that this was exactly what I needed to take my thoughts off of things.

I glanced at the parchment, mentally preparing.

Farming meeting.

Winter Ball planning.

Bow Men meeting.

Council meeting.

Infirmary rounds.

All in all, it was a light day.

With that, I finished my breakfast quickly and stepped into my farmers' meeting.

"Hello, gentlemen." I smiled.

They all greeted me, and I settled into my day, only thinking about Raife every minute or so. Was he in Embergate yet? Did Drae say yes? Would they go right to Thorngate, or come back here for a few days?

I broke for lunch after the Winter Ball planning meeting, and then stepped right into the Bow Men meeting. Raife's top six commanders were there. I nodded to Cahal, Ares, and a few of the others I knew well.

"Hey, guys, I'm taking notes for Raife so I can fill him in when he gets back."

Cahal nodded. "Alright, let's get started. We left off last week talking about preparing for the big war with the queen. His Highness wanted a thousand arrowheads forged per month, but we've had a shortage in metals."

I scrawled down the notes. "Can we melt down impractical items like sculptures and use that metal?"

Cahal inclined his head. "That was going to be my suggestion, but it will have to be by royal decree, and then we'll have to compensate—"

The door flung open and Haig burst inside with a messenger who was panting, dirt caked in his hair like he'd fallen off a horse.

"Queen Zaphira rides with her army to the east wall," Haig said in alarm.

Chills rose up on my arms, and I knew that Raife would never forgive me for urging him to leave. Because in the worst possible time, the queen of Nightfall was attacking. Had she been watching? Waiting until he left?

The messenger had finally caught his breath. "Over five hundred men march this way. Half on horseback, some ride on fast machines, like horseless carriages. The queen leads them."

My heart hammered in my chest as every single commander stood and looked from Haig to me.

Haig stepped into the room and sat beside me, leaning in to lower his voice. "Elvin law states that you are in charge in the absence of your husband. You must call an emergency war meeting with the council."

Holy Hades. Was this seriously happening?

"I'd like to call an emergency war meeting with the council. Bow Men, ready the troops for battle," I told them.

They saluted me and left. Haig ran out as well, presumably to get the other councilmen, and I sat there in absolute shock.

What the Hades was I going to do? Lead a war on our border? How? This was too much. I couldn't think.

It was in that moment that a line in *The Nature of War* came to me.

In times of war, staying calm is one of the most important things you can do. Others will look to you to lead, and the less nervous you are, the more faith they will have in your ability.

I inhaled deeply through my nose and shook out my limbs, rolling my neck.

I got this. Just a little skirmish at the east border with the witch I was just plotting to kill. If this went my way I might even be able to put her out of her misery and Raife wouldn't need to assemble all of these other kings.

The four councilmen burst into the room then and Aron looked right at me. "Zaphira was clearly spying on King Raife and saw that he left. She's choosing now to attack because she knows we are weak without our king," Aron said.

"No we're not," I said calmly. "Raife is an amazing leader and healer, but a single person being gone does not weaken an entire realm."

Haig stared at me, impressed, but Foxworth shook his head. "We can't let her get deep into the borders. Her army is larger and can conquer the entire realm before the king even gets back. He'll come back to burning fields, dead men, and enslaved women."

His words were sobering. I thought better on my feet, so I stood.

Stay calm, I told myself, taking in a deep breath as the council rolled out a parchment map on the table. I knew Nightfall and its people better than anyone here. I didn't exactly know the queen's battle plans or anything, but plenty of my friends had dated men in her army since every male above the age of sixteen was forced to join the reserves. I knew that they were heavily dependent on their machines.

The council was arguing about evacuating the highborns into Thorngate and begging the fae king for help when I cleared my throat and stepped up to the map.

"Bring the people from these outer fields into the safety of the palace walls." I pointed to the area on the map with the highest population of our farmers. Their knowledge of growing food was invaluable. We could afford to lose some crops but not the farmers themselves. "Then we set bear traps at the perimeter of the East wall to capture their horses. And we flood the field with as much wine and liquor as we can find."

The men frowned, staring at me perplexed. "Liquor?"

I nodded. "The queen's machines are all electric and electricity and fire don't mix."

"Fire? You're going to..." Haig suddenly looked impressed.

I could see the approval in their eyes as they glanced at each other.

"Are you saying we stay and fight the queen of Nightfall?" Haig asked me honestly.

I dipped my chin. "Are you really suggesting we abandon an entire realm over the fear of one woman? We can do this."

"One woman with five hundred men!" Foxworth barked. "I think we should take the highborn families and elite healers into Thorngate for safety."

Now *that* pissed me off. "Fine! Go and be a coward with the rich highborns. I'll stay with the Bow Men and the lowly farmers and fight for our home!" I snarled, pushing the table over and bursting from the room.

I'd never been so mad in my entire life. I knew that I'd probably just broken a law or something. I believed there needed to be a vote, but I didn't care. I wasn't running to the hills with the rich while the queen burnt Raife's home, our home, to the ground and killed the poor.

Footsteps fell in behind me and I readied myself for a fight. When I turned it was Haig, Aron, and Greylin.

Haig bowed deeply to me. "My queen, I'll bring in the farmers and people from the outlying villages," he said, and then took off down the hall running.

Aron bowed then. "My queen, I will get a group together and set the bear traps." He then left as well, and I tried not to let the emotion show on my face.

Greylin bowed, giving me a smile. "I will have villagers help me fill buckets with liquor and meet you at the stables with the Bow Men."

Once he left, I wanted to cry for how they just respected me, calling me their queen and backing my plan, but there was no time for that. Later I would drink an entire bottle of elf wine and cry myself to sleep, hoping to forget the trauma I was no doubt about to experience. But for now I had to go to war.

I had learned from my aunt's escape that dresses were not convenient to wear when doing nefarious things. I donned one of Raife's black suede trousers and the shortest, smallest tunic of his I could find, which was still pretty large on me. I was pretty crappy with a bow, but better with a sword, so I strapped that onto my waistbelt and then met the Bow Men lining up by the dozens outside the stables.

When I reached Cahal, he took a long look at my outfit but said nothing.

"How many do we have in all?" I motioned to the Bow Men and Archmere citizens that were being given weapons and conscripted to fight.

"Two hundred fifty," Cahal said.

Half of what the queen had. I remembered a line from *The Nature of War* then and it gave me an idea.

Play to your strengths.

"Take fifty of your best Bow Men and hide them in the trees of the Narrow Valley. We can funnel her men in and take out at least a hundred men before they can retreat."

Cahal grinned. "Yes, my queen." He turned and started to gather up men and I swallowed hard.

The Nature of War also said, *Out of all the things you do to be ready for war, inspiring your army is the most important.*

I'd have to give a speech.

With the help of two Bow Men, I stood on the back of my horse and put two fingers in my mouth, letting out a big whistle.

The murmurs stopped, and everyone turned to look at me, causing the nerves to burn in my stomach.

Stay calm. Inspire them.

"Queen Zaphira waited until our king was gone before she attacked!" I snarled. "That tells me that she's afraid of his leadership. She thinks we are weak without Raife Lightstone. Are you weak?" I asked.

Murmurs.

"Are you WEAK!?" I cried.

Screams responded with a resounding *no!*

"She has no idea what she's just walked into! No idea the shitstorm we are about to fling her way. I will die bloody on that battlefield before I give one inch of elvin land to that monster!" Spittle flew from my mouth as I bellowed across the entire field.

The men went insane then, screaming and waving their weapons in the air with grimaces.

"Let's ride!" I called, and then allowed the Bow Men to help me down.

"Shitstorm?" Cahal was back and grinning at me.

I shrugged. "It's a human expression, I guess. Let's go be her worst nightmare," I told him, and he spurred his horse as we rode off to war.

WE ALLOWED the queen to smash through the east wall. Her army trampled a few of the outlying farms, including the one with the yellow barn, but nothing we couldn't recover from. The most talented of the Bow Men were currently hiding in the trees that flanked the Narrow Valley. The Narrow Valley led to the most populated part of Archmere and the castle. Our civilian volunteers had soaked the dry grasses in alcohol at my request, and now we waited. Part of me couldn't believe this was happening, and the other part of me was running on instinct.

Remain calm.

I could freak out later. I had a war to win and a people to protect. Raife's people—my people too. I might be a fake queen in Raife's eyes but I loved this land, the land of my father, and I would not let it fall to the queen of Nightfall on my watch.

A messenger on horseback rode towards where we were stationed at the end of the Narrow Valley and I braced myself for his report.

"The queen's army rides this way!" he yelled. "She's sent some of her army through the Narrow Valley but most around it. She suspects an ambush."

I nodded. I'd prepared for this. Any smart woman would know that if you went through a valley between two large hills filled with trees, it could be a trap.

"Hold to the plan!" I screamed at our men and began to back up my horse. Going around the valley meant going around the hill, which took more time and was rocky and not an even trail. She'd struggle to get even a hundred men through there in any good length of time.

I rode over to Cahal, who stood ready for my word. "When her men get into the Narrow Valley, light the match and let it burn. Kill anything left moving with arrows."

He nodded. "You're going to the open hillside?"

I grinned. "I want to see her retreat with my own eyes."

Cahal gave me a crooked smile. "It's an honor to serve under you, my queen. Raife chose well when he married."

My throat tightened with emotion, more so because my heartbreak was so fresh. Still, his sentiment was genuine, and I thanked him before riding off behind and around the hillside, dismounting my horse to climb up the side of it where my team was waiting with the nets.

Civilians had volunteered to fight for their land in droves when they'd heard I had declined Foxworth's plan to flee.

I knew the Nightfall queen would suspect a trap at the Narrow Valley and so I'd had the civilians grab whatever rocks and boulders they could and shove them into fishing nets. Now we stood crouched behind bushes and makeshift camouflage as we waited for the queen and her men to cross the path at the base of the large hill. From this vantage point I could already see her army. I'd made it just in time. The past two hours had been the most rigorous and pulse pounding of my life. Mobilizing an army, preparing for war, it was nothing I'd ever experienced and so I was pleased that even though I could see the banner of Nightfall waving in the distance as they neared, we had a plan.

The sheer sight of over four hundred men, dozens of machines, trebuchets, and men flying in the air with mechanical wings, was enough to make terror crawl down my spine.

Another line from *The Nature of War* came back to me in that moment, and I thanked the Maker I'd read the entire book and committed it to memory, as I did most books I read.

People will die. As a leader, you need to worry about minimalizing the losses and tending to the wounded.

People will die.

People will die.

I looked around at the elvin men and women gathered, most of whom had brought their bow and arrow from home and wore makeshift breastplates made of cooking pans. A sob formed in my throat and I spun so that they wouldn't see me break down. Putting my face in my hands, I wept softly. Suddenly hands were on mine, ripping them away from my face and drying my eyes. My eyelids snapped open to see Haig standing before me.

When did he get here? He should be hiding in the castle with the rest of the council.

"My queen, the people look to you now for strength," he reminded me.

I cleared my throat, nodding, and then pulled him down to take cover with me behind the brush. I wiped the remaining tears from my cheeks and spun and faced the task ahead.

"Ready the nets," I whisper-screamed. The queen's army was quite far below at the base of the hill, but still I couldn't lose my element of surprise. She passed the hill, her archers shooting randomly up at it as we all crouched and hid, not firing back.

Shouts of alarm and screams rang out behind us on the other side of the hill, within the Narrow Valley, and I knew the war there had begun. They'd funneled right into our trap and our Bow Men were picking them off before the—

Smoke filled the air and I wrestled with climbing over the ridge to look down and see how the field burning idea had gone. But by the sounds of men screaming and machines exploding, I knew we'd won the Narrow Valley and they were surely retreating from there. Whatever men were left alive that was.

The queen knew too. I saw her then, leading her men. She wore her customary red battle leathers; mechanical wings hung from her back as she rode her black stallion. Strapped to her arms were the usual fire thrower and bolt shooter. She was as powerful as a dragon shifter from Embergate, or as deadly as a Bow Man from Archmere.

In all my planning, I hadn't thought of the flying men. The mechanical wings were relatively new. I'd seen men testing them around Nightfall City, but seeing six grown men fly towards where we all hid crouched on the hillside now had bile rising in my gut.

We needed the queen and her army to walk deeper past the hillside. But she'd stopped, no doubt seeing the smoke of her burning people and hearing the shouts of alarm. If we shot her men out of the sky she'd know we were here. If she doubled back for her men and then they all came at us, my boulder idea was gone and we were dead.

Press forward. You're not afraid of anything and you wouldn't have sent those men into the valley if you hadn't already prepared to lose them.

The ground they walked on was rocky but for a sandy flat path that hugged the base of the hillside. I watched as indecision warred in her gaze. She looked up to her flyers who were now ten feet from us. No one on the hillside moved. We were covered in leaves, bushes, moss sheets, and anything brown or green we could find. I had a perfect view of the queen's face from between the cropping of thick bushes I squatted behind. I saw the moment she sealed her fate. A cocky look of superiority washed over her face and her nostrils flared. The scent of burning flesh, of her men dying, filled the air, and then she grimaced.

"Attack!" she screamed.

They charged forward, funneling three by three down the narrow sandy walkway in an attempt to pass the hill and attack my army from behind as they waited in the Narrow Valley. The flyers, distracted with their queen's orders, veered away from the hill and sped towards the back of the Narrow Valley, where our entire army lay in wait.

Maker be with me.

Once the queen had gotten as far as my last net, I stood and screamed louder than I ever thought possible. "Now!" The bellow ripped from my throat, my voice cracking at the end.

Our civilian army burst into action, letting go of the taut, boulder-filled nets they'd been holding this entire time. At the same time, our Bow Men erupted from bushes and shot at her flyers and any of her archers on the ground.

Giant rocks and boulders tumbled down the hillside and slammed into her army. They knocked men off mounts, they crushed machines, they spooked horses, which ran off wildly without any direction, bucking their riders.

"Reload!" I yelled but it wasn't necessary, the people were already transferring the second stack of backup boulders behind them into the nets and then releasing them. There weren't as many but it was enough to cause so much chaos that the queen had lost control of her army. They scattered like a pile of frightened ants.

The queen.

I scanned the ground but could no longer see her. An explosion suddenly rocked the hillside and then I was thrown backwards, my head cracking the hard ground and my teeth snapping together.

Fire. Screaming.

Stay calm. I breathed.

She'd bombed us. One of their trebuchets must have been set up in advance as if she expected an attack. I rose to my feet and a shadow blanketed me from overhead. I looked up just as the queen aimed her bolt shooter at me.

Everything happened so fast then I could barely comprehend it. She flicked her wrist right at me and a bolt left its thrower. Then a blur moved in front of me as Haig threw himself in the path of the shot.

"No!" I screamed. The bolt was fired with such force it went halfway through his chest, knocking him backwards into me before he hit the ground at my feet.

Something wild snapped within my chest and I

burst from the ground, leaping over him and into the air. I grasped the ankle of the Nightfall queen and dangled from her leg for a second before she lost balance. She flapped her metal wings wildly as she tried to stay aloft, but they weren't made to carry the weight of two people.

With a grunt she fell from the sky like a downed bird, hitting butt first and then her back. I wasted no time crawling on top of her, unbridled rage roiling through me.

I didn't know what I was doing. Driven by pure instinct, I grabbed her cheeks and then hovered my mouth inches from hers. Her eyes went wide and she froze for a second, no doubt thinking I was going to kiss her.

Then I inhaled. My magic ignited, and instead of breathing life into the dying, I *took* from the living. I sucked her life force right from her mouth. Shocked to see the white mist flowing from her open lips and into my lungs, I was simultaneously freaked out and fascinated by the discovery of this new gift. I watched in awe as a chunk of her hair turned white in the front.

I'm killing her, I thought for a wild second, then something pierced my shoulder blade and agony ripped through my arm, causing me to lose my hold on the queen. She used the distraction to ram a knee into my crotch and shove me off of her.

I lay on my back, arrows flying every which way, and watched in wonder as she took to the skies again. Her wings glinted in the dying sunlight as I grappled with what I'd just done. What I could do.

Maybe I wasn't *blessed*, maybe I was also *cursed*. This gift seemed to be able to go both ways.

"Retreat!" the Nightfall queen bellowed into the sky, and Nightfall's deep horns blew throughout the valley.

Relief crashed through me at that sound, and I wondered if I'd weakened her. She was flying wobbly, her voice hoarse. Had I taken some of her vitality? Weakened her life?

I pulled my ponytail in front of me and inspected the darker brown chunk. Was there more of it than before? Had the queen just given me more life?

The pain in my shoulder brought me back into the moment and I looked down at my wound, and the arrow sticking out of it, and it was in that moment that I remembered Haig.

Scrambling to get up, I crawled over to the old man. He was lying on his back, bleeding heavily from the stomach as healers tried in vain to save him. This was beyond a simple healer. Maybe if Raife was here, but...

"Step back," I commanded. I didn't know how many breaths I had left. Definitely one. Maybe two.

Maybe three if taking from the queen added to my life force—I didn't know how it worked. When I hovered over Haig, opening my lips, his hand clamped over them, gripping my face forcefully and keeping me from breathing over him.

"I'm an old man. I've had a good life," he said weakly. "And dying while watching the Nightfall queen retreat is a death well earned. Don't take that from me and don't waste your precious gift on me, child."

My tears spilled out of my eyes and over his fingers. I wanted to thank him for saving my life, but his fingers were still positioned hard over my mouth like a steel trap. As if reading my mind, he stared at me. "Trading my life for yours was an honor... my queen."

The tears flowed faster now. He sucked in one large final breath before his eyes went glassy and his chest moved no more. His hand fell away from my mouth and flopped to the ground. It took every ounce of self-control I had not to try to save him. I wanted to honor his wish. A man should be able to choose how he dies.

"My queen!" Cahal screamed and I stood, wiping my eyes. I'd fall to pieces later; my people still needed me.

My shoulder stung like Hades, but I followed his

voice and found Cahal climbing to the top of the hillside.

"We have many wounded, and the valley is still on fire, but the troops have retreated," he said, slightly out of breath.

I nodded, turning to the royal guard that stood behind him. "Heal the wounded! Put out the fires! Send scouts to make sure the entire army leaves," I yelled and they scrambled. Then I turned to the civilians. "Gather our dead for burial. Burn the Nightfall soldiers." They too scurried off to do my bidding.

Cahal hadn't moved. He was staring at my shoulder. "My queen, you need a healer."

"No. I'm fine. I will be healed after the last man is," I stated.

The Nature of War had a very poignant line that had stuck with me. *On the day of the battle, be the last to eat, the last to rejoice, and the last to be healed if you can help it. This will earn you a respect among your army that you cannot buy with jewels and coins.*

I wanted these men's respect. I wanted their forgiveness. I led them into a battle where some of them had died. Fathers, sons, brothers. I didn't do that lightly, and although we'd won, the losses would forever stain this day in our memories. I wanted to honor that. The wound wasn't bad. I could move my fingers, so the tendons were intact, and the bleeding seemed plugged with the arrow so I knew no artery was hit. The pain was manageable.

Cahal put a fist over his chest and bowed before leaving.

I followed him, slowly hiking my way up the hill to peek over the other side. When I saw the carnage I took in a sharp intake of breath, and then coughed as the smoke entered my lungs. The entire valley was filled with dead Nightfall soldiers. They'd been burned, and the ground was black with soot. Farmers and soldiers carried buckets of water to put out the fire at the edges that threatened the trees.

The healing tents we'd erected ahead of time were filled, and there was a small pile of elvin bodies to be taken for burial.

I tried not to count, but I couldn't help it.

Twelve. Twelve men died because of decisions I made. If Raife were in charge, would it have been less? Would it have been zero? Would he ever forgive me for going to war with his army and killing twelve men?

As I made my way down the valley to check on the healing tent and see if anyone needed help, the first person started to clap. Then another. Chills rose on my arms when I realized they were clapping for me as I passed them. It was a sign that even though I saw the twelve dead bodies as a failure, they were pleased with how everything went and they saw this as a win.

I waved to them as I passed but couldn't bring myself to smile.

War didn't deserve a smile, even when you won, because no one really wins in war when even one person dies.

It took five hours for the healers to treat all the wounded and then me. Luckily, every elf had some healing ability, so the women and even young children came out to help tend to the wounded. My arrow wound sealed right up and left a tender pink pucker mark. I told my healer not to fully take the evidence of the injury, to allow it to scar so that I could remember this day that I'd found the strength to be a true queen, not just a fake one.

In the middle of the night I sat in the meeting room

with what was left of the council, Aron and Greylin. Foxworth had fled, and Haig was gone.

"I'm sorry about your father," I said for the tenth time to Aron.

Aron looked sad but was holding it together well. He nodded. "The old man always wanted a worthy death in battle. He wasn't really made for being stuck in a room all day and having meetings."

I inclined my head. "The latest messenger reported that Zaphira and her men are fully gone and our people are already repairing the wall, working in shifts."

Greylin rubbed his face. "I'm exhausted, but not sure I can sleep."

I knew what he meant. What if the queen came back with an army three times the size? What if she wasn't done?

The door burst open then and I jumped a little at the sight of Raife. He looked totally clean and not injured, which I was grateful for, but his eyes were wide, chest heaving and he appeared... livid.

"You led my army onto the battlefield?" he growled.

Of course he would have seen it coming in—the burnt earth, the piles of bodies. He'd probably already spoken to Cahal and gotten a full rundown.

I swallowed hard, trying not to think of the letter he'd left me.

Aron stood and looked Raife in the eye. "My lord. She did our kingdom proud, she did your crown proud. The people are safe and—"

"I need to speak with Lani privately. Get out!" Raife screamed at the council.

Greylin scowled at him. "You have no reason to be upset with her. She drove off the Nightfall queen when others wanted to flee!"

"Get. Out!" Raife said through gritted teeth.

They left, casting me worried glances, but I waved them off. I was covered in dirt, blood, and soot. I still wore Raife's tunic, which had been cut off the shoulder and tied under my armpit to expose my healing wound. If Raife wanted to punish me, I would take it. I stood, and faced him with my chin held high, ready for his wrath.

Did he know Haig was dead? I tried not to think about Raife's note. Making this as professional of a conversation as possible would be best.

Raife turned on me then, eyes raking over every inch of me, and I could almost feel their caress. "You went on the battlefield? You *led* a war?" He sounded like he was in pain. I was so confused I couldn't process it.

I simply nodded.

He reached up and grabbed the sides of his jaw in agony. "You could have died. I can't do this anymore."

My stomach dropped. "Do what?"

"Friends. I hate being your friend. *Screw* friends," he declared.

I couldn't breathe. It was as if his outburst absorbed all of the oxygen in the room.

My mouth popped open in shock. I wasn't sure if I should be hurt or... something else.

His hands fell away from his face and he stepped towards me, eating up the space between us. "I can't go one second longer pretending I'm not desperately in love with you, Kailani. Pretending this marriage is fake. It's not fake, and I can't fight it anymore. I'm too tired and I care for you too much." He leaned his forehead against mine. "You *consume* me," he said, and I gasped as his lips fell on mine.

It was like the dark hole he'd burrowed into my heart with all of his rejection and pushing away was suddenly filled up with light. I felt like I was buzzing, floating; my body couldn't process the elated feelings, and I couldn't tell if they were coming from him or me. It was from us both, I realized, a heady mixture of love and desire.

He pulled back then, looking at me with a vulnerability. "If you still want me."

A smile pulled at my lips and I cupped his jaw in

my hands. "Raife, I've spent every day since I met you wanting you."

His lips were back on mine then, as his fingers slipped up the backside of my tunic and I fumbled with the belt of his trousers.

I needed him, needed to make love to him to solidify that I was in fact *not* his damn friend.

But first he had to know something. I pulled away from him and he froze, looking into my eyes with uncertainty as to why I stopped.

"Raife, Haig died, people died—" My voice cracked and he nodded, stroking my cheek.

"It's okay. All that matters is that you are alive and the Nightfall queen fled, and the people are chanting your name in the streets, my love."

His acceptance of the loss of his people was exactly what I needed to heal. In that moment my guilt fled and I let my trousers and tunic fall to the floor.

His gaze raked over my naked skin, eyes going half lidded. "I heard you had some needs that required satisfaction?"

I tipped my head back and laughed and his mouth landed on my throat, sucking the skin there and causing me to moan.

Raife pulled back and looked me in the eyes. "Your aunt was right. Family makes a place a home, and you're my family now, Kailani. Forever."

A single tear slipped from my eye and Raife swooped down to kiss it.

Being Raife's family, after knowing how much he lost all those years ago, was a bigger honor than just being his wife and queen. I wanted to be his everything, and now I was.

Raife

When Kailani told me she was unsatisfied and wanted to take a lover, I nearly bent her over the couch and claimed her right there. That woman had owned my heart since the day I laid eyes on her in the slave trader room.

The night I learned I was falling in love with

Kailani, she was plastered on elf wine, so I couldn't tell her. Most men would be thrilled to be falling in love with their betrothed, but this horrified me. I'd barely survived losing my family. I thought about ending my life constantly for the first three years. To love another that the Nightfall queen could kill, would break me.

The night I kissed her while she was drunk on elf wine, I barely slept. I was wracked with nightmares of Kailani writhing on the floor and foaming at the mouth. So instead of loving her, I pushed her away, I fought the insane attraction I had to her, I protected her but hurt her with my rejection. Something I hoped she would forgive me for one day.

"Good morning, my love." Kailani rolled over in bed and kissed my neck. It was the second night we'd shared a bed together and the anxiety that I had expected to come with fully letting my guard down with her, with fully loving Lani, never came. Instead I just felt healed, felt whole. She was the missing puzzle piece all along. The person I could lean on and start a family with.

"I heard there is a liquor shortage because of you." I kissed her nose and she laughed, stroking my chest.

Maker, I loved that laugh.

Did she have any idea how intelligent she was? Funneling the queen into the Narrow Valley that she'd soaked with liquor and burning it, was genius. I was married to a genius.

My mind wandered then. A week. Drae wouldn't meet me for a week. That was a long time after just having the queen attack my people. Did I have a week? Would she be back?

"What's wrong?" Lani asked.

I both hated and loved that she had my mother's gift of being empathic. It reminded me of my mother, which I loved, but I hated that I could keep nothing from her. I didn't want to worry her unnecessarily. "Nothing. Just that Drae said he wouldn't be able to meet me for a week. His wife had twins."

Lani smiled. "That's wonderful for them... but a week is a long time. Especially after—"

There was a knock at the door.

I stood, throwing my tunic and trousers on, and opened it.

Mrs. Tirth was there looking flustered. "The dragon king is outside with his men."

My eyes nearly fell out of my head. His men? "What?"

Mrs. Tirth nodded. "He said you would be going to Thorngate, and I should pack your bag."

That bastard was bossing my lead housemaid around? I couldn't help but grin. He'd come early.

I looked back at Lani, who rushed forward and planted a kiss on my lips. "Go. I've got everything taken care of here."

She did. I knew that now, and as much as I didn't want to leave her after just professing my true feelings, I couldn't keep Drae waiting. We had to take out the queen before she got too powerful.

I ran outside, to the front of my palace to see Drae Valdren and what looked like nearly half of his army. The Drayken made up the first three rows of men and stood tall with their black dragon scale armor. They held banners bearing the Embergate logo, and I was honestly in shock at the sight.

"Speechless?" Drae approached me with a smile. "I didn't think that was possible."

I grinned. "You came early, and you brought friends."

Drae's smile broadened "I heard that bitch attacked while you were away. We marched right through the Narrow Strait on our way here. I want her to know we have your back. That we're amassing against her. I figure my men can remain in Archmere while we get Lucien and Axil. I hear there's good hunting here."

He was a damn good friend. He might have deserted me before when my parents died but he was just a boy then. Now he was a man, and a good king, and he more than made up for it in this moment.

"You're welcome to hunt wherever you please," I told him. "How are the girls?"

Drae chuckled. "I told Arwen to rest but she's probably already got the babies strapped to her chest while she practices her knife throwing."

I tipped my head back and laughed. Looked like he'd married the perfect woman for him. "Sounds like you've left your kingdom in good hands."

He nodded. "Shall we go and see Lucien?"

My expression became stony then. Lucien nearly killed me last time. I'd tried to play it off for Kailani's benefit, but I'd seen it in his eyes—he would have done it had she not been there.

"He's not the same friend we remember. Life has hardened him." I didn't know if it was just what I'd done, sleeping with his love, or something else, but he'd gone dark. All traces of the laughing jokester were gone.

Drae inclined his head. "Then we will have to remind him of who he is."

With that, my oldest friend in the world pulled out a metal box, rusted at the corners and caked in dirt.

My mouth dropped open at the sight of it. I'd totally forgotten about it. "You dug it up!" I scolded him. It was something all four of us were supposed to do together when we all became kings. I didn't even remember what I'd put inside. I was eight years old at the time.

Drae shrugged. "We're all kings now, and none of us talk to each other anymore, so I thought I'd take initiative."

I was actually excited to open it. I remembered that night vaguely. We'd all been roasting sweet potatoes by the fire at one of our annual retreats, and the memory box had been Lucien's idea. He said we should bury something to remind us of who we were as happy children because one day we would become angry old kings like our fathers.

Taking this along was a good idea. The box might just bring Lucien back from whatever dark place he'd gone to. If I had put him there, I'd never forgive myself.

I guess it's time to find out.

THE END

Captivated by *The Broken Elf King*? The story continues in *The Ruthless Fae King*, book three of four in the Kings of Avalier series

Lucien Thorne is the most vile monster in all of Thorngate. As Winter King, he rules our land with an iron fist and a cold, dead heart. **And my father has just informed me that I am betrothed to marry him....**

As the Princess of Fall, it is my duty to marry whatever suitor my father chooses for me, but even duty can't make me spend the rest of my life with someone like Lucien. However the more time I spend with this mysterious man, the more I wonder if the rumours about him are even true.

As I get to know the real Lucien, I start to discover the secrets and dark history of his family. A history that explains his ruthless behaviour... And one I plan to expunge if I am ever to live out my life in the Winter Palace in peace.

As much as I want to hate Lucien Thorne and everything he's done to our realm... **I cannot deny my heart.**

Captivated by *The Broken Elf King*? The story continues in *The Forbidden Wolf King*, book four of four in the Kings of Avalier series

Axil Moon broke my heart when I was fifteen and I've dreamed of getting revenge ever since. So when he becomes the king of all Wolven and summons me to compete for his hand in marriage in the deadly Queen Trials, I gladly accept. I want nothing more than to defeat the competition and leave him cold and alone when I slam the bedroom door in his face every night. Axil Moon will regret the day he thought he could discard me and get away with it.

But the Axil I expect isn't the one waiting for me. This grown Axil is different from the teenage boy I loved. This Axil begs me to believe it was never his choice to leave me, and my heart is torn.

Now I have to try and stay alive in order to see what could be between us, but all the while there is an enemy in our midst and war on our border that could overturn the world as I know it, and all I can do is fight to keep that world alive.

The story began in *The Last Dragon King*, book one of four in the Kings of Avalier series

The Dragon King is looking for a wife...

The news causes a frenzy for the women in my village. The king will be sending out the royal guard to bring women of childbearing age to his castle in Jade City.

There is only one requirement: his wife-to-be must carry enough magic to produce an heir for him.

I know I won't be chosen: I'm only human with a mere ten percent dragon magic lineage, but for some reason the magic sniffers command me to present myself to the king as a possible wife.

I'm ready to go to Jade City until my mother tells me a terrifying secret. A secret that could get me killed... by the king himself.

ACKNOWLEDGMENTS

Always a big thank you to my amazing readers! I truly could not do this without you. It still amazes me that I get to be creative and do this for a living and someone actually wants to read what I write. Thank you to my Wolf Pack who is so supportive. To my editors Lee and Kate, I am a sloppy mess without you. And always to my husband and children for sharing me with my art. <3

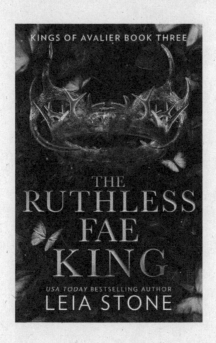

Have to know what happens next? Turn the page for

an exclusive extract from *The Ruthless Fae King*

ONE

"I won't do it, Father!" I screamed.

"Do you want the entire realm to be plunged into winter? Or our crops to fail?" my father yelled back. "When the winter king asks for your daughter's hand in marriage, you don't say no!"

I was so angry I was shaking. I'd never been this mad at my father in my entire life. I loved him, adored him, worshiped the ground he walked on, but I would not relent to marrying that monster.

"Well, that's exactly what I'm going to say when he gets here. NO!" I shouted, and wind picked up inside the house, causing the papers on my father's desk to fly into the air and form a funnel.

He sighed, as if he were used to my outbursts, but that wasn't fair. I didn't have them that often, only when being forced to be married off to a heartless jackass!

"Daddy..." I softened my voice and the wind died down immediately, bringing the papers to a slow descent to the floor. "I love you. I respect your decision-making.

But I will not under *any* circumstances marry Lucien Thorne. *Ever.*"

My father looked up at me with sadness in his eyes and I knew then that it was already done. Arranged marriages were common among royalty, and I always knew as the princess of Fall I would one day be called on by a royal suitor, but Lucien, the winter king?

It was unthinkable.

"No." A strangled cry came from my lips and my father could no longer meet my gaze.

"I'm sorry, Madelynn. There's nothing that can be done," he said. And that was that.

My fate was sealed to the most vile man in all of Thorngate. Lucien had only been king for six winters and yet I had over a dozen stories of his evil doings. He once froze the entire Summer crop when they protested his raise in taxes. I also heard that he took the tongue of his favorite chef for serving him bland food. He hated flowers, so he had them all destroyed for miles around his palace. He was dead inside. *Evil.* Ever since his father abdicated the throne to him on his sixteenth birthday, there had been nothing but rumors of his darkness.

"What if he beats me?" I tried to reason with my father. "You've heard the rumors, Daddy. He's unkind."

My father looked stricken. "He would not hit his wife." He didn't sound sure though.

Maker help me.

My father was kind, *too* kind, and always trying to please others. Now I was going to have to deal with this myself. I would have to be strong so that King Thorne knew I was not the type of woman to be crossed.

"When does he arrive?" I asked through gritted teeth.

"Later this afternoon." My father's voice was small.

"Today!" I bellowed, and the wind was back, blowing through the open window and swirling around me. My powers were the strongest seen in generations, and I knew that's why the king had chosen me. I'd never met Lucien Thorne as an adult. We Fall Court fae stuck to ourselves mostly. I'd briefly seen him as a young boy back when his mother was still alive, but I must have been six winters old and he only eight or so. I barely remembered that. He'd handed me a sunflower and told me my dress was pretty. A sweet boy—before the darkness took him over.

I stormed from my father's office, taking the wind spiral with me.

How dare my father tell me hours before the king was to arrive! It gave me no time to find a way out of this arrangement. And maybe that's what he wanted.

The palace staff hugged the walls as I passed, my wind blowing their dresses left and right. I needed to go outside and blow off some of this anger before I collapsed the entire house.

Bursting out the back doors, I ran past the gardens

towards the meadow I often went to when I wanted to use my power without destroying anything.

Once in the safety of nature, I let loose. I sucked in a huge lungful of air and the wind pressed in on me like an old friend. The grass bowed, dust kicked up, and the sun darkened as my little wind tunnel grew stronger.

Maybe the king was on his way right now. It was late afternoon and he might be en route. If I sent this little windstorm his way, it might blow his horses off track and he could be injured, delaying the engagement...

I shook myself from those dark thoughts, knowing such a thing would be traced back to me.

Balling my hands into fists, I looked up at the sky, into the eye of the storm I'd created, and let loose with an agonizing scream, aiming it at the sun as if it was his fault I was upset.

All at once the wind died out and I was calm again. Unleashing my power would not help me. I needed to keep a level head if I was going to find a way out of this.

"Your father told you?" My mother's voice sounded behind me and I spun on her like a snake ready to strike.

"Mother, how could you?" I whimpered. My father was the leader of this court, it was his duty to make such an arrangement, but my mother? She gave me no warning.

Her eyes filled with tears. "The winter king can be very convincing," was all she said.

4

I scoffed, stepping closer to her. She had the same bright red hair as I did, and today we both wore lime green dresses without knowing the other would be doing it. We often did this and I liked it. I'd felt a closeness with my mother my entire life, but now I just felt betrayed.

"Mother, he's awful," I pleaded.

She sighed. "Don't say that. He was a boy who lost his mother and he... acted out."

She was defending him?

"He lost his mother *six* years ago," I growled. "What's his excuse now?" His mother died in a tragic accident. She was riding with young Lucien Thorne when she was bucked off her horse. She fell on her neck and it snapped, killing her instantly. Because they were on an innocent horseback ride, there had been no healing elf present. I did feel bad that a young boy had to see his mother die like that, but it was no excuse for some of the stories I'd heard about him.

"Mother, he eats raw meat. He's killed with his bare hands. Not to mention what he did with the Great Freeze. He's a monster."

My mother sighed. "We don't know if *all* of those stories are true." She didn't sound too sure about that.

"Is it the dowry he's paying? Because I can raise my own money and pay you and Daddy back—"

My mother cut me off with the shake of her head.

"No, honey, it's law. When the reigning king asks for a royal's hand in marriage, it cannot be refused."

I frowned.

Law? A stupid little legal edict was standing in the way of my freedom? It wasn't that I was against duty, or marriage. My parents were arranged and had a wonderful marriage. I knew my day would come soon. I was just against the idea of *him*.

"Why does he want me?" I crossed my arms and tipped my chin up. "I'm from Fall Court. Duchess Dunia of Winter would be a *much* better match. They grew up together, she knows him. Their offspring would be better suited."

My mother sighed, stepping forward, and grasped my hands in hers. "He has heard of your power and beauty. He wants *you*, Madelynn, to be his wife and the mother of his children. Your son could be future king."

My heart sank. My power and beauty were not things I thought would one day seal my fate to an evil prick, but here we were.

"I'm sorry, Mother. I can't. Anyone but him. Help me say no. Say I am betrothed to another, or—"

"Madelynn! That would embarrass your father and our entire court. You've already been promised." She looked at me like I'd grown two heads. Her perfect eldest daughter. Most powerful with wind magic. Top marks in school. Never stepped a toe out of line. Sure,

I was independent and headstrong, but I never disobeyed my parents, or a royal edict... until now.

"I'll see you later, Mother," I said cryptically, and then ran to the horse barn to find my mare.

There was no way in Hades I was marrying Lucien Thorne.

I RODE INTO TOWN ALONE, disguised under the hood of my cloak until I came to one of my favorite courtier's houses, Maxwell Blane. He was handsome, rich, funny, and a total lothario. It would be perfect for what I was about to ask.

I knocked on his door hurriedly, as the street beyond his house in town was bustling and I didn't want any rumors. I'd never been alone in another man's presence without a chaperone, but I didn't want a witness for what I was about to ask of him.

When his housemaid opened the door, I slipped inside without being asked to do so.

She squeaked in shock, backing up, then I pulled off my cloak. "Sorry for the intrusion, Margaret."

"Oh, Princess Madelynn." She bowed, seemingly relieved that she knew who was barging into her home.

My lady-in-waiting, Piper, and I came to Maxwell's house once a week for one of his famous cocktail parties. He was the courtier to know, and put on the most entertaining parties I'd ever been to. There was singing, games, and drinking. I didn't drink of course, it wouldn't be proper but I played the games and we always had a wonderful time.

"Is Maxwell around? I have an urgent issue."

She nodded. "Right this way. He's in the study." She looked behind me at the door as if nonverbally asking where my chaperone was. I said nothing, only letting the heat of my cheeks speak for me. Without a word, she took the hint and asked for my cloak.

Maxwell's parents came from old money, and when they died in a boating accident they left him everything. He was a spoiled brat and a dear friend. I knew he would help me with my request.

She walked me down the hallway. We came upon an open door and the maid knocked on the casing. "Sir, Princess Madelynn is here."

His face lit up when he saw me. "What an honor. Come in, darling."

Darling. Beautiful. Honey. He never addressed a woman without something sweet at the end. He'd bedded half the court, I was sure of it.

The maid left us. Normally, she would stay to make sure my reputation was intact, but I think she had gathered this was going to be a private conversation.

I shut the door behind me and then turned to face him.

He wore a red silk smoking jacket and held a lit cigar along with a cup of coffee, a large diamond ring on his pinky. He was twenty-three years old. The town gossiped about his single status weekly but he'd informed me once that he had no intentions of getting married. Ever.

Out of politeness he extinguished his cigar and stood to kiss my cheek. I accepted the kiss and kissed him back in the affectionate way I would a brother or beloved uncle. I'd never been attracted to Maxwell. He was handsome, but his flagrant flirting and the ease at which he bedded women turned me off. Now I realized it was exactly what I needed.

"To what do I owe this secret pleasure?" He beamed at me, looking at the closed door and my lack of chaperone as he sat back down in his chair.

I took a shaky breath and leveled my gaze on his. "My father has just betrothed me to Lucien Thorne."

His coffee cup stilled on his lips and he set it back down. "Oh dear, that man has a nasty reputation. But you will be queen, so that's a plus."

I shook my head. "I obviously can't marry him, Max. You have to help me."

Maxwell had long, dark-blond hair and ice-blue eyes, and his skin was softer than mine. Sometimes I studied his face wondering how he could be so... beautiful. I did this now while he considered my fate.

He nodded. "I see. I can give you money, you can pay your father the dowry—"

I held up my hand and interrupted him. "My mother said he won't take it.

It's not about the money, it's about reputation."

Maxwell chewed his lip. "Well, you could take some money from me and run away."

I scoffed. "And leave my family? My home?"

He shrugged. "I don't know any other option, Madelynn. He's the winter king," he said, and took a sip of his coffee.

I tapped my fingers nervously on my legs, my cheeks going red with embarrassment. "As you know, there is a purity test before marrying the king. I was wondering if you could help me… fail it."

His coffee spurted out of his mouth and in my direction. I barely had time to move before it covered the seat behind me.

His mouth was agape and I winced.

"Are you trying to get me killed?" he exclaimed. "Your father would kill me, then your mother, and then the king. I'd be thrice dead!"

"I'm desperate!" I sobbed. "He's a monster. You know this."

His gaze traveled down my body, then he reached up and bit one of his knuckles before pulling it from his mouth. "I will admit I've thought of bedding you, Madelynn, but you're royalty and I don't do drama." Maxwell looked at me with pity. "I can offer money that does not need repayment, but it's all I can do."

It was a nice offer, but I wasn't leaving my family and my home. I frowned. "Max, I don't want to marry him."

Reaching across the desk, he grasped my hand in his. "Be the strong, bold, and independent woman I know you to be and maybe he will reject you."

I laughed, but then thought maybe that was a decent idea. If I was nasty enough to him, he would realize my beauty and power were no consolation for the kind of nightmarish woman I could be.

"That's brilliant. Thanks, Max."

He took one more longing look at me and waved me off. "Go, before I change my mind."

I wished him farewell and then grabbed my cloak from his maidservant. When I got to the front door and flung it open, my mother was leaning against my horse.

Hades.

That woman knew me too well. I tried to act calm, like I wasn't just caught doing something I shouldn't.

My mother shot me a glare as I approached. "Going off to the local seducer without a chaperone? You wouldn't be trying to tarnish your reputation, now would you, daughter?"

I huffed. "He wouldn't have me."

"Madelynn!" my mother scolded, reaching out to whack me on the back of the head for good measure. "Your father has betrothed you to the winter king, the ruler of all fae. You could do no better."

My mother and father seemed to have blocked out all of the horror stories of Lucien Thorne.

"You gave me no time to prepare for this," I growled, suddenly feeling ashamed with what I'd just done. If word got around that I was alone in Maxwell's house without a chaperone, I would have *no* marriage prospects from *any* man.

My mom rested a hand on my shoulder and looked me in the eye. "Because we know you too well." She eyed Maxwell's house as if to make a point. "Listen, honey, we raised you to be a leader," my mother said. "At King Thorne's side, you can make a difference. As his wife and our queen, you will influence law and carry out rulings. You can give back to your community and even talk him down from war. A woman has an important place beside a king."

Her words touched me, touched the place inside of me that wanted to sacrifice my happiness for that of my people. I had naïvely assumed I could have both happiness and duty, but now I knew that not to be true.

I sighed in resignation. "If he hurts me, I'll kill him. Consequences be dammed."

My mother flinched as if I'd slapped her. "If he hurts you, *I'll* kill him."

Her shock at my mention of him being abusive made me wonder if I was being too harsh on the winter king. But the stories I'd heard—that he once dragged a courtier through the town behind a horse—they were all dark and brutal, and told the tale of an unhinged king who I wanted *nothing* to do with. Tears suddenly filled my vision and a gust of wind passed over us,

picking up my hair. "I'm going to miss you."

I barely got the words out when my mother pulled me into a hug.

THE WINTER KING would be here any minute. After we negotiated my dowry, he would parade me around Fall Court like a prized hog. We would announce our engagement publicly and then go on a tour of the four courts, inviting each one to our upcoming wedding. And all of this was before I'd even met the man or agreed to it.

In the end, I relented to my father's begging and my mother's tears.

I was the most powerful princess in all the realm, and the king wanted powerful heirs, so it was an obvious pairing.

A part of me sort of always knew this day would come. I'd just hoped he'd marry a woman of royal lineage from his own court and leave me alone. I didn't want to leave Fall. Orange leaves, crisp cool air, the scent of change. I'd grown up in my father's kingdom my entire life. We were one of the most prosperous of Thorngate, growing half the food for the realm, and

even selling excess to Embergate.

I sat in my room as my beloved lady-in-waiting, Piper, finished curling my hair, and I gasped at the sudden realization that I would no longer have her company. I was nineteen winters old and she was twenty. We practically grew up together. Her mother served as my mother's lady-in-waiting and she'd become my best friend.

We'd been quiet since we both heard the news. I wasn't sure she knew what to think or say to me. Marrying the winter king was more of a curse than a blessing, so congratulations were not in order.

"What's wrong?" she asked me finally.

Unshed tears filled my eyes as I looked up at her. "I just realized I would be losing you. I could never ask you to leave your family and follow me to the frozen Hades of Winter Court."

Piper smiled. I loved that smile. She had two crooked teeth in front that pressed onto her bottom lip like fangs.

"Oh, Maddie, I would never leave you to marry that bastard alone. I've already asked your father to be dismissed from Fall Court. I'm going to Winter with you."

Tears lined my eyes and I pulled her in for a hug. "I don't deserve you," I told her.

I released her and she nodded, her long brown hair shaking around her shoulders. "That's true. And I hear the winter king is richer than your father, so maybe I should ask for a raise…"

I grinned, loving that Piper knew how to get me out of my rotten mood.

There was a knock at the door and I stood, squaring my shoulders and tipping my chin high.

It was time. He was here.

As I strode towards the door, Piper caught my wrist. I turned to look at her and there was a fire in her eyes. "Remember your worth, Madelynn Windstrong. You have a lot to offer. I don't care if he is king. You're worth more than a bag of gold."

My heart pinched, and I thanked the Maker for such a loyal friend. Squeezing her hand, I nodded and then opened the door to find my mother waiting for me. The dowry negotiation was always done in person after the male suitor met the prospective wife. He would want to make sure I looked as pretty as he had heard, or last seen, and that I was as powerful as rumor stated. The prettier and more powerful, the more money and land my father could ask for.

Because I would be giving him power in his kingship and future heirs, he would pay my father for the right to marry me. It was a practice as old as time in our culture, one that if I stopped to think about felt a little offensive, but was necessary to keep our court funded. My father didn't ask for many taxes from the people, and fifty percent of what we got we had to give to the ruling monarch, the winter king.

"You look beautiful, dear," my mother said, and extended her arm so that I could hook mine into hers.

"Thank you." I took her arm and then looked back at Piper, who gave me a thumbs-up.

I loved her for saying she'd would go with me. Truthfully, I wasn't sure I would be able to survive in Winter without at least one friend.

As my mother and I traversed the hallways of my family home, I felt reality settle in. I couldn't believe I was doing this. The man who was rumored to have killed a servant for not making his bed correctly was about to be my husband.

Could I marry a man who would make me miserable for the rest of my life just to honor my duty and make my family happy? Was duty above happiness?

Unfortunately for me, it was.

"Maddie!" My little sister's voice came from behind me and my entire body went rigid. If I saw her right now I would fall into a puddle of tears. I couldn't imagine leaving Libby.

"She doesn't know yet," my mother whispered, and relief rushed through me.

I spun, plastering on a fake smile, and let her rush into my arms.

"I got top marks in archery! Master Bellman says I'm as good as the elves!" she shouted excitedly.

I grinned, smoothing her frizzed red hair with my palms. She had mine and our mother's red hair coloring but my father's texture. She looked like a wild lion half the time. "I imagine you are."

"You look pretty." She took in my gold embroidered dress and fancy hair and makeup.

"Thank you. I have… a meeting, so I will come by after and talk with you, okay?" Saying goodbye to her would kill me. I couldn't even think of it right now.

"'kay!" she shouted, and then ran to our mother to hug her before she was bouncing off down the hall to her room with her nanny running behind her.

I shared a heartbreaking look with my mother but said nothing.

Libby and I had a special relationship. I'd watched as my mother had cruelly gone through seven miscarriages before Libby was born eight years ago. When she came into our lives, it was the breath of fresh air we all needed. She kept things fun and light in the palace. She was the joy in my mother's heart after so much sorrow.

When we reached the door, I looked at my mother to hit her with the truth. If I was going to marry this man with the heinous reputation he had, I wanted to have control over certain things.

"I want to negotiate my own dowry," I told her boldly.

She almost choked on her own spit, coughing and clearing her throat. "Honey, that's not done. It's between King Thorne and your father."

I tipped my chin high. "If I'm going to be sold to a monster, I will state the price I am worth, no one else."

My mother's cheeks burned with shame and I felt

awful for saying it that way. Her curt nod was all I needed before I opened the door.

When my gaze fell on Lucien Thorne laughing near the fireplace with my father, I knew I was in trouble.

I'd built up a deep hatred for this man. The things he'd done were inexcusable, and yet when my gaze fell on him, I couldn't help the tightening of my stomach and the warm wash of pleasure that rushed through me.

He was the most attractive man I'd ever seen. I faltered as he turned to look at me.

Oh, Maker, have mercy.

Lucien Thorne was nothing like the boyish paintings hanging in meeting halls. The man before me was chiseled perfection: steely gray eyes, a sharp nose and strong jaw. His lips were pursed and thick. He wore the hairstyle of royal warriors, his long black tresses shaved at the sides and then pulled into a ponytail, braided at the very edges. His charcoal-gray tunic hugged his muscular body, leaving little to the imagination. I didn't know what I was expecting, but not this, not to feel attracted to the man I hated. It threw me for a second, as the king and I just stood there and stared at each other. His gaze raked over me slowly and I felt my breath hitch.

He was evil incarnate, and yet wrapped in the most delicious package I'd ever seen. I wasn't sure I could resist whatever he would offer as a dowry.

I can't marry this man.

Shaking myself, I pulled out of whatever spell he'd cast over me and remembered his reputation.

"My king…" I curtsied the least amount possible to still be considered polite and then stepped closer to greet him.

My mother curtsied next to me, deeply and overly respectful.

He watched me like an animal tracking prey, and I swallowed hard. "Madelynn Windstrong, you are far more beautiful than the songs written

about you," he stated, and stepped forward, reaching for my hand. I offered it to him and he kissed it lightly, a zap of cold traveling up my arm as he did.

A charmer too. Great.

I gave him a curt smile. He then kissed my mother's hand as well. Because he was so handsome, I took this time to remind myself of every horrible story I'd heard of him, and then turned to my father.

"I've spoken to Mother about wanting to negotiate my dowry myself and she agrees," I told him right in front of the king.

My father made a choking sound and my gaze flicked to the king to see what he would say or do, but he just watched me with amusement. His hands were clasped behind his back calmly and his eyes crinkled as he assessed me. "That's not done. It's men's work," my father said, and then gave a nervous peal of laughter before looking at the king. "I'm sorry, my lord, I think

I raised her to be a little *too* independent and head-strong."

The king was still watching me, his steel gray eyes boring into mine. "I think I'd pay extra for independent and headstrong."

His comment shocked me. What the Hades did *that* mean? Was he joking? I didn't like it if he was.

My father didn't even know what to do with that, so he remained silent.

"I would be happy to negotiate your dowry with you, Madelynn," the king said to me, and I gulped. Saying I wanted to negotiate my own payment was one thing, doing it was another.

I hadn't actually expected him to accept. I'd hoped he would have seen the move as too pushy and domineering and called the entire thing off.

I looked to my father and mother, knowing that if I were about to actually agree to marry this man I needed to have a private conversation with him first.

"Mother, Father, if you will excuse us, I need to speak with King Thorne alone before I can agree to marry him."

A panicked look flashed across my father's face. He knew me too well, and was probably imagining all of the horrible things I would say or do.

"You cannot be alone with an unmarried man. It's not proper," my mother reminded me, giving a nervous laugh.

I nodded. "Go fetch Piper. She can chaperone."

My father was frozen by the fireplace as if unsure he could break protocol and allow this. We all stared at the king for guidance, but the king appeared to be perfectly calm and enjoying himself. He leaned against the brick wall of the drawing room casually.

"I look forward to our private chat," he stated to me.

My mother scurried off then to look for Piper, and I started to grow uneasy with the winter king's accommodating personality. Surely the monstrous king I had heard of would forbid such a thing. A woman negotiating her own dowry was unheard of, yet he looked as if this amused him, which infuriated me.

What was he playing at? It seemed if I'd hoped to turn him off with this behavior, I was mistaken.

A moment later my mother appeared with Piper, who bowed deeply to the king and then stood in the far corner of the room to be a silent spectator.

My father cleared his throat, obviously out of his element.

"You may leave us," I told my father. My mother was already standing in the doorway.

My father looked to the king, who nodded, and then my parents reluctantly left. As soon as the door shut, I stepped closer to Lucien Thorne. I decided to be as honest as possible so that he knew where I was coming from. "I've heard the stories about you," I told him. "You're a cruel man who is unkind to staff members, and severely punishes people for the smallest infraction. I would be lying if I said I was excited to be your betrothed."

There, I'd done it. I was completely honest to him, and allowed there to be no pretenses between us that I was going to be some doting wife who was in love with him. It was a bold thing to say to a king, and I awaited his angry response.

Instead, the bastard just smiled at my verbal account of his reputation.

I crossed my arms and pinned him with a glare. "And *furthermore*, I'm not interested in giving you children right away, so you will have to wait until I am ready."

His gaze went half lidded and he licked his lips as if imagining having children with me.

Heat traveled to my cheeks and I flushed. "And I will not bed you unless we are making a child. You can take a mistress, or a whore, I don't care." I tipped my chin high, then a bark of laughter erupted from his throat.

The sound shook me. It was deep and gravelly and filled the entire room. "Are you laughing at me?" My hands balled into fists and a light gust of

wind filled the drawing room, causing the fire in the hearth to increase its flame.

A sudden flurry of snow drifted into the hearth, down the chimney and dropped onto the fire, causing it to crackle.

Was he displaying his power because I had? What the Hades was this?

Were we in some sort of showdown?

He just watched me, smiling and seemingly entertained as I wrestled with all of my emotions.

Reaching up, he grabbed his heart. "I think I just fell in love."

I rolled my eyes, groaning as the wind died out in an instant. Was this man going to be an insufferable charmer the entire time?

"I tell you that I think you are a horrible person and you fall in love with me?" I asked. "You sound unstable."

He stepped forward quickly, causing my heart to quicken as he suddenly strode to within two inches of me. "I'm not known for being stable, am I?" he whispered, his warm breath washing over me.

Holy Maker.

I stepped back a pace, looking towards Piper in panic, but she was statue- still, an observer. She played the role well when she needed to, but we would no doubt be talking about this for days when we were alone.

He took another step, closing the distance I had just gained, and lowered his voice. "I have a confession to make," he murmured.

My heart was in my throat and I swallowed hard. "What?" I breathed.

Why did he have to be so handsome?

He looked down at my lips, and then at my throat before finally meeting my eyes. "I saw you in the meadow by your house last full moon. I was traveling with some of my soldiers in the woods. We were searching for a lost hunting dog. You were dancing in the garden with your sister and..." He took in a deep breath, reaching out to catch a lock of my red hair. "I thought you were the most beautiful woman I'd ever seen. I knew then I had to have you."

It was as if all of the air had been sucked from the room. I couldn't breathe. What was happening? The evil king was... complimenting me?

"Name your price, Madelynn Windstrong, because there isn't a piece of gold in the realm I wouldn't pay to be able to wake up next to you each morning." He smiled sweetly then and I had to swallow a whimper. It was the sweetest thing a man had ever said to me and... it was coming from the bastard who'd caused my family so much pain in the past. I didn't know what to say or feel. I was... at odds with myself. What I had initially assumed were a charmer's flirtations had quickly become a serious confession.

"When you first became king and you brought the Great Freeze across the entire land, my grandmother died," I blurted out.

A darkness cast over his face and I almost regretted saying it. I was already getting used to his smile.

I was now staring at a man devoid of all emotion.

He'd retreated somewhere, a place I couldn't follow, a place I didn't want to follow.

"I'm sorry I killed her," he stated. "Others too. Thirty-seven people died in Summer Court that night. Twelve in Spring. They weren't prepared for that kind of cold."

My brows knotted together as he confessed the horrible things he'd done without an ounce of emotion.

"You admit it?" We'd never gotten an apology or explanation. Just an extreme cold that ripped across the land and the next day it was back to normal.

"I do." He stood tall, his back erect and his chin up, his smile gone. "My powers are tied to my emotions. Same as yours. I couldn't control them." He was speaking about a moment ago when I couldn't keep the wind from entering the room.

What kind of emotions did this man have that he would end up freezing the entire realm for a full day and night? I was thirteen at the time, and it had been one of the scariest nights of my life. The cold crept into the house like a shadow and lingered no matter how high we built the fire. I didn't sleep; my teeth chattered all night. I stood outside with Mother, pushing the frost back with our wind power. My grandmother came out to help us, but she was too old for that kind of exposure. She passed the next day. A weak heart, the healer had said, but we all knew what weakened her.

The Great Freeze.

Since he was being so open, I wanted to ask him

what had happened that night to make him lose control, but I wasn't sure I wanted the answer. I didn't want to know what kind of man I was marrying. A scary man who could freeze me solid if I made him angry.

I didn't know what to say. This was supposed to be a dowry negotiation and it had somehow turned into something else.

The king stared at me then and there was something deep in his eyes that brought a pain to my heart. He looked… sad. Like maybe deep inside of him there was a desolate little boy who just wanted to be loved.

"I know arranged marriages are not ideal anymore, but they are tradition," King Thorne said. "That being said, if you do not want to tie your fate to mine, I can cancel the whole thing. I will tell your father we are simply not a good match. No harm will come to your reputation."

I frowned, my heart thudding into my throat. He was giving me an out? A seriousness descended onto the room and I warred with what I wanted before I'd met him, how I felt now, and what my mother and father expected of me.

"Honestly," the winter king said, "I feel like I should be asking *you* to pay a dowry to be married to this." He gestured up and down his body and laughter erupted from my chest.

He was funny.

Funny. Charming. Sweet.

Slightly unhinged. What could go wrong?

His offer to allow me to back out of the arrangement was noteworthy, but my father had already told the elders of the Fall Court. Not to mention the king rode up here with a full contingent of royal soldiers. Half the town probably already knew what was going on. If we were to cancel, rumor would spread and people would say that there was something wrong with me, that I was impure or too independent. This would tarnish any potential future suitors.

No, I had to do this now. My family's reputation was on the line. This would impact Libby's prospects as well. As much as I'd wanted him to back out before, now I saw the ripple effect that would have on my family.

"We can proceed with the arrangement." I smoothed my dress in a nervous gesture. "I just wanted you to know where I stood."

He nodded, assessing me coolly. "You don't want children right away, will only bed me for children, and I can take a whore. Got it."

I winced when he said it like that, and then gave a nervous peal of laughter. "Okay, the whore comment was a little strong. I'm sorry. This is… a lot for me all at once. I was only told today."

He regarded me with a grin. "Does this mean you are taking away my promised whore?"

I reached out and slapped his shoulder like I would

an old friend, forgetting for a second I was in the presence of the king. But he caught my hand, holding my fingers lightly, which caused my mind to race.

"I would never do that to you... take a whore, or a mistress, or anything in between," he promised, and my stomach flipped over itself.

He was so... not what I thought he would be.

"How much dowry did your father pay your mother's family?" I asked him, pulling my fingers from his and trying to get a feel for what was a good amount to ask for.

The mention of his deceased mother caused his face to fall a little before he regained composure. "A hundred gold coins, ten acres of land, and a dozen horses. But that was a simpler time." His voice was monotone, and I wondered if speaking of his mother after so long was something he didn't like to do.

A hundred gold coins was how much my father made in a year, and King Thorne would be taking me from my father for life.

"I want a *thousand* gold coins," I told him, ready for him to whittle me down to five hundred.

"Done," he stated without missing a beat.

I froze, and then swallowed hard. He was awfully agreeable. "And I want my beloved lady-in-waiting to come as well." I nodded to Piper, who stood erect in the corner.

"Done," he said again.

My heart hammered in my chest. "Also, I think a hundred acres of farmable land for my people is a fair price for the two heirs I will give you."

The king looked my body up and down slowly, his gray eyes caressing my skin so that I could almost feel it. "I was hoping to have more children than that, especially since you stated you will only lie with me when making children."

Piper's snort-laugh came from the corner, and I turned over my shoulder to glare at her. Heat traveled up my cheeks and I knew that they probably resembled the color of my hair.

"The number of children can be discussed later." I fanned myself and stepped away from the fire.

"A hundred acres. Done," he said.

"As far as horses, we have twenty elders in Fall Court. I would like you to gift each one a new stallion. They do most of our farming and this will help—"

"Done," he interrupted me. "Anything else?"

I looked at him incredulously. That had been way easier than I thought. He was saying yes without hesitation. "Will I be able to see my family?" My voice broke as I thought of Libby.

"Of course." His lips pulled into a frown. "Whenever you like. They are welcome at Winter Court anytime. We have a lovely guest house I can have ready at a moment's notice."

I had planned to tell him that if he ever hurt me I

would tear his body in two with the strongest wind imaginable, but now I felt that might be too unkind of an assessment. Had he done bad things in his past? *Yes*—he admitted to the Great Freeze. But there was something else there, a gentleness I couldn't describe, an eagerness to please, to be loved. It held me in confusion and tempered my anger towards him.

I knew that dowries were sealed with a handshake, so I stepped forward and extended my hand.

"I look forward to the upcoming nuptials and serving our people as queen," I told him.

He smiled then, taking my hand into a strong, firm grip and shaking it. "I look forward to spending the rest of my life with you, Madelynn. I hope I can make you happy."

I stopped breathing for the umpteenth time. The way he spoke was… so intense, so real. He leaned forward and pressed a small kiss to the top of my hand before gently dropping it, and I was almost sad to see it go. The winter king then crossed the room, tipping his head to Piper as he went. When his hand rested on the door handle, I called to him. "King Thorne!"

He turned back to look at me, and I met his steely gaze. "I could have asked for more, couldn't I?"

The slow halfcocked grin that spread across his face made my knees go weak. *Good night*, he was handsome. "There is nothing I would have denied you."

He turned then and shut the door softly. Probably

to go in search of my father and put all of this in writing.

I stood there stunned as Piper peeled herself away from the wall and stood before me.

"Do we still hate him?" she asked with a frown. "I'm so confused."

I shrugged. "What the Hades just happened?"

She chewed her bottom lip. "I kind of liked everything about him." So did I.

So. Did. I.

ONE PLACE. MANY STORIES

Bold, innovative and
empowering publishing.

FOLLOW US ON:

@HQStories